Circus Planetaria

Robert Tyler

TABLE OF CONTENTS

COUNTING TWO JOKERS

BLOWING LEAVES

With one foot, Nicolas Nesbitt props open the south door of the observatory. He bends down, slides his fingers into the cut-out ovals, and lifts the cardboard box into LA sunshine.

Inside the box there is a desk lamp, a stapler, six plastic lunch containers, a three-hole paper punch, two commemorative coffee cups, a deck of post cards, and a dander of little objects, bewildering in their variety, that appeared thirteen minutes earlier as Nicolas removed and inverted his desk drawer.

The lamp is of the formidable drafting kind, its double-strut neck accustomed to holding vulturesque postures as it peers over people and their plans. But here outside in the bright sunlight, suddenly and immensely outshined by a close star, it presses its coned head against Nicolas's shoulder—a frightened damsel in his arms. The other objects are more predictably inanimate and simply wait in the hull of the box to see what will happen to them next.

In a few seconds, a few slow and tiny steps, Nicolas is almost upright and far enough into the bleaching yellow sea for the door to close and lock behind him. Minutes ago, he surrendered his key, and so he is cleanly on the other side of a wall now. So abruptly his world is so different. A kink in his lifeline. From a climate-controlled office and stable career, in there, to being rebirthed, out here, into a big bright world. He has felt the adjacency of this bigger world for some time. Heard its high-valence activity beyond the moat of administrative meetings. Smelled its broad spectrum through the windowed offices of his bosses. But these are the first frames in which he sees it. He is reassured to find that he can breathe the atmosphere on this new planet.

And then, three steps into the sunlight, Nicolas stops. Dallies, perhaps. The light streaming into his eyes assembles into a pattern that doesn't make sense. And so he squints. Hardly an illuminating response, but perhaps this reduces his susceptibility to distraction. Nicolas sees that his truck looks different today, and so he squints to discover why.

The young truck is parked on its chewy tires beside a yellow bus. The truck is two years old and has spent the daytime half of its life parked precisely in that space. Precisely in that way. Never once backed in. So

Nicolas has viewed his truck in that posture, from this position, at least half a thousand times. He has by now a well-engraved, all-weather image of the truck over there in its reserved space. As observed from precisely this observatory staff exit.

But today the truck does not at all appear to comply with that encompassing image. It's defiant. Completely different. Currently casting toward him an image that is an outlier by many standard deviations. Is it significant that this very last view of his truck parked this way in that space is by far the most deviant in his historically compiled set? Or might it be simply typical that the first and last in such sets deviate more than the inner members...and end effect? Today, the final day Nicolas Nesbitt shall leave work through this observatory door and observe, from here, his truck parked over there...it looks different. Very different.

Because it's covered in rectangles. Quite completely. Over the painted surfaces. Over the glass windows. Even over the door handles. A constellation of peculiar rectangles in various orientations that cause Nicolas to think he is seeing something other than his means of transportation. A steamship travel trunk. A relic perhaps.

Within the constellation of rectangles crouches a woman. She wears an elegant summer dress with purple polka dots. She has a matching parasol, and her cloth gloves loll over a forearm as she squats near a mud flap to work with something delicate in her lap. High-heeled dance shoes give her knees an unusual rise above the ground and her parasol rests back on her shoulder, revealing struts that are normally hidden from view.

Nicolas reaffirms his grip on the box and decides that the rectangles covering his truck might be bumper stickers, and that the woman he sees right now so busy in her own lap is, in fact, releasing another of the bumper stickers from its backing. Confirming his suspicion, she next has two items—one that she holds carefully by the end with two opposed fingernails, and another that she wads up and tosses into the back of his truck. Holding the remaining item with fingertips, she leans back to take a look. After cocking her head to the left side, she attaches the sticky rectangle—orientation landscape—to the mud flap in front of her. She replaces her cloth gloves.

Nicolas stands still.

She stands up and rights her parasol. She glances in his direction. She is looking at him or maybe just toward him. In any case, she turns back to admire her work and then mounts the banana seat of a small purple bicycle and sets her dance shoes to its pedals.

Nicolas still holds his box in the sunlight three steps away from the south exit of the observatory. He and his lamp watch her slowly pedal across the parking lot in a direction that is maybe toward him or maybe away from him.

The purple seat of the bicycle was manufactured with glitter, glitter that scatters sunlight in random directions and causes the long seat to twinkle now like a sliver of boreal sky. A sissy bar rises from the tail of the seat like a croquet hoop and sways with her slow pedal. Tassels jiggling at the ends of the handlebars report on details of the asphalt over which the purple bicycle travels. Indeed, an abundance of information describing bike, rider, and environment are being broadcast on a variety of channels. Broadcast for anyone around to receive and interpret. If they wish.

Nicolas lunges, but his feet remain in place. If all this information were coming from a far-away star, he would know what to do. But these celestial emissions are arriving from very close range, and he hesitates.

As she rolls by him, the clicking sound of spokes slapping against a face card held by a clothes pin in her front wheel makes Nicolas feel like he is watching her as an old movie from his own future. And during the few frames in which she turns her head and smiles brightly, he experiences something transcendent. As disorienting as a peek at the sun through a deep-space telescope, it wraps around his head. It is dizziness. Sort of pleasant, warm, and a little worrisome. He has lost even the conviction that he will fall downward if he faints. The laws of the cosmos are not being obeyed right now. Even the right now is not being obeyed right now. The moment is simply and curiously absent; it has rolled away and escaped the present, escaped the past, escaped the future. Gone West or something. Now waiting in a sod hut for its prairie to be recognized as a state in his union.

There she goes, the woman of purple polka dots, somehow both mysterious and familiar. And neither. Nicolas finds no linear rule for measuring the experience. If he were to make a long, graded number line, the kind of number line he once made out of colorful construction paper in early grade school, a number line with a ticked axis to sequence, order, rank, and align all experiences he has ever witnessed, progressing from the most familiar to the most mysterious, and if he were to bow this number line in a giant loop and connect the ends—then there, there under the shard of sticky tape is the tick mark to describe her. The tick mark of overlapping mystery and familiarity. Now she pedals away from him down the driveway.

Nicolas rushes toward his truck. Because he still carries the box, it looks like he is trying to hold up the pants of somebody running in front of him. The cone of the lamp ratchets faces down.

The many stickers are thoughtfully positioned over the surfaces of his truck and carry, utopia-bold font, such messages as "I'm helping to warm the planet, ask me how." And "But it's for school, Mom!" Nicolas stares at the truck, the truck that now looks like a trunk. He suddenly wonders why he bought it. It has never been off-road. It has never even had anything dirty in its bed. Like the sports-utility vehicle, it exists in great numbers only because of crafty marketing and a loophole that strangely classifies these luxury vehicles as farm equipment. It suddenly occurs to Nicolas that he has been driving around Los Angeles in farm equipment. Just he and a plastic lunch container most of the time. Driving around Los Angeles. A victim of a fashion that fuses winches, rivets, and engine snorkels with disappearing drink caddies, lighted vanity mirrors, and electrically heated seats. He is suddenly aware of the four-thousand extra pounds he has brought to work with his lunch each day. Of the small but finite increase in global temperature added by the fumes of his transportation. Of the change in the earth's rotation rate and the shift in the timing of sunsets and sunrises over the globe because his massive truck has sat business hours at a slightly higher distance above the earth's rotation axis. He is suddenly aware that the timing of sunsets depends a little bit on the whereabouts of his giant truck on the globe.

Turning his box, Nicolas looks at the woman becoming small with her parasol. Then he looks at his truck. Then back at the parasol. The desk lamp that earlier followed his gaze now looks downward over the box edge, anxious of falling.

The sound of a leaf blower makes Nicolas turn in a new direction. The machine is strapped like a rocket pack to a gardener working on the observatory's panoramic walkway. The noisy, two-stroke engine bullies leaves off the walkway and leaves them to flutter down onto the city below. Somebody else's problem then. This noisy activity takes place beside a small and empty yard-waste trailer.

Nicolas stares at it. The trailer. He walks toward it, the trailer, slowly and with cautious wonder. As an early native might. He arrives beside one of the plywood sidewalls of the trailer. He shifts his box to one arm. He stretches a hand out. He touches the trailer's wood.

The rip of the two-stroke engine lowers to a gargling idle and the gardener turns. Nicolas takes a half step back from the trailer, returns his free hand to his box.

The two men face each other. About the correct separation for a shoot-out. In two hands, the gardener holds a long nozzle diagonally across his erect lap. The other, Nicolas, stands in the driveway with his box drawn and nervous fingers twitching in the cut-out ovals.

Something is then exchanged between the men that immediately reverses their apprehensive postures. Perhaps it is a mutual recognition that they now both hear the voice of Earth. And that they thereby can only strive to participate in actions consistent with this enormous awareness. Perhaps it only establishes that this trailer does not belong to this gardener; not his concern. The trailer's tailgate is down, and Nicolas slides his box in. The gardener responds through modulations of the growling leaf-blower nozzle in his hands; he seems to approve.

Grabbing hold of the back ends of the side walls, Nicolas Nesbitt begins to push the trailer, slowly at first and then skipping into a run where the observatory parking lot drains into the long drive down the hill.

SELF INFLICTION

Gary Saar stands in the grocery line and wonders if he will ever have kids. Two perhaps. One of each sex would be best. A pair of self-inflicted injuries. Perhaps as severe as those on the woman up in the front of the line. The woman wearing crayon marks on her blouse, a pen cap in her mouth and a Nemo hairband around her wrist. And just one earring. The woman struggling to monitor the trajectories of her little comets and block—with a leg extended behind her—both their midair collisions with the candy rack and the passage of their little feet over fallen chocolate while, with a fist clenching a pen in her open checkbook, she tries simply to remember her name.

Gary's direct contact with the outside world has become essentially just this: a several-minute foray through grocery aisles followed by a much longer wait below a handbasket filled with everything he might swallow, brush his teeth with, shave his face with, wash his clothes with, or wipe his butt with over the course of a week. And Gary doesn't use carts. In Gary's mind, carts are slow and extravagant. Carts are for people who do not understand the virtues of streamlining their lives, for people who spend no part of the day in contemplative reflection about the things that really matter. This is his contact with the common world. A quick foray through bright aisles that carry more words than food, and then the inescapable vignette, the wait behind some impossibly contingent gymnastic involving leaky fruit juice, price checks, and unswipeable credit cards. All pasted together in a sequence to precisely defy any rational attempt to choose the shortest line. The outside world, as Gary understands it, is the world beyond a federal building. The world beyond a microcosm designed by analysts. And the world beyond a one-bedroom apartment with a small kitchen, a counter bar, a living room with a sofa and a coffee table and an electronics console and several other things—all of which stay put while he is gone during the day because he lives entirely alone.

Although Gary has little direct contact with the real world, he is immensely engaged with a virtual version of it. Through cameras and screens and microphones and speakers and pretty much any and every indirect way in which information can be conveyed through space, Gary interacts with a vast and tangled virtual reality that he evidently prefers over the real one. Since a young age, the kinds of puzzles in the world that most interest Gary are not the peg-in-hole baboon kind that require hands on; they are more like chess, which is already so abstracted that distancing himself further from the puzzle through electronic conduits adds little extra challenge or isolation. In compensation for not really being present, Gary Saar participates in some of the most secretive and officially important puzzles on the planet.

EVANGELIST'S MIRROR

The Reverend Jimmy Pea mounts a pointed index finger at each of his temples; he bends at the waist, and gallops into the back of her skirt. Mrs. Dougherty bangs her head against the file drawer and turns around, appearing more saddened than offended. Jimmy continues toward his dressing room, walking sneakily on the edges of his feet, as if he is silent and invisible. Side to side through the office, stopping behind furniture like a crab dodging behind rocks to reach a scent upstream. The Reverend is not well.

He sits down at his dressing room mirror. He looks at the face in front of him. His tongue comes out and an eyebrow goes down. He juts out his lower teeth. He giggles. But a faint aspect of his image is also in there trying to figure out what in hell is going on.

With hard work over two decades, Jimmy has amassed the world's largest televised assault on paganism and idle retirement accounts. His televised sermon has spread far and wide, with Jimmy's church erected in the center of the thing like a fanged spider. The dressing room in which he sits is nearly as big as the Alabama church of his first sermon, and his empire has just kept getting bigger.

At least until about six months ago. As anxiety over the planet's health turned to guilt and fear, Jimmy's business increased. Guilt and Fear are the Reverend's business associates. In fact, they run the show. But only Jimmy looks good in a blue suit.

Then something started to go awry. Jimmy began to suffer strange mood imbalances. Powerful mood imbalances. He doesn't know if it is because he uses a cell phone without an earpiece, or if it's because his church is built near a high-voltage power line. The Reverend just finds himself behaving in bizarre manners and isn't sure why.

Before these episodes started, Jimmy sometimes joked with his staff. Harvesting the exploding crops watered by Guilt and Fear has given him such a hectic work schedule that he sometimes feared that he was going mad. But this was an unfortunate misuse of the word. For now that madness has really arrived, Jimmy no longer has a word for it. It isn't at all like what he would have expected. He never guessed that going mad would feel so willful, so voluntary, so elective.

CHECKOUT STAND

The woman at the checkout stand closes her checkbook. She isn't finished signing her name yet, but she has to stop to pry something out of her young son's hand and explain to him what people do and don't do in the grocery store. Gary Saar, his basket, and the space-time continuum twist together and sag at the event horizon. The checkout stand has become a distant singularity that Gary needs to pass through to return to his familiar universe of motion. He is on the back side of a black hole and there are no fast-forward buttons like there are in his virtual worlds. He can only wait and watch as the slow space ballet sucks up all surrounding motion—as it draws the energy out of the shopping carts, swallows the last shuffles of feet, and deflates the orbits of children. He watches as the confined lane funnels soup cans, cereal boxes, and broccoli onto a conveyor belt and deposits their last momentum into a paper or plastic bag. And then, once the singularity has counted everything and made appropriate deductions, the motion is returned to the carts, and the cans of soup, and the cereal boxes, and the broccoli, and the kids, all of it then rocketing away toward the parking lot at relativistic speeds.

But Gary is still on the inside, on the back side of the black hole, not close enough yet to even imagine the acceleration on the other side where gleeful people and their food speed away to freedom. It is a zone that the tabloid, diet, and self-help publishers understand well, and one they have long exploited. A zone where temperatures approach absolute zero, brain waves slow, and people are forced to contemplate their own existence. A magical and horrid vacuum of meaning where one sees the absurd contingency in their own life, society and culture, and the world around them. All of it hanging suddenly and stupidly before them like smiley ornaments on a Christmas tree. All of it pretending to be preordained.

TRAILER PARK

Stumbling out of an invisible orchestra pit in the center of the planetarium, the first banjo notes climb up and dust themselves off. After a wondrous look around, they invite up their kin folk. Notes, chords, and soon the whole clan of "Foggy Mountain Breakdown" spreads over the reclined young spectators as they watch the Universe unfold above them. The groans, colors, and contrasted brightness associated with the birth of Everything is displayed above them on a bulbous projector screen that is deep enough to portray Deep Space yet shallow enough to tuck around the edges of the planetarium's event horizon like a paisley toilet-lid cover. The Big Bang, the big birth of space and time…light, and mass, all flying wonderfully apart. Bright light exploding in beams, radially perfect except for the slight blemishes required to create the entire material universe.

The explosion that started with leisure is soon prodded by the music to understand that it must fit the whole universal creation into a single hillbilly song. A fast and jerky coalescence of particles, atoms, molecules, galaxies, igniting stars, accreting planetoids, all accelerating into a comical thumb movie of the Encyclopedia of All, and then all finally coming to a strange and skidding halt with the sudden pulsating image of, in the moderator's nasal voice, "…the Blue Planet as seen from space, children."

The silence is accompanied by the slow brightening of lights in the planetarium, and a question from one of the sky-tilted seventh graders: "Um, who took the pictures? Did they have to wear a space suit?"

Outside in the sunshine, the sound of a now distant tailgate scuffing against the asphalt can still be heard. But the planetarium is well insulated. The important learning about the birth of the Universe continues. The education of these school children has not been harmed. Their grades in no way affected by the man outside riding an unhitched yard-waste trailer down the hill.

Right now, Nicolas is noticed only by the motorist beside him. Mouth open behind air-conditioned glass, the motorist needs consoling. Nicolas has just had his whole reality blown up; he has just been reborn, and he would most like to share this, first with the adjacent motorist. A veil over reality has been towed off by purple polka dots and it has been revealed to him that miracles do happen, if at a rate commensurate with collective expectations. Nicolas Nesbitt is certain now that he can fly. He has only been waiting for the world around him to allow this to be possible. And it is this he wants to convey to the man in the car. But their time together is brief. The motorist has locked his brakes.

Nicolas has found that he can steer by shifting his weight on the tailgate. After the next curve, he sees her—a patch of polka dots coasting in the road further down the hill. Her right foot rests on her kick brake. He listens for the sound of the clicking card in her spokes. The clicks should be at a higher frequency now because her wheels are rotating faster. He doubts

8

he will hear this above his own noise, but he listens hard anyway.

He passes her. Their encounter is short but fulfilling. As he came alongside, she gave him another bright smile. And he gave her a bright smile back, a bright smile posted atop an elongated neck that contracted as his head screwed clockwise to compensate for the fast advance of his horseless chariot beyond her purple bicycle. After another curve she is gone again. Behind him now.

As Nicolas approached her from behind there were nuances beyond the sissy bar and tassels. The tassels, the banana-seat glitter, the folded parasol in her pink macramé bike basket, even the much-anticipated frequency of the playing card in her spokes—these things merged and mated in an appreciation beyond their simple addition. He had simply never seen anything so compellingly beautiful, so invincibly vulnerable by means that remained so far overtly hidden. And so, Nicolas Nesbitt knows that in this new world he is bound to her. Bound to serve and follow her...despite having now just passed her by.

Further down the road and within his wide slalom sweeps, Nicolas knows since a while that he has no real brakes. So he considers the hedge. Or maybe it should be hedges. He thinks about this but isn't sure. Is it one hedge if, no matter how long, it remains unbroken? So then there are two hedges—one on each side of the observatory drive? But what if they wrap together at the top? Despite having been around the hedge or hedges since years, Nicolas isn't sure how many of them there are.

This hill has become as familiar to Nicolas as a pair of his own slacks, he thought. Now, the zig-zagging trailer feels like the head of a descending zipper in his very own fly, unpacking him in an intimate sort of way. Unzipping the symmetric hedge or hedges of what are they—oleanders?

Nicolas gazes at LA, the city beyond the green blur of shrubs, the hedge or hedges, which flash in front of the city like a train of moving boxcars. Plants in LA are sootier than they should be. Sootier than they would be in nature. Normally, they would get a bath each time they get a drink. In nature, that is. But these plants are irrigated. They get a drink without getting a bath. Just a drink. No bath.

The curve ahead is too sharp, and Nicolas can tell he is moving too fast to stay on the road. He observes again the oleanders. Floating his eyes across them he sees that they are all about the same size. They have probably grown up together. In their line along the road, they seem to hold hands. The image of one of them suddenly missing is disturbing and upsets the already difficult enumeration of hedges. While seemingly plentiful, like teeth in a zipper, the loss of even one of the plants could be a tragedy. He enters the curve hugging the inside shoulder.

Not a car but a large sports-utility vehicle—a black Lincoln Navigator. Such enormous vehicles populate the streets in such great numbers and at such a time when we should by now know better. The SUV is suddenly seen by Nicolas as the flagship ill of the world and also possibly a singular explanation for the Fermi Paradox. If it is simply the propensity of technology to disastrously outpace any culture appropriate for controlling it, and if this is the explanation for the surprisingly unchatty cosmos, then he sees now that his larger mission is to help try to make this blue planet be an exception. The arrival and significance of the woman of purple polka dots is now clear and Nicolas understands what he must do. Nicolas shifts his weight on the grinding tailgate, glides across the yellow dashes, and brings his trailer tongue crashing through the grill of the SUV.

The trailer tongue rams through the radiator and crashes to a halt against the engine block. Twigs, dirt, a few leaves and Nicolas's box slide forward on the trailer floor. The trailer frame begins to buckle and the air in the tires compress before the road pushes back and the wheels rebound toward the sky. Nicolas gazes over the row of dirty oleanders and sees the view of the city far below. Little ants everywhere. All very busy. Tracking along their networks of roads and freeways in neato contraptions they have built for themselves. Zipping around every which way, spewing out obnoxious gases while they haul their important little loads around. Though tiny, they form together an assembly that covers the landscape as aggressively as ants on a fallen caribou. The frantic mindlessness that Nicolas previously held in quiet contempt is for the moment, however, just a bunch of little ants doing their little ant things. Looking over the smoggy city, a strange admiration arrives at least for the exploded absurdity of it all: we are a very accomplished species.

Nicolas feels his momentum beginning to diverge from that of the trailer. He watches the personal possessions from his box begin flight. He sees the deck of Bigloo cards explode from the box as it collides with lunch Tupperware overhead, and he loosens his hold on the plywood sidewalls to avoid splinters later.

The vaulting trailer continues to rise. Free from his piloting duties, Nicolas is now the owner of his morning. Time is of his choosing and he chooses his experience of it to be long enough to include the slow, gentle motion of his hands as he releases his hold on the trailer side walls and brings them together in long-arm prayer posture above his head. As he floats out of the trailer and into the air, he thinks for a moment that he hears Christmas music...but then decides it is something else, perhaps the safety chain of the trailer hitch. He observes again the city below with its ants and tries to remember what it looks like at night-time. The lunch containers have left the crumbling trailer to accompany him in his flight, but the desk lamp is less resilient in adapting to the new situation, its long, worried neck accelerating forward toward decapitation at the front trailer wall. Nicolas looks back toward the landscape. He sees the thickness of the hedge, hedges, the age and color of the leaves, blossoms, and some litter. He sees a black hood, a brief pine-tree shaped air freshener under glass, and then his chest, knees and feet tops skid across the roof of the vehicle. And then he is in the air again.

Over and beyond the oleanders there is a slope of ice plant, ice plant the succulent. Nicolas observes it carefully as he can see he will be landing in it. There once was a proposal to send ice plant to Mars to prepare the Martian atmosphere for man's arrival. Some expected that the red planet covered with this blue-green plant could one day provide a place to escape from our squandered Earth. If things get bad where we are, we can just rocket over to Mars and eat ice plant.

The landing is relatively gentle as he meets the succulent downslope. It takes a long distance for him to stop. Then, face down in the waxy plants, he hears a bee. It buzzes right over to him without any delay, as if this sort of thing happens in its ice plant all the time. Or maybe from the bee's perspective, the whole thing occurred so slowly as to not seem particularly alarming.

Clicking. Fast but slowing until the bicycle parks in the oleanders. The squeak of a kickstand. The buzz of the bee, the drone of the city, and then a woman's voice. From very close. She is making word play with the words "trailer" and "park." While audibly chewing gum, she laughs. Nicolas rolls over and finds himself under the polka-dot parasol of the woman with the polka-dot dress. Not truly under, however. She is in fact higher up in the ice plant than he is, but she's making her way down to him, while she bends to collect post cards that have just fallen from the sky. Barely bends. She just suggests a reach downward and the cards electrostatically jump into her hand.

Counting two jokers, there are fifty-four post cards in the ice plant. The woman collects the whole deck in no more time than it takes her to pick her way through the waxy plants in such shoes. When she reaches Nicolas, she hands him this deck, this deck of postcards doubling as playing cards, this deck of photographed wall art. This deck of fractal poems now in his hands, precisely fifty-four, precisely in order, precisely the poems that got him   fired   this   morning.   She   smiles.

IN-LINE LOCK

WIDOWER AND FREE

Mrs. Dougherty adjusts the tie in Jimmy Pea's light blue suit. "Are you ready?" She backs away from him.

Jimmy and the camera lens stare at each other for a moment. And then the preacher erects a still-life smile and holds it while he looks at the reflection of his teeth in the lens. He turns his head in an attempt to center his gold tooth.

"It's reeling, Jimmy—so any time you want to start," says Mrs. Dougherty.

"You know," Jimmy begins with his slow voice from the South, "I think this morning I was allowed to see, even if for just a brief moment..." Jimmy's ten fingers crawl over the pockets of his blue suit. He finds what he is looking for in an inside pocket and smiles compassionately as he pulls it out. "I was allowed, this morning, to see into the soul of our planet." He begins to unwrinkle the ball of paper.

"This morning, after my meditation with God, I drank tea and opened a letter, a letter I received in the mail from a Mr. Ferguson...a Mr. Ferguson who was, up until recently, an inmate over in the Jasper Penitentiary." Jimmy examines the crinkled paper respectfully. "Mr. Ferguson watches our show...and is much closer to God than he was a few years ago." Jimmy pauses. The letter is difficult to read.

"Mr. Ferguson wrote me a poem...it's of a personal nature...but I think he would want me to share this with our viewers." Jimmy now holds the paper in his flat hands like it's an ancient papyrus scroll.

"I think Mr. Ferguson would have wanted me to read this for you...his message..." Jimmy gazes at the papyrus scroll again. "I think he would have wanted me to read his message to our wide world of worshipers, the generous hearts that fill this congregation. I think Mr. Ferguson would want to remind us all, each and every morning as we get up and get busy with our day...busy with making our coffee...while we're sipping our tea...while we're buttering our toast or toasting our bagels, while we're pouring milk over chunks of sugar pressed into entertaining animal shapes. Or while we're simply fisting the box for a better prize." Jimmy looks moved. "While we're frying bacon." The last words come out in a whisper. His face is sober as he tries to proceed.

"You see, Mr. Ferguson spent four-thousand, fifty-seven days in Jasper and just got out this week...And what I want to say is Mr. Ferguson's loving wife—April's her name—she waited four-thousand, fifty-two days for her husband. The name of the poem Mr. Ferguson sent me, the poem I'd like to read for you. It's called, 'Since five days a widower and free.'"

"Jimmy..." It's Mrs. Dougherty interrupting—and in no sort of whisper either. Jimmy throws her a quick, constipated smile to remind her that the camera audio is picking up her interruption. He continues:

"I should probably warn you all that Mr. Ferguson's poem ladled up something tremendously emotional...from deep inside me..."

"JIMMY! Let's get back to work."

Jimmy remains facing the camera. "Before I begin, let me just ask my lovely assistant for some water to clear my—"

"Jimmy, I told you, we're not live!"

"...Not live? What do you mean?"

"We're not live." Mrs. Dougherty glances unwillingly at the crumpled paper in Jimmy's hands—some Chinese take-out menu or something. "We're not live, Jimmy."

"What do you mean? Jimmy's always been live!" says Jimmy.

Jimmy's baby-blue suit sleeves have risen, and Mrs. Dougherty comes over and pulls them back down. "You can't be trusted anymore, Jimmy. I'm sorry. Since you got sick you just can't seem to stay decent on TV— that's why we have to do it this way. That's why you have to tell them. About our pause, remember?"

Jimmy laughs. "Well from what you've told me, the only part of my flock still watching me are the gore and guts ones—the ones that enjoy watching my fiery crash. Are you asking me to abandon their needs?"

Mrs. Dougherty doesn't respond.

Jimmy senses her frustration. "Okay, all right, enough horsing around." He centers himself in the chair again in front of the camera and when he begins again, despite his slow and sad posture, he begins abruptly, before Mrs. Dougherty can get out of the way of the camera. And on a different topic:

"I was only nine years old when I gave her my word. I sat...sat holding my mama's hand for several hours...and then I went into the next room to tell everybody she'd passed on, over to the Kingdom. That's what she'd been waiting for, I guess. Because, you see, you see as soon as I made that promise...as soon as I made that promise, well, I felt her hand become cold in mine."

Mrs. Dougherty closes her eyes. Jimmy notices this.

"That was the first promise I ever made, and it's been my single-minded devotion to fulfill that promise that has shaped my life and led me to the deceit and wretchedness you've witnessed."

Mrs. Dougherty, eyes still closed, begins to shake her head from side to side. Jimmy notices this too and looks pleased.

"You see, I was the youngest, and my mama didn't want me to turn out like my boozing brother or my sleep-around sister; she wanted me to go out and be the best!

"I told her, 'Yes, Mama! Yes, Mama! I'll go out and be the best! I promise!'

"But to tell you the truth, I didn't have any simple-minded idea in hell about what I'd promised my mama. The best? What did that mean? Best at what? Did that mean I had to get first place? Or would any ribbon do?"

Mrs. Dougherty gets up from her chair and comes over to squeeze Jimmy's arm forcefully. "TELL THEM, JIMMY!"

Mrs. Dougherty has raised her voice, and now Jimmy looks less willing to cooperate. His mood has changed, and now he doesn't care about the camera. He turns his knees and sighs. "Mrs. Dougherty, do you think I ever tugged anyone's chain?"

"No, Jimmy...or maybe..." She tries to say whatever will truncate his digression, but she isn't sure what that should be.

"You see, the way I see it, it's a lot like walking my dog, Farpie..."

"You have a dog?" Mrs. Dougherty asks with curiosity and irritation.

"Ah, nah. So Farpie's a big dog, and well there's only one way in which I've ever been able to get his big furry butt swinging through the air..."

"Why in the world would you want your dog's butt—" Mrs. Dougherty suddenly catches herself. Even sick, Jimmy is still able to make people immediately interested in stories that they immediately know are not true. Mrs. Dougherty struggles with her own vulnerability in this regard. Meanwhile Jimmy addresses the camera again.

"I've recently been getting a lot of criticism. I'm told that I'm very good at pulling on people's leashes. Especially some kinds of people: old ladies scared because they see the end of their lives coming at them fast; sick folks wanting to be healthy again; folks wanting God to get them a new car or a better house...or to help them get back at their ex-husband. All kinds of folks. But mostly the insatiable masses of people who would just rather pay me to think for them. Pay me to pray for them. The sad, pitiful souls that must have gotten so beaten up in grade school that they don't even think they can figure out something as simple as putting their two hands together to pray to God for themselves. They think there's going to be a god-damned test afterward if they do.

"I'm not talking about the people that had a hard time in math class. I'm talking about the people that had a hard time in art class. I'm talking about the ones scared of even finger paints. I mean the ones that when the teacher told them to draw their favorite animal, they decided their favorite animal was whichever critter from the illustrated encyclopedia book they could see the best through the tracing paper. I'm talking about the ones that somehow came to think that their wheelbase was not quite wide enough for the curves the art teacher was pitching."

Jimmy is mixing metaphors, but Mrs. Dougherty collects herself and does not point this out. Without raising her face to look at Jimmy she says calmly: "It has to be *you* to *tell* them, Jimmy. If you don't, you'll lose the little trust left in your followers. And you won't be able to even go back to your eight-pew church in Alabama."

Jimmy gets up, his eyebrows bent with thought. He seems to weigh the plausibility of Mrs. Dougherty's argument.

"Let's say you're right," he says as he opens the door and enters the hall. His words have the tone of a prelude to a more cooperative chapter. Mrs. Dougherty waits eagerly for Jimmy to return from the men's room. But Jimmy Pea has left the building.

CAKE FIRE

Why am I here? Gary Saar asks himself.

This is an insidious question that if called with desperation will find license to move in and unpack itself like a cartoon mother-in-law. And the slow approach to the checkout stand provides such desperation.

Why am I here? Gary asks again.

The difficulty with the question is that it has too much luggage—an endless stream, it seems. This prevents the question from being well posed for at least two reasons. The first is that in order to properly consider a question one has to do more than just open the door to let it in. One has also to unequivocally close the door behind it in order to adequately define what has arrived. But how is this possible for a question trailed by an endless stream of luggage?

The second reason—which Gary figures might be equivalent to the first—is that with endless luggage there is endless unpacking. How can one properly consider a question that is forever busy unpacking? And the unpacking doesn't obey physical laws—patio sets can be pulled from a small valise.

To stave off the existential chill of the checkout stand, Gary decides to consider a severely pruned version of his burning question. This amounts to closing the door at some arbitrary point, realizing that most of the luggage is still outside. Gary shall consider a restricted, local form of the question, one with just a carry-on bag allowed. Gary shall consider the question:

Why am I here—here in this store? As opposed to some other store, presumably.

Gary inspects his now tractable question. The first thing he can see is that the entire essence of the problem he initially wished to address must be in the bags that were left outside. But because there might be some incremental worth, he proceeds, proceeds to ask himself the truncated but tractable question of how come he shops here.

Gary knows that he shops at this grocery store because it has the reputation of being eco-friendly—or more "natural" than other stores. But Gary has always been too busy to find out why that is. Why is the store eco-friendly? Why is it more natural than other stores? There is a wider selection of organic foods. Is this why? Or is it because the cereal aisle is shorter and less colorful?

The truth is Gary doesn't really care. Whether the store is eco-friendly or just looks the part, his part of the bargain is the same: by simply buying his food here, he has become an eco-friendly shopper, socially responsible, somehow elevated over others.

Gary observes a small box through the grated wall of the shopping cart that is being unloaded in front of him. Under a proud "all organic" statement, the box is labeled "Bunny Bites" and includes illustrations for the illiterate, illustrations of grinning rabbits, which probably correspond with grinning cookies inside.

What reason do these rabbits have for grinning? They look tremendously happy. Likely, the little den of bunnies has traveled very far and are now ecstatic over nearing their destination, stomach acids close at hand.

Previously, Gary was an environmentalist. This happened when he donated money once to save the bobcats and the bears—wherever it was they were, the bobcats and the bears, and whatever it was they needed saving from (he hadn't read the pamphlet thoroughly). But as a result of his donation he was sent a massive amount of paper from various other environmental organizations. This made him decide that his piddly donation had caused the environment too much harm. So as an environmental measure, he has abstained from any further donations.

Gary's difficulty in taking any of this shit seriously is that he has a problem with inconsistency. Gary is a good observer and what he observes, here, is that people aren't all that different from people elsewhere. They drive AWDs instead of 4WDs. They want to eat chickens that once ran free and enjoyed a social life. They know what kind of bag they want. But they sure aren't doing without very much. In the last seconds of their history, Homo sapiens suddenly require aisles and aisles of things, must-have things produced by ripping and shoveling up various segments of the earth's surface and pressing these segments of nature into unnatural Bunny-Bite shapes, grinning rabbits that seem to understand the absurdity of their own creation better than the gods that have given them form.

Whatever a truly consistent eco-friendly approach would be about, Gary strongly feels that it involves handbaskets rather than carts. Carts simply hold too much—there is always room for more. And once one adopts the cart mentality one loses contact with the weight in the basket; the load becomes merely a pecuniary abstraction.

It is true that Gary doesn't have a family—like that poor woman in front of him. But even taking that into account, he still doesn't understand the arithmetic. A family of five should have no more than the equivalent of five baskets. Gary lives on one, albeit very full, basket; why do they need to roll up to the cashier with a shipping container?

The little girl in front of him starts to cry. She is about five years old, by what Gary observes. But she is already using the same principles of symmetry used by physicists in developing Grand Unified Theories. Arguments rooted in these principles are arriving in her head and are causing her to expect that because her brother got to maul a chocolate bar and put it back on the shelf, that she should also get to maul a chocolate bar and put it back on the shelf—she *just* wants to touch it. But her mother is not respecting the symmetry the girl expects.

Deciding what is right and what is wrong is too high level for Gary—but he can definitely form an opinion when the practice and preach don't line up. When someone says one thing and does another, Gary arrives at the conclusion that they don't have their shit straight. They don't yet know what they are talking about. Not someone he can regard as a teacher.

The family of Bunny Bites are now upright, grinning with excitement at the approaching scanner.

Really, the primary difference Gary feels in shopping in an eco-friendly store is that he can be more critical of his fellow shoppers. As a visible member of the basket clan, he is elevated—more eco-friendly than even the people who read through the bobcat bear pamphlets. And, of course, the merit of his self-imposed, one-basket limit would be lost in a normal grocery store, where it is understood that people should get as much as they can afford, and no less. People with baskets are simply too poor to fill a cart.

Perhaps Gary is in this store because he is waiting to see an example of a qualitatively different lifestyle. Yes, perhaps that is it. Perhaps his reason for being here has not yet arrived. It's pretty clear to him that the mindless development and expansion cannot go on forever—the spherical geometry of the planet simply doesn't allow that possibility—and it is clear that sooner or later the modern world with its misdirected infatuation with consumption will have to come splattering back down in a soapy mess, into some kind of configuration that is truly more sustainable. Gary can see all this mess coming, but he doesn't consider himself to be the one to lead a cultural revolution. He expects that the logical leaders for such deep change should be the people most invested in the outcome—the people with kids.

But Gary sees that people with kids are typically some of the most short-sighted. From what he can see, they are very busy people, and like most very busy people, they easily fall out of consistency with their own values. They simultaneously show enormous concern and indifference over matters that are essentially the same ones. Gary finds this peculiar. It is as if anything that makes it onto their radar screen is taken very very seriously, but when there is an offer to improve the resolution of their screen they decline. They don't want a better radar screen.

Because Gary doesn't have children, he watches the whole thing from the outside. It seems like a circus show: a mother, frantically concerned about the flame-retardant capacity of the current pajamas on her kid, but with only a dingy, myopic regard for any concern involving the next pajama size up; a father, working late into the night under a trouble light to restore a muscle V-8 before his kid's sixteenth birthday, generously sacrificing even his sofatic football time, but giving only a stingy glance beyond the glowing tines of the coming cake fire.

There is little question that such parents love their children. They typically love their children more than each other or even themselves. For they can be seen trudging from school bus stops off to cubicles and car seats and counters and cash registers—off to a variety of configurations involving the maintenance of an unnatural stance or body position throughout the day, contortions their physiology never expected to encounter. Allowing blood to pool in their calves as they hold stiff positions to focus on objects less than two feet away. Heroically pulling on neoprene wrist sleeves, and metallic back braces, and murky eye wear, patching themselves up and continuing without complaint as they, chin up, hold the course to provide for their little darlings.

"Paper or plastic?" the cashier asks.

Approaching the singularity, Gary has crawled up into his head to keep warm. The question from the cashier helps to bring him back and prepare him for the acceleration out into the parking lot.

"Whatever."

GREEN DRAGON

The skirt of Eve's polka-dot dress pumps up and down over his lap. Nicolas holds her waist in his hands and his face expresses excitement and pleasure.

But he also feels uncomfortable. To keep his feet from dragging on the ground, he must hold his knees high and spread apart in a way that is neither manly nor ladylike. What's more, the curvature in the banana seat gives his pelvis a vulgar pose. Eve pedals the bicycle up to a newspaper rack in front of a streetcar diner and stops.

They both get off. She pulls a sheathed chain out of her pink macramé basket, rotates the dials on an in-line lock. Then brings herself down to the level of her dance shoes as she turns to fasten the chain to the leg of a newspaper rack and expose, for a momentary solid angle, her beige panties.

Nicolas observes the glittering banana seat. He observes the in-line lock, the leg of the newspaper rack, and the beige panties. Especially the beige panties. These several images hold a residing overlap of last frames that merge into some kind of instructions.

The gathering motion of Eve's hem, as she stood to pedal, has collected him to a spot below her on the bicycle seat and from now on that's where he wants to be. He has found his place. From here Nicolas finds he understands the essence of the yin-yang and its embodiment of meaning. The instructions for how he should participate in the time left he has to patter around on this planet are clear, and he also understands complexity theory better than he previously did. He sees the mercy of forest fires and the health of extinctions. He sees the forces that shatter stagnation as suddenly something embraced by life. He finds the address of creation as it lives at the interface between order and chaos. He sees that it *is* the interface. He also hopes to see her beige panties again. Eve climbs up the steps to the diner entrance. Nicolas follows—a few steps behind—to watch her body climb stairs.

The diner is small—only six little tables long and barely a grill wide. It is a Red Car left over from the early LA transportation system. LA's good start toward mass transportation that was soon run over by oil and Detroit. Nicolas is behaving very crudely right now. He's overtly staring at Eve's ass. He is maybe even ready to open his mouth and flitter his tongue. But his vulgarity contracts as he approaches to sit next to her stool—in her stool, if he could, but without her having to move. He would like both he and her to sit in her stool. He sits down beside her and erects an incredibly sleazy grin. It seems his own face is rented right now.

"I know what that's like." Eve says this to him over the top of her arm. The glance that goes with it is all-knowing. All understanding of the huge transition suddenly and still going on in Nicolas's soul. He is certain she is deeply compassionate on the inside. She understands what this is like. She has just said so.

"Right there, I bet." She grinds her elbow into a sensitive spot on his outer leg. It hurts and feels wonderful when she does this. She understands exactly what has happened in his body as he sat on the banana seat painfully holding his legs above the asphalt.

The only other customers in the diner are two police officers. Their backs are turned to the window where several dark vehicles with flashing blue dash lights zip by to climb the observatory drive.

"What'll you have?" asks the grill cook.

Eve turns toward him. "Two black coffees, please."

"Anything else," asks the cook, turning toward Nicolas.

"The same, please."

"Ahm…do you mean another two coffees? So four?"

Nicolas turns finally to give the cook an uncommitted circular nod. "Yeah, please."

Eve leans down the counter to reach a paper pad attached to a flashy cardboard box. She picks up the pen attached to the box. "What's your phone number?"

This catches Nicolas by surprise. Pleasant surprise. This is going so fast. You can tell by his face. He is delighted to provide her his phone number.

She starts to write the number down but stops and gives the pen a small jerk. The box that the pen is tethered to takes a jump toward her, and then the leash sags more comfortably. She finishes writing and then leans to insert the slip into the little slot of the little box.

As Nicolas watches the slip with his phone number disappear into the little slot in the little box on the counter of the diner that once was a Red Car of the early aborted LA transportation system, his expression changes. "YOU MAY ALREADY BE A WINNER!" This is printed on the front of the box—above the slot for depositing the entry form for the "VACATION GIVEAWAY!"

"Four, right?" the cook asks as he fills the mugs. He docks the coffee pot. Then slides a tub out from a low shelf, groans, picks up the tub, and disappears into the tiny pantry with it. Meanwhile, Nicolas gazes at some skin visible through the sleeve hole of Eve's summer dress. He considers it to be part of her breast.

"He probably had to go cut potatoes," Eve says, looking over her arm at Nicolas.

Nicolas straightens his posture and then leans back on his stool. "When were you born?" he asks.

"Why?"

"Because I want to check something."

"Something what?"

"I need the date and precise time."

"Why?"

Nicolas's eyes become small and glossy, and his mouth melts into a grin: "Because I think astrology can be completely dismissed if the constellations lack a supernova at the moment of your birth." This feels seedy, and his hand instinctively comes up to check his shirt buttons.

"Very ugly," she replies approvingly.

Nicolas takes in her response, like lovely air drawn deep into his lower lungs. He feels that very soon his perfect communication with this woman will abandon words altogether. He wants to ask her about kismet, about the nature of reality and the future of the planet. He is somehow orbiting her stool.

"A garage sale," she answers.

"A garage sale? A garage sale what?" Nicolas asks.

"You were wondering where I found the bicycle."

Nicolas stares at her. Exactly. Exactly this question he was also thinking about just now. A side effect of this miracle he is experiencing is evidently an ability to grant serious attention to sundry thoughts while still feeling fully preoccupied with the patch of armpit she holds open for his view. "That's right...I was. I was thinking about your bicycle." He takes this as evidence that she can read his mind. "It reminds me of my *Green Dragon*."

"A pet?"

"No, my bicycle. The name of my bicycle."

"Your bicycle has a name?"

"Well that one did." Nicolas rubs his palms on his thighs. "The one I've got now doesn't."

"Did *Green Dragon* come with training wheels?"

"*Green Dragon* came with training wheels...but my Uncle Bob took them off before I ever rode it. I never used training wheels."

"Did you come up with that name?" Eve sets her back against the open counter in a way that makes her look strangely cornered.

Nicolas's presence in the diner grows cloudy as he leaves his stool. "No, the name was already on the chain guard when I got it." He accelerates toward her.

"Chain guard? Why do chains need to be guarded? Are they often stolen?"

"Think 'guard' like 'prison guard'."

"Oh." She raises her eyes to her left brow. "You mean they try to escape."

"They sure do." The distance between them disappears; his momentum folds the air in her dress as he meets her mass and pushes it up onto the counter. Somewhat unconscious, he has sweaty fistfuls of her polka-dot dress. Rolling condiments, falling shakers, and strewn sugar he plows her backward down the countertop.

A flat piece of metal intervenes as his lips are to land on her face. It burns and tastes like bacon. He discovers this though his eyes are closed. Eve studies his face with curiosity. The cook slowly lowers the spatula, returns it to the grill. "Officers?" he says, without turning. The police officers have already noticed the woman forcibly pushed up onto the counter.

Nicolas pulls himself off her. He lets her get down from the counter. Everybody in the diner seems to be looking now at the green ice plant streaks on his white dress shirt. His reddening lips. There is mutual awkwardness. The police are uncertain of the correct direction of duty right now. Until Eve suggests they could simply give her a ride when they leave. That would be a solution. To get her away from this crazy man with the strangely stained shirt. This man she seemed to come in with but who has also maybe just assaulted her a little bit. The officers are already done with their meals.

Before Eve joins her new escorts, she nods toward the purple bicycle on the other side of the diner window. Then to Nicolas. "You'll need the combination," she whispers. "Last four digits of your phone number. Give all the dials a full twist first."

PERSONAL HOLIDAY

Gary has four fingers hooked to four plastic bags as he shuffles across the parking lot of the grocery store. He is a third of the way across when his path is suddenly interrupted by a black sedan. Doors quickly open and two men in suits and sunglasses confront him. Mr. Saar is needed immediately at work.

Given the importance and urgency of matters often facing the federal agency for which Gary works, it is understandable that employees may be unexpectedly called into work. But in fact, today is Gary's Personal Holiday. He tells the men this, sure that they too are aware of this provision in the annual leave component of the federal benefits package, the orientation seminar for which they too, assuming they are also federal employees, must have attended. The men do not respond to this and instead usher him toward the open door of the back seat.

Gary won't get in. He needs to talk with these men more. He needs to help them appreciate the unreasonableness of their request. They need to understand that a Personal Holiday is not just some Saturday or Sunday. There is only one a year and it is, as the name suggests, personal. It must be respected. While Gary is not, himself personally, into any religion with an annual holiday that must, as a matter of god choice, be observed, this could indeed be the case for others called into work on their Personal Holiday, and he feels a strong need to instruct these two men before him on why they should respect the integrity of this self-assigned day of rest.

The men are very big and have orders. They are to bring Mr. Saar in immediately and without any delay whatsoever. By any means. At least where such expedition does not breach other instructions or protocols they have been given. Stuffing Gary and his groceries into the back seat does not, evidently, constitute a breach, and so this is what happens. This is partially explained to Gary as it happens and Gary, understanding now parts of this, still tries to insist that they just let him follow in his own car—it's right over there. And, when that fails, he requests that they at least let him walk the rest of the fucking twenty feet to his car to drop his fucking groceries in the fucking trunk. But these extra twenty feet—forty when you count the round trip—do not fall within the exemptions allowed by the orders the men have been given and soon Gary sits with his groceries in his lap and gazes out the back window of the sedan as it speeds away through the Seattle streets to the Global Information Bureau nine blocks away.

Inside the lobby of the Bureau is a heavy security check. Gary's escorts look on, now with infinite patience, as Gary loads his grocery bags onto the belt of the scanner. There are several tuna cans that spark a complete unbagging and individual rethreading of the groceries. It takes considerable time to check the security of even his modest one basket amount of groceries. The escorts stand with folded hands and relaxed face.

As Must Any Lobster

Plain View

In the building, there's an underground wing that nobody is supposed to know about. This is where GIB does its darkest business. More specifically, the Global Information Bureau (GIB) includes the division of Information Security (IS)—a powerful element of which runs a very black operation in the basement. Not the kind of basement that you get by applying some slush money to dig a secret hole while the regular building construction crew is on Christmas break. More the kind of labyrinth you get with huge untraceable funds and a schedule that excavates and then reburies the secret complex years before any paperwork even shows a federal interest in buying the lot.

Whereas upstairs there are Gibbons, down here there are Apes . Gary's two escorts, neither of whom have offered to carry even one of his grocery bags, are clearly Gibbons, not Apes . They're down here only to make a delivery. Sort of light thugs for Cornbread, Associate Director of IS. These two come with paperwork. Bona fide federal employees. Eligible for Personal Holiday. Everyone upstairs, Gary included, is a GIBbon.

Apes, Apes are different. Gary doesn't know as much about the Apes because they don't officially exist. He has heard rumors but doesn't know if all employees within the Aperture program can be considered Apes, or if it's just the ones born from a vat with enhanced data collection and combat skills. Because they are probably not paid in a traceable way. Apes may even be ineligible for Personal Holidays.

Such thoughts chatter in Gary's mind as he trots between his escorts down the long hall of the underground secret wing. If Cornbread is bringing him here, then that means Cornbread himself was summoned by the dark lord. Something's definitely up.

The doors along the hall have no numbers. They all look the same. But one of the Gibbons has a small wand that tells him which door they should go to. He finds the door and Gary is brought immediately inside.

Dark and then not. An Aperture situation room. A front wall of flat screens shows real-time surveillance streaming in from field-deployed Apes. A half dozen analysts sort through this from their…well, they seem to be stations. Or consoles. Desks. Gary isn't sure what to call

24

them. Each straddles a skimobile seat and leans slightly forward into a wrap-around cove of screens and windows. The wrap of screens could be to reduce stray light in the room, but the reason for the Ski-Doo seat is so far a pretty weird mystery. Cornbread stands stiffly in a dark corner, back turned and a cell phone raised to his ear. He turns to see Gary and says into his phone, "He's here now, sir."

In the IS director's preference, his name is in fact spelled a little more Germanically. And Gary recalls several memos where his high boss has expressed exasperation over the misspelling of his name, particularly as it has entered agency documents and internal messages. But here Director Cornbread appears to have far more serious concerns on his mind. Gary sets his grocery bags down against a dark wall.

Director Cornbread has received such extensive leadership training that even in the best of meetings Gary has had a hard time understanding what the big boss is saying. Here the situation is further complicated by the fact that Cornbread needs to speak with Gary in a room that doesn't exist and about a topic Gary shouldn't know about. Another immediate complication is that Gary hasn't yet today been online or even listened to the news. In his own defense, and if the communication channel with his boss was only a little crisper, Gary would like to clarify that on most any other day there would, in fact, not be this lapse; he would, by this hour of the day, at least have heard the news. But today happens to be his Personal—

"Heist? Why do you say heist?" Gary asks. Along with his own internal chatter, Gary was also listening to Cornbread describe the breaking scandal of the day. But the term *heist,* or even the more complete *data heist* that arrives in one of the director's sentences, is confusing to Gary. At least within the context of the story Cornbread provides. It seems more of a *leak* than a *heist.* And even if it was a *heist* the people who did it are not *terrorists* In the interest of speeding things up, Gary wishes his boss would communicate more clearly.

In time, Gary learns from his boss that Plainview has been compromised.

Oh shit.

Plainview is another project Gary is not supposed to know about. But many upstairs at the sunlit level of the Gibbons do know about Plainview because it was mostly sunlit Gibbons who coded it. A big project evidently contracted by the big black money down under. Ape money---they seem to have as much of it as they want. Plainview was supposed to provide a secure communication and transaction platform for Aperture. Some novel and ingenious software design dismembers the sensitive records into unintelligible fragments that it splays in plain view over the

World Wide Web. Some gobbledygook could be added to the whisker pixels of somebody's cat picture. Senseless words could appear in the critique of a novel draft on the site of a writing workshop at a retirement center. Only someone with the specific Plainview key could find and turn such senseless pieces into a shipping receipt, signature of consent, or diabolical plan to take over the world. In any case, there was no way to know what was hiding in Plainview without the key. Is what Gary understood.

But this morning this seems to not necessarily be true. Evidently some fragments are being assembled without a key. Complete documents are not yet the result, but it seems clear that this is coming soon with the exponentially growing number of amateur hackers around the world sharing and lacing together the delicious tidbits as they are uncovered. All of this abrupt and emergent order seeming to stem from some strange graffiti recently painted on the interior wall of a retired planetarium. Gary isn't sure he heard this last part right and has Cornbread repeat.

Cornbread repeats that Plainview has been compromised by some "poems" recently painted on the interior wall of a retired planetarium. A trial art exhibit at a historical observatory above LA. The exhibit was temporary. It wasn't supposed to have become a success. After the city's observatory had built a new, modern planetarium, the observatory's steering committee decided that as stalwarts of reuse and waste reduction, they could not just immediately tear down the old planetarium to build the better parking they all so much wanted. They had to first fail with some attempt to repurpose the structure. And after some thought by the board members, an unbrilliant astronomer turned unclever administrator at the observatory was tasked to direct the observatory's new art hall—art dome, really.

The budget Nicolas Nesbitt was given to put art in the new art dome was really not very much, but he found an elderly woman who would paint on the walls for free. If the observatory paid for the paint. Unexpectedly, Anita Fray's fractal poems splayed over the interior of the big igloo ("Bigloo") were a sudden and huge success. Gary remembers seeing a headline, maybe even part of an article about this in the paper. The "Bigloos," as they are being called, are maybe poems or maybe pictures or maybe just frames of graffiti. Gary didn't get a clean understanding on this. From what he is hearing from Cornbread now, whatever the Bigloos are, they are being used as search tags for uncovering information Plainview was supposed to keep secret.

The newspaper article Gary saw included examples of Bigloos. Gary didn't understand the poetry, but he can appreciate now that the strange word sequences are unique enough to provide, at the very least, unique keyword axes for a community collectively assembling a very large and difficult puzzle. He also understands now how inconvenient it must be for Cornbread that postcards of the poems have already been sent all over the world by thousands of tourists. He also understands now a potential design flaw of Plainview in which its secrets cannot be washed from the web without declaring their location. Of course, the most sensitive secret, exposed this morning, is that Plainview exists and that its secrets are, for the amateur puzzle-solver with free time, much more accessible than one would think. But Gary still does not understand why he is here.

Although the painter, Anita Fray, was not with any absolute assurance involved in the data heist, IS wants to immediately find Anita, talk with her, maybe apprehend her a little bit. She was up at the observatory this morning and may still be there. That's where her car is. But Cornbread has Gibbons up there, and the Gibbons can't find Anita. She may have already come down the hill in some other way.

Aside from the deployed Gibbons, there are now also twenty-two Apes in full sensor gear holding a large perimeter around the hill of the observatory. The radius of the perimeter reflects the maximum distance Fray could have traveled by car or any other available transportation between the time she gave back her utility-closet key up at the observatory and the time Aperture got its Apes in place. This is why the analysts are frantically sorting through all the data streaming in from the perimeter. But Gary still does not understand why he is here. Here on his Personal Holiday.

What follows gets awkward. Regarding why Gary is here, there is some important enlightenment Cornbread seems to not want to provide Gary. He thinks Gary needs first only to understand that he is special, not like other analysts. Gary's special talent is needed right now, and Cornbread feels that Gary can surely provide this while they both respect the important need-to-know restrictions of the operation.

But the speaker of Cornbread's phone evidently disagrees with this approach. Cornbread turns toward the wall to respond. Something seems very terse and tormented in the one-sided conversation. Whoever is on the other end of the phone makes the director speak in subordinate whispers. Cornbread puts up only a moment of resistance. Then finally turns, sighs, and reveals to Gary that Gary has long been a carefully studied lab rat.

His pattern recognition ability. Cornbread has had analysts teaching an AI filter in the Algs to sift through data and pull out the kinds of things Gary does. Mimic Gary's method, his talent. Evidently using records of Gary's behavior. Certainly, his cyberbehavior at work, and maybe his porn surfing at home. No, not maybe but certainly. Without knowing it, Gary has been invasively spied on by his own employer. Without knowing it, Gary has been training software to recognize what's wrong with this picture. Without knowing it, Gary has been training a computer to take over his job.

This is indeed a disturbing revelation for Gary. A voice, sub-audible for now, demands to know what mother-fucking right his boss has to suck his mother-fucking brain without him even mother-fucking knowing about it. But "So why am I here?" wisely steps back in before any of these more important questions can arrive in sound.

"Well, Gehr-ree…" Cornbread begins. By simply lowering his phone, the director immediately returns to his dick-self. Gary notes the pronunciation of his name at this moment. How on occasions Cornbread has similarly slandered other employee names in this subtly offensive way. How this choice of address might hail from some miffed little piece of shit in Cornbread's subconscious retaliating for the agency-wide joke on his own name. Gary has recovered from this thought midway into Cornbread's explanation that the filter—Virtual Gary, let's call it—has been screaming all morning that GAIA's signature is all over this, this Bigloo scandal. The data heist, he means.

Virtual Gary (VG) identified in the data stream a GAIA pattern, and even more specifically a pattern it attributes to the high-value GAIA terrorist Braid. But VG evidently isn't as completely helpful as Cornbread would like, and that's why they have brought MG (Meat Gary) into work on his Personal Holiday. Cornbread needs MG to help explain what the fuck VG is saying.

"We need to find Fray," Cornbread says. Because of the data heist this morning we really *really* need to find her." Cornbread wants Gary to know that the other analysts have not been able to confirm or even understand the GAIA flags coming out of Virtual Gary, and that he really *really* needs Meat Gary to look at the data now.

"Look for what?" Gary asks.

"Well, Geh-ree…" Gary hears the director's diss is a little lower now. That's because Cornbread has momentarily lowered the dark lord to his thigh. Cell phone muffled, Cornbread so much better steps on Gary. "We need you to confirm the GAIA flags the Algs have been throwing."

Gary Saar understands why he is here now. An adequate explanation has been provided. As he sits down at a console—Ski-Doo—and begins clawing through the data stream, his neural network switches to calmer coherent patterns. Without a challenging puzzle in front of him, Gary's mind is like an angry woodchipper into which he must combine his own mental yard waste to avoid the internal clanking sound of his own big brain gobbling twigs. He is at his most serene searching for painfully subtle things wrong with otherwise reasonable pictures.

Most of this session in the Ape room is dedicated to educating Gary. He figures. Gary must first see the data, the same data the Algs have seen. Then Cornbread can ask him if the GAIA flags that the Algs threw seem right.

So VG—the digital shit stolen from Gary—is already subroutines in the Algs. Great. Now Gary's supposed to, fucking can you believe it, evaluate the performance of the fucking distributed robot he has been unwittingly training to take over his fucking job!

"We need to know if GAIA is involved." Cornbread is clearly stating an order.

An exciting curiosity blossoms for Gary. Hell, it goes two ways. Gary wants to see what data VG and the Algs flagged as GAIA. Of course, you want to see the picture of someone pretending to be you. And a teacher gets to see what questions a student gets wrong.

Gary goes immediately to work and, oh my, yes there are indeed very *very* many things wrong with these very many pictures. Even in the bowels of this black basement wing that doesn't exist, even with his boss wringing his one free hand as he paces around behind him, into the puzzle Gary is lost.

Aperture is monitoring all traffic through the periphery that has been set up. By design, Aperture can immediately access public and private surveillance data. Given a situation such as this one, the Algs—a name used to indicate the distributed computing system supporting Aperture—examines all the surveillance data available to determine the smallest perimeter that must still contain the target. This is no easy feat, as the surveillance data must be instantly pulled from sources ranging from security cameras and social-media posts to spy satellites and the illegal remote operation of people's personal electronic devices. The Algs know about this data. The Algs know about Apes available for field deployment. The Algs know about the target's last sighting and how fast the target could be moving. The Algs combine this information into an evolving optimization problem to determine the most efficient perimeter around the target.

In this case, the Algs were asked pretty late, and so the perimeter it can set up is not that small. But the Algs are coded with a conservation-of-people rule, from which it is expected as a hard constraint that Anita Fray cannot simply disappear; She is still inside the perimeter until they see her come through it. And when they do see her come through it, then the Algs will immediately set up a new, smaller perimeter. When enough Apes are in position, they will then boa-constrict down on the target. The cybernetic design of the Apes allows not only this capture ability but also, as an option, the assassination of the target once they find it.

This room of analysts is here to help the Apes. Help them boa down on their target. The analysts monitor flags and tags raised by the Algs; they monitor the surveillance images appearing on the giant wall in front of them. Everyone is carefully pounce-poised on their Ski-Doo seat, monitoring the perimeter for any sign of Anita Fray.

Evidently, Virtual Gary has been screaming GAIA since the Bigloo opened weeks ago. VG has been claiming the GAIA pattern is all over this. In particular, the high-value GAIAn terrorist Eve Braid is implicated.

Gary understands now that VG, for whom he now holds conflicting feelings of competition and compassion, was not taken seriously. The analysts were getting GAIA flags from VG since the Bigloo opened but were ignoring them. Considering that GAIA is regarded as a top threat by the agency, this is surprising. But perhaps initially understandable, because the flags make no fucking sense.

Gary understands why he is here. He is here to find the fucking sense where the other analysts cannot. The fact that whatever fucking sense there is to be found is modeled after his own brain should give him an advantage. Why is the GAIA pattern being flagged in the data?

Gary leans into the Ski-Doo fairing. In minutes it is clear why. There are not just many weird and freaky things going on in this data, but weird and freaky things of a very GAIA sort. Global Awareness In Action—GAIA. Its signature is so loud, and yet the other analysts swing through the data forest without hearing it somehow.

"That, for example," Gary says to the director, magnifying a satellite image up to a grainy resolution, and then leaning aside so the director can see better into the fairing. "You say that's an accident?" He nods negatively while showing a smirk of admiration.

Cornbread pulls the phone down to his shoulder, steps over and shows a face of irritation toward Gary. "We've already looked into that, Gary. Yes, even our GIB officers can be involved in a car accident. Right now, what we really need you to look at is—"

"Accident? Heh heh." Gary turns and descends back into the data.

Cornbread looks even more irritated as he considers his phone as well as the necessity that he take Gary seriously. The director is ultimately responsible for having ignored the GAIA flags so far, and that must be very embarrassing. He lowers his head toward the light between screens and Gary. "So Gehr-ree...are you implying GAIA may have been involved with this vehicle accident?"

Gary doesn't turn. "Oh, yeah. Definitely."

"Let's be clear. You're saying you are sure?" Cornbread knows when to pin people down. Useful later.

"Yeah. Braid all over it. She might as well have left her card on the windshield."

"She. Let's be clear. You just said 'she.' Correct?"

Gary nods without looking up.

"You know the Braid to be a she?"

"No, not *know*, really." Gary slides up two images and searches the database for a marker he sees. "Just sort of know." He enters another marker. "The pattern seems feminine to me." Slide, expand. "Maybe girly."

Cornbread raises the phone muted against his leg. Not to talk through it but evidently so that Gary can be heard through it. "You're claiming, Mr. Saar, that a girly pattern somehow rolled a trailer down a hill to disable our team driving up to apprehend Fray?"

"Ah, nah, I wouldn't necessarily say that."

"Well, Gehr-ree, what *are* you saying?"

That pronunciation of his name is so annoying. Gary finally turns from the screen to his boss. "I'm not saying anything...or I don't know what I'm saying."

"Now just a moment ago you said, and confirmed, that you were sure this was GAIA. And that 'Braid was all over it.' Did you not?"

This is unpleasant now. Gary just wants to get back to looking at pictures. "Yeah, but...all I'm saying is...just look." He enlarges the satellite image of the accident again. "Come on! Look at it." He laughs. "You got a trailer sticking out of the engine of one of your trucks! That doesn't look GAIA freaky to you? Not just sticking out; the trailer bed's flopped over the windshield like a sleep mask. It's freaky."

Cornbread is trying to understand. At least for the sake of the phone he holds, he strives to show patience for the muddled thoughts of his junior analyst. "Are you saying that 'free-key' is GAIA's signature? That's your assessment as a GIB analy—" Cornbread is interrupted by his phone. He listens. "Yes, sir." He puts the phone down to his leg, breathes, and leans again between Gary and his fairing. "Okay, Gehr-ree...what else can you find that looks free-key?"

Gary nods. Almost chuckles. Then gets back to work.

While Gary is surfing through the pictures—ones on the wall now, ones from an hour ago, ones from archival—while he is sent every which way and that, time traveling as he scrambles to raise and lower windows—he overhears the other analysts as they confer with one another and bring to Cornbread's attention things they think he might find important. It seems Gary's colleagues don't so much surf through the pictures on their own but rely on the leads being supplied by the Algs. The Algs in fact are the collected electronic wisdom supporting Aperture, so they may be justified in focusing their attention on only the data the Algs have flagged, and perhaps the subset of that makes some fucking sense. Still, Gary reaches a point where he needs to lean over and break into their conference. "Is that…?" Gary points to an image off to the left lower corner of the wall that has just appeared.

The image is a street view of a squad car passing through the Ape perimeter. In fact, there are a few frames, though largely redundant. Just an unremarkable squad car passing by. Unremarkable except for the polka-dot parasol open in the back seat. The car window is up, of course, and so it could be easy to miss the pale dots under glass. Even the umbrella is not certain but instead only suggested by the small part visible. The frames taken together seem dreamy and unhurried. The police car quietly drives its dots through the Ape perimeter.

The analysts are discussing something among themselves and mostly ignore Gary's question. He has to ask again before one of them nods up to confirm that yes, this is a GAIA flagged image. The Algs just dropped it on the screen now.

Gary understands that it is pointless to try to get anyone else in this situation room to understand why the image is so freaky. So GAIA freaky. He could describe how he feels about seeing the open umbrella in the back of a squad car. What this image does to him internally. He could insist that it is really *really* weird. And as fast as he would be saying this, one of the other analysts would run an instant data search and present evidence for the statistical abundance of umbrellas open inside of vehicles. Then Gary could demand more nuances of those statistics, showing that most examples were inside school buses, not squad cars. And even if Gary then spent more time to try to get them to understand that the weirdness he wants them to see is really the colocation of umbrella and squad car. And maybe the purple polka dots. Not just an open umbrella in a vehicle. But Gary knows he would be wasting his time because (a) he just now partially tried the above to little avail, and (b) an essential problem with the people in this room is that they are unwilling to see what he is pointing at. To show that they are hardcore analysts trained in rigorous pattern recognition methods, they are much more willing to decide that Gary and his methods are ridiculous.

Of course, this work environment makes Gary, when he has time to think of it, envision various ways in which his coworkers could come to harm in some freaky accident they never saw coming. Some demise they refuse to believe possible even from their hospital bed. But Gary is distracted now, and so these fantasies are light for the moment.

Distracted by the larger and more important consideration: a computer has just assimilated his one singular talent at the agency. A computer has flagged the same freaky image that he would have flagged. Gary wants to go home now. He demonstrates his shared concern over the freaky image by simply enlarging it a bit for all to see, but otherwise leaves it in the same corner of the wall.

Cornbread has retreated to a back office with his phone when Gary sees another image appear in the ignored GAIA-freaky section of the front wall. He enlarges this one similarly, and similarly he must immediately agree with VG, with the Algs. Yeah, GAIA freaky. A man on a groovy little bicycle, stand-cranking the pedals as he too passes through the Ape perimeter. The man's face seems newly rugged. There are strange green streaks all over his dress shirt. And what happened to his lips? Next to this image, a third pops up. Of a truck driving through a northern point of the perimeter. The truck is covered with stickers. Even over the windshield. How can someone drive like that?

Gary does make a further attempt now to call alarm. He doubles the size of the three images and moves the group to the center of the wall.

"Your filter, yeah," says one of the analysts, tersely as he reduces Gary's images and returns them to the corner. He and the other real analysts are real busy right now. They are all in hot pursuit of a red truck. Red truck, red truck. Fray's car is still up at the observatory and the observatory employee who hired her, Nicolas Nesbitt, his truck, red truck, is gone. Fray must be with him. Red truck, red truck. It hasn't come through the Ape perimeter yet. It has sort of just disappeared in the satellite images. Red truck, red truck. They can't find it.

SEA BOOGER

Nicolas Nesbitt is delusional. Always has been. At least when it comes to love. Because he makes up and then firmly holds exotic excuses to explain to himself why he is still a virgin. Why it has been that every girl he starts to kind of like in that way never starts to kind of like him in that way back.

The simple explanation he avoids is that he is not sexually attractive. Maybe to anybody. His chest is squirrel-like, his hands too big for the tiny wrists. His feet are similarly disproportionate, with squeaky little calves that support overlength femurs. A thin man with hips unnecessarily wide. Self-chapped lips caused by incessant licking. Fingernails and square teeth often nibbling on face flakes, cuticle, and skin burrs. He can behave like a cleaner fish in public places. And remain completely unaware of the cost of this to his sex appeal.

Which is to say that right now he sits on his toilet and can stare right

33

through the open door into his living room. He does not share this bathroom with anyone and can sit here with the door open for as long as he wants. From here he admires the groovy bicycle tilted on its kickstand in the middle of his living room. He is probably done with his specific business here in the bathroom, and yet long he lingers. The bicycle is simply so beautiful: the longhorn handlebars tipped in dazzle tassels; the frisky sissybar sticking up like a cat tail above the banana seat that grins Cheshire. The pedals are posed in a kick-brake posture, and the rug under is carefully and deliberately crumpled to suggest a sideways slide of the back wheel has occurred.

The news has been on in the background, but Nicolas was not really listening until just now, this breaking news on the scandalized Reverend Jimmy Pea. Nicolas has been a follower of Jimmy, though he would not be able to articulate why. Of course, in any literal sense most of what Jimmy claims is verifiably false. But Nicolas finds that he can enjoy Jimmy's sermons when he takes them as some kind of Aesop's fable. Where the claims are deliberately preposterous such that one must assemble on their own any moral to the story. Most preachers also provide this unfoundedness in their storytelling, but Jimmy is so over-the-top that he might be somewhere else than them, than most preachers. Jimmy is very likely somewhere else. It's probably this that appeals to Nicolas.

And now the news is that Jimmy has abandoned television, abandoned his church, abandoned god. The news is also that Jimmy seems to have gone crazy. And that he has just released a new sermon, over the world-wide web this time, and it has gone viral.

Nicolas has been waiting in his apartment, waiting for the next sign, and now this could be it! He claws at the virgin toilet paper roll like he's doing so with a fishing gaff from six feet away. He pulls up his pants as he jogs out to his computer in the kitchen, turning off the radio along the way. In a moment, Jimmy's new sermon is piped from a laptop to the speakers that sit on top of the kitchen refrigerator:

Evidently the Reverend Pea is peeing. The video shows just a still ceiling and part of the top of a stall partition. Maybe from the camera of a phone that currently rests on a toilet paper dispenser.

You know, he unzips, *when I was young...when I was young...uoh,* zip...when *I was young I could piss like a dolphin beak going through a pool ring!* Unmistakable crack of a fallen toilet seat. Then the sound of uncinching and heavy settlement. *But now...now I can't even keep my forking dribbles off the seat and floor. I'm a sit-down pee-er now.* The sound of a muffled tinkling. *Life stage transition I wasn't happy about.*

So let me just start, start by saying...well I've got an admission to *make...and I should just...well I should just put the string on the tooth and rip off the Band Aid right away. Folks, I've got an admission to make...*The reverend's voice is both husky and ceramic...*I'm in the men's room of a truck stop.*

...and I've left God.

Nicolas's jaw is slack as he stares at the freezer door of his refrigerator. This is a big development. The size of the mega church Jimmy just blew up makes any message he has now immediately spiritual.

...Suppose I'll kick and scream, the reverend chuckles, *kick and scream like hell when the next step comes. I'm sure not going to like it. But some day it's going to come.* The reverend swallows, *and it will be all too soon enough...diapers, I mean.*

With the reverend's last word, Nicolas raises his stare several inches to the adult diaper that lies between the speakers on top of the refrigerator. In a flash he is suddenly aware of the two years that have passed since he received it as a birthday prank from a coworker. In a flash he is aware that he has not moved the diaper from this initial spot where he first set it down when arriving home. In a flash he is aware that the absence of any guests in his home in two years may be the cause of his long complacency with having a diaper atop his refrigerator. He is aware that these words from the reverend coming to him right here right now must be pointing to a coming participation of this object in his life. The diapers, he means.

Jimmy is continuing and Nicolas is listening, but suddenly there are one, and then two important distractions. Nicolas realizes that these distractions may in fact be alternative possibilities for the important sign he has been waiting for, the call he needs to go forth, the signal from Eve suggesting his next action, and with this hopefully a description of when he can expect to see her again. Just as the phone in his pocket begins to ring, the intercom buzzer beside the refrigerator also goes off. Nicolas continues to listen to Jimmy but also opens the phone, picks up the intercom receiver, puts each to an ear: "Hello?"

Reverend Pea, meanwhile, begins painting a deeply meaningful description of a molting lobster. In Nicolas's right ear there are GIB officers who want to come up and talk with him. In his left ear is Jeremy from Vacation Giveaways. Jeremy is asking, very friendly bubbles in his mouth, to speak with Ms. Penny Market!!! Penny is a winner and he is calling to congratulate her!!!

Nicolas is aware that an apartment intercom distorts even the most cheerful voices to sound submerged and robotic, but he does his best: "I'm sorry but I'm very ill at the moment. Housebound ill. I'm not receiving visitors right now." Nicolas lowers the intercom receiver from his right ear and returns it to the wall. "You have the wrong number. But thanks." He flips shut his phone.

...and so what do you suppose would happen if that lobster didn't want to climb out of that old shell? What if he refused...said no...no way...won't no way...I'm not going around like an undersea booger. I don't care if it's just while I'm waiting for my new shell. I refuse. What if he says that?

Nicolas hears the intercom buzzer again.

And he'd have a point. The lobster's shell is also his skeleton. That's what holds him up. Lobster can't stand straight without it.

A long, sustained buzz now.

Without a shell, that old lobster, well, he's just a helpless sea booger. In the bathroom with Jimmy, there's another man's voice suddenly. A brief misunderstanding about who Jimmy is talking to. The voice seems to leave the bathroom. *Now I know noobody wants to be a sea booger. Sea booger's something we try hard not to be.*

There is knocking on Nicolas's apartment door. Jimmy's voice lowers; he speaks more slowly:

But sometimes...sometimes you jess got to be a booger. Can't grow if you don't. It's like when you grow, and your clothes get too small. Just the way it is. Doesn't matter how much you like those old clothes. How familiar and cozy they are. Can't highwater your way through the rest of your life blowing buttons. Gotta get new ones. New clothes. New shell.

There is now pounding at the door. The diaper has been here on the refrigerator for so long because Nicolas has never been sure what to do with it. Until now. "Just a minute," he yells. He changes into the diaper.

The chain is on the door. So when Nicolas opens it, he can see in hyper portrait two men in suits. Though their vision into the apartment is tall and narrow they can see quite enough of a naked man in diapers. They have questions for Mr. Nesbitt. But Mr. Nesbitt is not feeling well. Not feeling well at all. He insists that he must be left alone right now. Not feeling well. But the two men in suits insist that they want to talk to him, they need to talk to him, they have the right to talk to him. They must come in and talk to him.

The diaper is not working. Or at least its role in a larger plan has not yet been revealed. "Okay, I understand. Just give me a moment to clean up and put something on." Nicolas shuts the door...but a little more completely than would be necessary if he were just releasing the chain to open the door. Immediately, the men are again knocking. Pounding. They want to wait inside while he changes. They insist that they must wait inside while he changes. They have the right to wait inside while he changes.

Sound travels four times faster in water than in air. That's why you can't tell which direction a sound is coming from when you're underwater. Your ears can't triangulate it very well.

Nicolas has known since graduate school the relative speeds of sound in air and water. And yet Jimmy knows how to wield this information. How to make it every-day relevant. How to weaponize it. Gary hears now the sound of his apartment door splintering.

Now when you finally get your bigger shell, I know y'all will like this part, when you finally get your bigger shell, your ears will be farther apart...your ears will be farther apart, and you'll, well, you'll be triangulating better than ever!

Nicolas slides the chair over, climbs atop the table...

Even underwater!

...and springs from the kitchen window.

* * *

The sound of his own splash reverberates off the pool walls, and so he stays awhile to listen, releasing his knees, relaxing his shoulders, unfolding the canon-ball posture he formed as he leaped from his third-story apartment window, re-securing his soggy diaper.

He comes to the side of the pool, climbs up the ladder. Squeezing water from his loin he looks through and beyond the fence surrounding the pool. He sees then his own truck pull into its parking space. It is still covered with stickers and appears to drive itself.

And there is a motorcycle in the bed of the truck. Nicolas knows he should take five steps over now to install his feet into two rubber boots he can see beside the pool shed. Holding his diaper, he waddles out the gate and moves under the parking awning.

Anita. She steps down and thanks him for the truck again—to get her paint and ladders back home this time—and hands him back the spare key she loaned him. She claims she could hardly see through all the stickers over the windows. She claims he should not put bumper stickers on his windshield. She claims they belong on the bumper. She claims that there could maybe be window stickers that are see-through he could use instead. She asks nothing about Nicolas's wet diaper.

Nicolas is meanwhile fixated on the motorcycle. Boosting himself up on one of the giant truck tires he leans into the bed to touch it. Pet it. "Is this for me?"

"Oh!" She laughs. "You wouldn't be able to even start it. I'm afraid the compression release is broken. XR 500. Need quite a kick. No, it's to get me home."

Nicolas turns to look up at his apartment window—where it would

37

be if he could see it through the parking awning—then back, his diaper sliding down a bit. "Can I go with you?" He stares at Anita.

It is the point of dusk when the lights in parking lots turn on. And as this happens, Nicolas catches a face between the shadowed and lit. A brief face of Anita he has not seen before. He seems to understand her better now. Anita has climbed onto the motorcycle seat. And then up onto the kick starter. "Sure. If you want." As her kick comes down, the engine comes alive. Her chin and fingers nod at the second helmet strapped on the tail. Nicolas climbs up and onto the rear of the seat, positions his diaper, boots, and helmet, and the old lady releases the clutch and launches the monster enduro off the tail gate.

PERFECT PART

Late in a day that Gary should not even fucking be at work, he waddles with groceries down a GIB administrative hall. Sent to go find some fucking taxi voucher so he can get back to his fucking car. They can send two Gibbons and six-cylinders to go get him, but they won't let him call his own taxi to get the fuck back. Instead he is sent off to go find some fucking obscure cubicle so he can waste a bunch of fucking time with some fucking administrator so he can get a fucking voucher to wait extra long for some fucking GIB-approved taxi, all so GIB can save a couple of fucking dollars. Of course, he could just pay the taxi himself and not worry about reimbursement, and it's only a mile back to his car. But his outrage at this situation, Personal Holiday and all, would be just too loud. Matter of principle.

And then, when he finally finds the right cubicle, it doesn't help that this Patricia Concept he is supposed to talk to is presently on the phone. Talking with someone else.

At least it doesn't help initially. But then as he stands with his groceries in the small space behind her chair, her face still turned toward her screen, he notices that this woman has the most perfect part in her hair that he has ever seen. A stupendously perfect part right down the center. Jet black symmetry. If the number of hairs on her head is an even number, he is certain that exactly half fall to each side of her head. Gary's net for what's wrong with a picture rarely fishes up a detail of perfection and beauty, but this does happen sometimes, and he welcomes it. His filter most often finds the ugly and awkward. But like samba lyrics, seeming opposites can live as neighbors where measurements are made with circular rulers.

He leans forward a bit to follow the part toward her forehead. He can't step much closer to the back of her chair on account of the grocery bags in his hands, but his neck takes it from there, cautiously elongating like a church snake through the air above her head, his tongue loaded behind his cinched lips as his cold, black eyes inspect the follicles of impossibility. And then—holy moly!

His inspection of her hair is abruptly interrupted by the appearance of her cleavage. The snap of his refocus brings a little recoil that starts at his eyebrows and propagates backward to dissipate in his own follicles. Large breasts in the white blouse of a petit frame are always noteworthy, but this is preternatural. Created somewhere else.

He is sort of spelunking in this natural wonder, quite content now to listen to her busy on the phone with somebody's travel reservations, his grocery bags craned backward to counterbalance the extension of his snake face...when he suddenly notices she can see him. Been watching him the whole time. There he is right there, reflected in her computer screen. Patricia Concept provides a date and airport code to her phone as she watches the snake head retreat from her air space.

RANCHO MIRAGE

Nicolas has forgotten about everything else. Or at least there have been no extended thoughts in his head as the warm Southern Californian air blasts over him, the engine wrestles higher gears, and the gritty pavement passes below like an upturned belt sander. Aromatic particles and pollution sift through both nostrils as he, for the first time in his life, comprehends the happiness of a dog in the back of a pickup truck. He has never been on a motorcycle before. And riding bitch isn't so bad.

Cars try to catch up for a second look at the man wearing a diaper and rubber boots, but the motorcycle glides past in the HOV lane. If not for the long, flapping ends, Anita's scarf, now x-wrapped around his torso, might look like ammunition belts over bare skin.

Unemployed, in diapers, and so excited to be alive, Nicolas has been born again, and he plans to ride this extended baptism wherever it takes him: presently, to a windmill. Anita yells over her shoulder. "Have you seen this, Nicky? This is what I wanted to show you."

She pulls the bike off the highway. It grumbles about the lower gears it is handed as she pulls down a dirt road, and then off the dirt road and out over the desert. They ride over a hill and leave the freeway lights behind them. In front of them, and soon all around them, towering over them—three generations of windmills. Anita turns off the motorcycle and glides to a halt. It's suddenly quiet.

Nicolas has seen the windmills—turbines—many times from the highway, but he has never seen them like this. A little motorcycle in the middle of them. The youngest so tall and milk-fed. The oldest so rusted and retired. Some fully stopped. Metallic sunflowers spreading over the shallow horizons lit by the young lunar crescent overhead. Turbines milling wind into loaves of electricity. Or perhaps powered like a propeller and pulling the planet toward a more thought-out trajectory. A better path. Somehow finding a hold on the tenuous interplanetary space. Steering our planet toward a better…

"Dear…Dear, I can't get off the motorbike until after you do."

SNOW DOGS

The waitress pulls the fur down to her brow, pushes through the door, and bends down to the leashes of her snow dogs. She looks back to Gary at the bar counter and makes it very clear to him that she is headed North and is taking his credit card and their unsettled account with her. He will have to wait at the bar until she returns in the Spring.

Factually, the waitress heads not North but just into the kitchen. Where she stays for a long time. Customer Gary insulted the waitress. Customer Gary must now wait.

The waitress—bartender, really—did not react to his comment as he had expected she would. She did not receive it very well. She does not at all understand that he is trying to help her. Gary is a regular customer here at the Faraday Cage, as are many from the GIB building three blocks away. He thought that the bartender—Dawn, is her name—would appreciate the notes he has compiled on her waitressing. The suggested steps she might take to increase her performance as well as the tips she receives.

Instead, she has left him alone during unhappy hour. Nobody else at the bar yet. His phone won't work in here, of course. Only a couple of old spooks at a table together. Swapping old spy stories, or whatever they do this early in the late afternoon.

A few men in suits come through the entrance and through the bar, through the few steps needed to get to the stairs leading up to the Gentlemen's Club. That club up in the penthouse—or whatever you call the top floor of this short building. Invitation only. And you have to walk through a scanner hall. Gary has heard that a whole lot of whoring goes on up there. But from what he has watched, that's very unlikely. There don't seem to be many women that go in or out. He has heard that card games go on up there. More likely. He has heard that the suggestion of whoring going on up there is just a front for poker gambling going on up there. Gary would have, on his own, guessed the reverse more possible.

A more parsimonious theory that Gary has just now put together, waiting for his credit card to return from the North, is that the card game and whoring going on up there are a front for clandestine business meetings going on up there. The men going up to the Gentlemen's Club wear expensive power suits. Up there is where they meet for their power meetings. Seems this is even an offsite location where black-op GIB managers meet up with their powerful clients. Gary has seen Cornbread go up there a few times. Up to the Gentlemen's Club. But because that piece of shit Cornbread could quite believably be up there for any combination of whoring, gambling, and organized crime, this data point is not very constraining on Gary's guesses.

More helpful testimony comes from Doug. "Dog," as the Australian says it. Dog has recently become a regular at the Faraday Cage. A regular upstairs at the poker table. He gets free drinks down here before going up there to lose his money.

It took Dog time to get an invitation to the Gentlemen's Club. For weeks he drank on his own dime down here, broadcasting to Gary, the bartender, anyone, the details of his personal fortune and prostate cancer. And his gambling addiction. How he has been left with so little time to lose so much. Now he gets an invitation upstairs pretty regularly. When Gary comes in, Dog is usually already here drinking. Later, Dog heads upstairs. You can hear him set off the scanner alarm each time. He carries a radioactive suppository up his ass and has explained the details of this to the security guards. More than they wanted to hear.

DIVING CLOWNS

The motorcycle arrives at the gate, the gate of the gated community. It is evening.

"It's me, Mom," Nicolas speaks into the intercom.

"Excuse me?"

"Mom, it's me, Nicolas."

"What was that?"

Anita turns the engine off.

"IT'S ME, NICOLAS!"

"Nicolas?"

"Yes, it's me."

"Nicolas...where are you? Oh, why I guess you're at the gate, aren't you?"

"Yes, I'm at the gate. Mom, I got a guest with me."

"You're here, and you've brought a... well I wish you'd called first. I just brought a box in from the garage, and I was going through it, and the whole place is..."

"I'm sure it's fine, Mom."

The mother of Nicolas is irritated. She likes visitors, but not drop-ins.

After some hesitation, an electric motor engages a slow screw, and the gate begins to move out of the way. Anita kickstarts the engine—Nicolas has to get off a minute—it coughs and seems reluctant but rolls through the gate.

Immediately inside the gate is a roundabout, a traffic circle of sorts. But there is not very much about the roundabout, no traffic around the traffic circle. The purpose of the island popping from the pavement is unclear. It sits like an oversize float in the Pasadena Rose Parade. A geyser in the center splashes water far up into the desert air, as if responding to a steady train of clowns diving into a bucket. Nicolas leans forward and brings a hand over Anita's shoulder to indicate that she should take the right side of the water-fountain thing. Anita takes the right side of the water-fountain thing.

The panoramic view from the rear of a motorcycle makes Nicolas suddenly aware of the peculiar environment in which his mother lives. By several yards into the community, Nicolas is aware of the flood lit Taj Mahal towers that support the gate closing behind him; he is aware of the slopes of low flowers screaming like stadium fans on each side of him; he is aware of the spurting island in front of him. These things are designed to be looked at in a parceled fashion, a view from one car window at a time. Without the automotive blind spots to crop out the distinct motifs, it all looks suddenly huddled and ridiculous. As if everything this community wants to say is bunched together and waiving from a parade float with an undersized wheelbase.

"LEFT AT THE BOUGAINVILLEAS."

What is the indelible aspect of a tract home that always bleeds through? Facade, arches, differing roof tiles, stucco color-coats—these have done a superior job at hiding the fact that the houses are all permutations on one of three floor plans. And despite this help in building individuality, despite the half-million-dollar price tag, each house remains tragically a tract home.

Cul-de-sac...huh. This isn't right.

Perhaps it is the curvature of the streets. In a natural setting, the road curvature is causally related to land topography.

"GO BACK TO THE COCO PLUMOSO. THE FANNY PALM TREE BACK THERE ON THE LEFT."

Here it is only casually related to the small fluctuations in elevation that have been afforded by piling up desert sand. This artificiality triggers confusion in visitors—people and vehicles alike. The motorcycle, usually the vehicle with the most intimate understanding of slopes and curves, topography, is here flustered. The curves are too perfect. And too constant. All road here is curved. By fiat.

"LET'S TRY LEFT THIS TIME."

Even though none of it really needs to be.

"YEAH, THIS IS RIGHT. STRAIGHT DOWN."

Organization.

The homes are organized by the lots, which are in turn organized by the streets. So that's it. The quirky layout of the streets sets the tone for the whole community. A Manhattan grid would have been supremely possible in this desert flatland, but they make the roads curved anyway.

"THAT DRIVEWAY THERE."

Anita wants shade for the bike and parks under a tree on the front lawn.

Skirting invisible topography. Mountains out of mole hills. Nicolas removes his helmet. It is as if the layout for the whole gated community has been stenciled from a model built by connecting two different sections of Hot Wheel tracks—one curved right, one curved left, but both with the same radius of curvature.

They ring the doorbell. There is the sound of little dogs but otherwise no answer immediately.

"My mother is probably cleaning up," Nicolas explains.

"Oh, I know how that is," Anita replies. "We really should have called first."

The delay gives Nicolas time to realize that he has not really thought this through. At the windmills, should he have even mentioned to Anita the proximity of his mother's house? Will his mother survive his appearance? It has been a while since she has seen him in a diaper. Also, what about Anita? Is he not arranging to put two incompatible species together in the same terrarium? Anita, a strong liberal. Probably an environmentalist. Perhaps for her this is the most offensive location in Southern California. A society of wealthy people are gleefully turning the desert fauna and flora into Scotland. They have already pumped so much water out of the water table that the whole area has sunk a couple of feet. The desert oases are now one of the top endangered ecosystems in the country. An unfathomable celebration of waste, and his mother is an eager participant.

This and most other matters are no longer discussed between Nicolas and his mother. She could no more appreciate his occupation with the vacuous, distant cosmos than he could her preoccupation with her air-conditioned microcosm. For her astronomy is at best an interesting motif for a child's room, and he finds her perfectly arranged house decor to be more sterile and vacuous than any patch of black sky he had seen through a telescope. The books on the shelf—all hard-bound and in similar color—are merely wallpaper. Even the fanned magazines across the glass coffee table are not reading material.

43

The ornamentation of his mother's home is standard for the context. Interior decoration carefully honed until it reveals absolutely nothing about the individuality of the occupants. Anything that might reveal what the occupants eat, read, wear, or how they pass their time, is militantly stowed away. Usually in the garage. Nicolas's mother probably has little choice in the matter.

Nicolas's mother appears among barking little dogs. Nicolas expects next the bar-code scan. But his mother stalls at a first annoyance. She is looking past the people on her doorstep; she is looking at something on her lawn.

"Nicolas, what are you...? Is that a...?" She frowns and looks up and down the street to see who might be looking.

"Hi Lady! I'm Anita. What's your name?"

Mrs. Nesbitt's eyes dilate from the desert night beyond her doorway, "Well, I'm...I'm Mrs. Nesbitt..." It takes her a moment to see that she is answering someone her own age. Then she takes back her response because it sounded a bit stuffy. "Susan. I'm Susan. It's very nice to meet you, Anita."

Susan is stationary for a second. There is something incredibly disarming about Anita's smile. It falls between a pair of thick, gray braids; and below a pair of blue eyes that are so youthful that they make Susan look again to be sure she isn't seeing a child through the holes in a Halloween mask.

"Oh please, come in!" she finally replies as she turns to lead the cloud of yapping dogs into the living room.

Nicolas is the last to enter. As he shuts the front door and turns, Anita and Mrs. Nesbitt are already down on the carpet inspecting the little dogs that jump around like hot gas molecules.

"Annette and Lucie, you say?" Anita is getting acquainted. "How do you tell them apart?"

"Yes, I know it's hard," Susan replies, "but if you look closely...look, see?" she says, capturing one of the Pomeranians out of the air. You see, Lucie has a bit of white on her nose."

"And you can see that little spot when they're bouncing around like that?" Anita asks.

"Well," she says in a whisper to Anita as if she were revealing a family secret, "Annette also eats a bit more."

Nicolas stands in his diaper and rubber boots at the edge where expensive entry tiles transfer path to the upgraded living room carpet.

"Mom...?" he asks, not sure if he really wants to draw her attention. "Do you still have some of Dad's clothes?"

Susan looks up from the dogs only briefly to point in a general direction. "Just whatever's left in his golf closet. In the garage by the refrigerator."

Anita laughs. "You have a refrigerator in your garage? You got someone living in there, Susan?"

Susan laughs. "Just some *Mexicans*."

Susan's way of saying "Mexican" is strange, and Anita cocks her head with interest. It seemed like she meant to say a different word.

Nicolas finds the closet in the garage. Inside is a ready bag. A golf get-away duffel. The handles are also shoulder straps. In case you want to wear the bag like a parachute. Nicolas removes the shoes from the side pocket. Throws them back in the closet. They're too small. He unzips the duffel bag and pulls out a pair of lime-green slacks. With an overprinted plaid that looks like woolly circuitry. Sewn into the waistband is a wide, white belt with a giant rectangular buckle. It requests that the shirt he now puts on be tucked in. Yellow and pink. Argyle, sort of. Nicolas observes the little golfer on his tit and wonders if on that golfer's tit is a tinier golfer, and on that tinier golfer's tit is a...and so on.

He pulls out a cylindrically symmetric hat and places it on his head. A sign to indicate that an experiment is underway. He returns to the living room. Susan and Anita are still on the floor talking about the dogs. Nicolas notes that his mother must be unusually enthralled with her guest. Otherwise she'd be at the ice tray by now showing hospitality rather than interest. He backs into a chair and watches them suspiciously.

"So when you wash them, I bet they shrink into little..." Anita looks to Susan's face for the right word. "...tennis-sock balls?"

"Yes!" Susan laughs. "Pretty much disappear. They're real tiny under all that hair."

"So what do you do then? How do you dry them? Do you just pop them into the dryer with a cling-free sheet? What do you do?"

"The dryer?...Oh, well almost!" Susan giggles, almost. "Actually, I use a blow-dryer."

"A blow dryer!" Anita laughs like a little girl. "A blow dryer!"

"Well, yes. I don't use the hottest setting, of course."

"A blow dryer!" Anita's eyes are watering, and she is looking toward the dogs, pointing an imaginary pistol their way and seeming to imagine their puffy pelts bent over in odd fashions. Her voice becomes shrill, "And hotdog tongs?"

"Hotdog tongs?" Now Susan *clearly* doesn't understand what this is about. And she would dismiss any further attempt to understand if Anita left her this option. But Anita continues to laugh, bent over the little dogs with her imaginary hot-dog tongs and blow dryer as they jump around and seem to share her amusement.

Blow-dryer...and hotdog tongs...Mrs. Nesbitt can see that even her dogs understand. She experiments with invisible tongs in one hand and a blow-dryer in the other, gesturing toward the dogs in a manner discreetly mimicking Anita's motions.

Humor assembles in Susan's face like a brass band for a centennial in the park. "Oh, pfff, you mean..." A sound check and in a moment she begins to laugh. She laughs. And then she laughs because she is laughing. Her torso even dips, but her eyes still look around apprehensively at the commotion. She isn't playing a concert yet, but most of the band has reached the gazebo.

"Oh you wouldn't get Annette or Lucie anywhere near a hotdog anything!" Susan's tone is snobbish but strangely playful now. Nicolas doesn't recognize her and stirs in his chair.

"Actually, they won't even go near canned dog food!" She turns from the bouncing dogs to Anita. "They come from a breeder in France...and it's only the finest for these ladies!" she says proudly. She puckers her face and looks down again at the dogs between her and Anita. "*Mais non! Pas des hoat-doags! Non, mais non!*"

"*Mais non!*" Mrs. Nesbitt repeats this many times with her puckered face. Until Anette and Lucie stop bouncing and cock their heads to try to understand what they are hearing. It's very nasal. "*Mais non!*" Susan says again. The dogs become excited and open their mouths strangely at times, but they still aren't able to repeat any of it.

Nicolas sits in the chair and listens to the women. They continue to discuss the dogs for over an hour. Anita appears genuinely interested in all the little details, which Susan eagerly provides about everything from favorite chew toys to the description of that frightful time when Lucie got caught in the electric garage door. Nicolas thought he'd heard the garage-door tragedy enough times, but now the story seems new.

And then something happens. Something that Nicolas has never seen before. His mother has run out of things to say about her dogs. She moves from the floor up to the couch. There is something peaceful and settled on her face. She voluntarily changes the topic.

CRITICAL DAMPING

BIG FLIES

Supplies…Surplus…the fucking TER. Gary has three chores. He is still thinking out the optimal execution sequence, but he already knows Surplus is first. Not carrying the chair around through more of the fucking building than necessary is a precondition on any execution sequence he will devise. So even though he has not yet optimally resolved the complete execution sequence, he can already head out in that first direction now. Surplus.

As it turns out, Gary doesn't need to carry the chair at all; he herds it. Down the hall, into the elevator. Its little wheels need some lifting over the floor gap is all, and then, back to elevator wall, it nicely rides the two floors down with him.

Supposing the distance between office doors is about the same…and everybody in this building knows the offices for which this does not hold…

The elevator doors open. Two men talking with each other try to get in, while a man and a chair are trying to get out. This is of course not right; enterers should yield to exiters. The two back up and watch the man and the chair get out. Down the hall the man and the chair go. He sort of has the chair by the back of the neck, like he's taking it to the principal.

Supposing the distance between office doors is about the same, Gary's estimation gives a clear win for Supplies next. Supplies next, then the fucking TER.

The hall is blocked. "Jacob my Man" passing "Paul in the Hall," the two slowing down to a hall clog to do their ritual exchange. Body motions and lots of eye contact—this is how alliances are built. Jacob my Man and Paul in the Hall, young Flies climbing Mount IS, part of the next generation of decision makers.

Gary is surplusing this chair because he doesn't want it in his cubicle anymore. He doesn't need a guest chair. The only people that come by Gary's desk are not the type to sit down as his guest.

Gary calls them Big Flies because they have big flies. A prize "what's wrong with this picture" puzzle.

The fucking TER. The Travel Expense Report. Rejected. So after

Supplies he has to go over to E208 to figure out why. Maybe he has to add more details to his explanation for why his destination was a grocery store. And eight administrators will have to read over it before it can be approved. Then ten weeks later the $8.80 taxi reimbursement will be deposited into Gary's account. Of all the paperwork concerning this reimbursement, there will be none so helpful as to notify Gary when the deposit is made. Instead, he can waste more of his fucking time watching his bank statements.

Their flies extend from up around the navel down to a sagging spot below the groin. Why so big? Ladies unpack giant asses out of skirt zippers smaller than that. If the lengthy fly is not merely a subliminal boast, it might be a secret marker of some kind. A marker showing membership in a club. Like the toe-cleavage loafers with the tassels, or the little American flags on lapels. The details of such markers are so strict that anybody outside of the club would have a difficult time forging them. If your little lapel flag is just there on your lapel but it isn't waving in the pretend wind, well you might wind up in the wrong club; you might simply be somebody announcing their nationality. Perhaps if Gary were to look more closely, he would see an intricate coordination of these zippers—number of teeth, whether the top tooth is on the left or right—beyond simply their enormous length.

Gary's existential crisis, the "Why am I here?" question that follows him around like a fat kite, making him bump awkwardly down even the widest halls, is certainly rooted in an identity crisis. And because he has no life outside of work, his identity is closely linked to his occupation, his occupation as an information analyst for the Global Intelligence Bureau. For this reason, understanding the organization of the bureau and the mission of its inhabitants is important to him.

After he drops off the chair, Gary takes the elevator back up two floors. He finds the office supply cabinet he is looking for. He heard it has just been restocked. He opens the cabinet doors, find this to be true, and pushes his head and torso inside. Even before his eyes adjust, he claws through the trays of paper clips, the gel-tip pens, the ball points, and the clamps, and the liquid paper. The different sizes of pencil lead, all the colorful sticky pads, the cannisters of compressed air for blowing dandruff out of the keyboard. Gary feels the strange adrenaline rise and looks down to see his guilty hands full of the goodies.

He slops the stuff down in disgust. Somewhere there are marketing armies that study just how to poke and prod the human brain—how to get brains excited over fucking office supplies. How to get people to pack their desks with all kinds of shit they can't possibly need. How to make the little monkeys always want more more, more...

But…Gary then begins to pick up the items again. It's been a fact he himself has observed that most of the time the supply cabinet—at least this one he is authorized to use—is regularly understocked. People grab everything when it's there to grab. And that becomes the reason it is not there later. Gary sees the absurd feedback loop.

But that doesn't mean he can decide not to participate in it. The situation, as it is here before him, however it got here, whoever's fault, is that if he wants some office supplies, he better grab them now. Grab as much of the fucking shit as he can, because it won't be there later.

"Mr. Saar."

"…"

"Mr. Saar."

Gary is aware that, torso in the cabinet, he presents his butt to whoever in the hall now addresses him.

"Mr. Saar, could you turn around please."

Gary pulls his head out of the cabinet, arms full of supplies. He turns around. It's Cornbread's hench Gibbons again.

PENNY MARKET

Nicolas left the city in a diaper almost twenty-four hours ago. But now he has come back in golf attire. After a latent realization, with some help from Anita, that "Penny Market" is not a vacation winner, not a person, but instead a place, a small business, they sped back to drop him off at the entrance of the market.

Penny Market is evidently the name Eve signed before she stuffed that little paper slip into the little box at the little Red Car Diner. Right there in front of him, she sent him his next meet. And in a clever way such that the instructions would arrive only after a delay. If those GIB men had gotten the chance to ask about how to find her, he wouldn't have been able to give them squat. He didn't know. Or, he knew, but he didn't know he knew. Until now.

Nicolas has gone from pegs to pavement and stands now upright on the sidewalk. He faces the late afternoon sun. Anita can't stay and clogs off on the XR, the giant single cylinder pounding quarter notes on the crankshaft as she accelerates away. Nicolas waves. Almost kiss waves.

The entrance of the market has an old-time electronic-mat door. A customer in front of him stepped on the mat and the door opened. Now the door is closing. The door damper has been tuned to critical damping. Too much damping, the door takes molasses seconds to shut. Too little damping and the door overswings. Critical damping is a sweet spot between these two. A selection of parameter choices that shut the door as quickly as possible. No molasses seconds, no overswing. Exactly the way you want a door to shut behind you. The door is now shut and Nicolas steps a rubber boot onto the magic mat.

The door opens. Air-conditioned breeze. He steps through. Pauses until the door has shut behind him. He takes a few more steps, then pauses again as he comes to be more centered in the store.

Soon Nicolas is, very slowly, canoeing through the aisles. He paddles while his eyes scan the riverbanks. A can he was pretending to consider fumbles out of his hand and his horizontal gaze is flustered. But he resolves the emergency and quickly returns to lookout.

It does not appear that Eve has arrived yet. But Nicolas feels sure she will soon. The world has so well made this Penny Market the right place that right now being the right time must come along for free. He feels.

His canoeing goes on for twenty-five minutes. He is drawn almost lastly to the wall of glass doors. The cool white light. He paddles over to it.

A yogurt. Berry Nut. It falls down when he opens the glass door that now returns shut slowly, subcritically. Molasses slow. Almost wet kissingly it seals. Nicolas bends and picks up the yogurt.

Berry Nut. Can there be such a thing? A berry nut? Sounds like a *lettuce fish* or something like that. Nicolas searches the trays for other berry nuts. He intends to return the fallen bird to its family. He finds the berry nuts and snuggles Berry into a place right up front. Nicolas backs up, the door shuts again. But right before the sealing pucker, Berry falls again. Gary opens the door, bends down, picks up the yogurt, repeats the delivery. Door closes. But just before the pucker...well...

Nicolas peers down at the yogurt on the floor, then up and through the glass door. There's a whole dark universe back there, and he couldn't see it because he had his face too close to the view finder.

There she is. It was the motion that caught his eye. Though she is barely visible in the dark, she appears because of her motion. She is smirking. Sniggering. Double-elbow wheezing with laughter. She motions for him to come back. Back there with her. He should go over to the left, through the double swing door, through the stockroom and back around over to her.

In seconds Nicolas enters the cooler and sees her. He pulls the door closed behind him. She is so beautiful. And she has dyed her hair. She also seems a little younger than before. She has tattoos today.

When she has finally stopped laughing, Nicolas says, "Hi."

She says "Hi" back. And laughs more.

"So, how have you bee—"

"Come on," she says. Smoke break. She grabs her cigarettes, his hand, walks down to the end of the glass doors, opens the last one. The lower trays have been pulled out. She bends, pushes the glass door on the other side open, and steps through into the market lobby. The outside is right there. She holds a cigarette up, nods for Nicolas to follow. She steps on the exit mat.

LOUNGEY LIGHT

Gary's eyes have not yet adjusted to the low, loungey light of the Aperture situation room. Here he is again in the apeshit cave. One of the analysts is explaining to boss Cornbread an important statistical feature he has found regarding GAIA. Gary sets his office supplies against a dark wall.

"That's not what the Conservation Index means, sir. It's not, like, whether they recycle." The analyst goes on to explain to Cornbread that the Algs find that GAIA has a remarkably low Conservation Index— meaning conservation principles seem not so much to apply to them. "Sir, the Algs think GAIA can make things and people disappear."

It's clear that Cornbread was getting impatient, and this last paraphrasing has been very helpful to bring him back.

"It doesn't mean GAIA *can* make things disappear. It just means that very often it appears that way in the data. And a computer can't possibly make a distinction between these two."

Cornbread looks down at his taller subordinate. "And that's exactly why we don't let the Algs give the orders."

Gary watches the analyst's face. Confused. What does giving orders have to do with the Algs giving a high-confidence prediction of GAIA capabilities? Is this just Cornbread auto-threading as usual? The analyst, still fully confused, gives his boss a gracious bow and returns to his work.

Aperture has Nesbitt pinned down. A parking-lot surveillance camera showed him enter a small market in Pasadena. The closest two Apes were immediately sent by helicopter.

Aperture is intended to provide the wider view. Synthetic Aperture would have been a better name, in terms of accuracy of metaphor. With Aperture, a bigger lens is provided than can be carried on one man. By growing the Apes in a vat, one can control many of their parameters. They not only loyally imprint on their master like a duckling, but they operate with each other and the Algs as a single organism. Their cybernetic implants and wireless connections give them photographic memory and an elevated group awareness. They are as selfless as a nuclear explosion, and as data logging as a high-quality weather station. Aperture is a deadly system.

The Apes are designed to take their time and boa-constrict down on their prey. The most important thing is that they do not take any chances that could let the prey get away. They take their time. Once they have their perimeter up, they take their time and boa down, tighter and tighter, blow everything through their baleen. Until they suck out their man.

The center of the front wall of the Aperture situation room is split screen right now. Everybody has turned up to look at it. Cornbread nods to Gary's escorts, and they finally go. Gary counts their steps and opens his eyes to full aperture when they open the door to exit. With the light streaming in, he gets more information about the faces around him. The door closes, and he looks up to the wall with everyone else.

It's an itchy moment. Nesbitt showed up on a security cam a half hour ago. Two Apes already control a perimeter around him. One controls the back door and loading ramp of the market. Nesbitt has not come out that egress. The other started at the only other egress—the market's entrance at the front. But that Ape has already boa downed to the interior push doors where he saw Nesbitt enter the stockroom. They have him trapped back there. Nesbitt's in the stockroom, no question. The two Apes will hold these two secure egresses until backup Apes arrive.

CLOUD CONDENSATION NUCLEI

The reverend is in a gym locker room. A tentative conclusion supported by the water vapor in the air, the reverberating sounds of naked men showering together, the man partially visible behind Jimmy with a foot on the bench while fervently drying his own dick and balls.

Jimmy's phone camera sits on a shelf inside the locker closely before him. A tentative conclusion supported by the sounds of Jimmy's elbow bumping the slim metallic door as he uses a thin comb to slick back his wet hair. With the reverse camera, this sermon also serves as his personal grooming mirror.

"Food, shelter, clothing, buwullshit!" The reverend's nipples raise as he begins with the bottom button of his shirt. "A man also needs to fight. Box. I'm talking boom boom boom." His gold tooth turrets center.

"See, boxing is where I learned about honorable deception." Jimmy wags his comb warningly. "Deception, now there's a word. And, well I know it's confusing, but deception isn't always bad. Long as you and the one you're deceiving follow the same rules. The honorable in Honorable Deception has to do with honoring the rules. First round, I get in the ring, Private Right comes up and then I slam down with Colonel Left. Know what I mean? Deception is the beauty of boxing.

"But say now, I, I come through the gym door, slip my watch onto the other wrist, chat up guys I come across as I limp to the locker room. I start unlacing my banker shoes, listening to what's going on, taking my time. And then I'm in my undershorts asking around the locker room for Bim. Anybody seen Bim?

"And when I find a sympathetic ear---and I don't mean somebody who's seen Bim; I'm fulling supposing there's not a Bim in the gym---and when I find a sympathetic ear, I explain that Bim's supposed to meet me here for a rematch. A rematch. He promised to give me a chance to win my five hundred bucks back.

"And then this sympathetic ear wants to know more. More from this middle-aged man struggling to balance on one leg as he changes into his gym shorts. This old fart will give you five hundred bucks to beat him up?

"Funny thing about deep, angry, insecurity is that it will make a man underestimate his opponent. Fall for the private and not see the colonel coming. That sort of thing."

Jimmy has dressed and is packing his gym bag. "Point I want to make, is that all deception is not the same. Only some of it is honorable." His face is close as his hand reaches into the locker shelf. "Hoh!" He recoils gleefully with a small stack of bills, Franklin visible, slides it into his shirt pocket. He reaches back into the locker, retrieves the phone camera. He slides it, too, into his shirt pocket, adjusts the lens clearance above his pocket brow, turns around. "What I really want to talk about...why we're...why we're in here, I mean...is this water in the air. See it? Steam, vapor, whatever it's called. Air's holding too much of it. That vapor is just looking for something to coalesce onto. Finds the mirror, see it over there? All those droplets dripping down. Finds the ceiling. See it up there?

"But what if you don't have a mirror or a ceiling? Like in the atmosphere. Well then when the vapor gets like that it's looking for Cloud Condensation Nuclei. CCN. Some little aerosol tiny doodad for the water to grab onto. Make a droplet of rain. Lot's a places across the world you got a whole bunch of water just hanging there ready to rain down. Only thing missing is CCN." The reverend's breath sets a slow tidal motion to his shirt pocket and therefore the picture frames. "Yea-uh."

"Now how about that graffiti everybody's talking about? The fractal poetry assembling meaning on multiple scales all at the same time. Paisleys within paisleys." Jimmy pauses to capture frames of soapy men in the shower. "My new bible. For the moment at least."

"The Bigloos are CCN, folks. Cloud Condensation Nuclei. We see right now a whole world of people trying to figure out what the Bigloos are about. The Bigloos are CCN. That's the holy message I have for you this sermon."

The reverend is not visible in this part of the sermon. His camera is left-tit forward toward the men slowly shuffling to escape him. As he strolls down the locker aisles and rolls out his sermon on CCN, his towel slowly coils as he approaches each new bare ass. It's a pretend snap, but the reverend makes sure towel tip touches cheek. The correspondence with each victim is surprisingly gracious.

"The Bigloos are CCN, yessiree. Onto which at the moment is coalescing only a bunch of deep dark classified secrets." Jimmy lowers the tip of his towel into a puddle beside a locker bench. "We'll do much better than that…" He stirs his arm cyclonically until his towel is again torsionally cocked, then continues his stroll down a new locker aisle. "…much better, yessiree."

"But even if that's not for you---" Snap! "---hoa, hey, how you doing? Let's say God, well he just didn't make you a very curious person. You honestly don't really give a hoot about the nefarious powers positioning themselves to rule the world. That sort of stuff." Snap! "Let's say. Well what I have to tell you right here is that you are really missing out on something pretty fun and special." Snap! "If you aren't following the Bigloos, you're cheating yourself. Better entertainment you will not find out there on the world-wide internet."

The reverend reaches the end of the locker aisle. He has a naked man cornered. The man is separated from his duffel bag of clothes the reverend has just kicked distant. "Now I'm not saying you gotta follow ALL the Bigloos…ALL the incredible cumulonimbus clouds forming right now from these magical CCN. Forming all across God's green acre." Jimmy's crank arm tightens the coil until the twisted towel hangs half its length. "Not saying you gotta do that." SNAP! "You can just pick one." SNAP!! "Maybe two." SNAP! SNAP!! "Just pick one or two of your favorite Bigloos and, well---" SNAP!!!---just see where they go. Hardly take much of your time at all." Jimmy lowers his towel and lets the camera absorb the naked man as he desperately pushes by to grab his duffel bag and run. He captures in detail the peculiarly delicate gait the man acquires as he scurries away naked over wet locker-room tile.

"See, me, my favorite card, at least right now, is the APERapTURE card." Jimmy tries to pronounce the "Ape Rapture" Bigloo in a way that anticipates where he is going with all of this. He describes this coal-black operation the government seems to have going on. Where they're making some kind of half-man half-robot combat zombies. "Apes, is what they call them. At least that's what the information leaked and linked so far is saying." Jimmy reviews the fragments of design specs so far uncovered regarding these creatures. He describes with partial or maybe complete embellishment the superpowers and sometimes sulky dispositions of these cyborg primates. And he wants his listeners to know that it seems that already at least one of these little rascals has murdered somebody. So they got to be watched. "That guy, remember him? That guy, Tom Guy? That poor fellow who tried to be a spokesman for GAIA but got his head blown clean off his shoulders instead. Hadn't expected some killer Apes would pack the mic with explosives. Just take a look-see and you'll find those travel receipts I was talking about. Pretty clear to me who killed old Tom.

"Well. Well, I'm taking over his job." The reverend straightens his blazer. Tom's job. GAIA Spokesman. Though I view myself more as Chaplain, I think I can do my new god's work with this title." Jimmy makes a bow with his towel, in honor of the loss of his predecessor, Spokesman Tom Guy.

APE RAPTURE

Earth's Alert! The Queen of Hearts carries this lone poem that was painted on the lintel of the Bigloo's egress. It's the sparsest card in the deck. The artist Anita Fray, by *Earth's Alert!* did she mean a global sentience? Or just an alarm?

The other cards are not as devoted. Multiple poems share the same card. But you can be more specific; you can say, like, Ten of Spades, lower left corner. Yeah, that thing about the bat. Never mind the tango shit above it. Just the bat. And everybody knows right what you're talking about. Of course, the partitioning of Fray's wall art onto a set of fifty-four cards was sort of arbitrarily decided by the observatory gift shop. Similarly, the cross-referencing of each with a playing card, while nonetheless maintaining a size that allows the cards to double as post cards, were simply business decisions. The result, in any case, has been very helpful. With the playing-card indexing, the Bigloos now have an address that can be referenced. And from there you can point more specifically if you want.

For example, if you ignore the elephants flying in the sky of the Two of Diamonds, then you are referring to the sub-Bigloo displaying the symmetric triads of tens and ones: TEN TEN pound bricks TENd to more easily move than ONE ONE hundred pound ONE. These words are painted like stone totems placed on a coastline. They observe us out at sea. Even avoiding italicization and punctuation, this Bigloo does not carry well into mono-font. Some sense of Easter Island is lost without the artist's original brush strokes. Although the discretization of the Bigloo's painted dome into 54 panels and their assignment to 54 playing cards is a convenience taken by the observatory's gift shop, at least on the cards the brush strokes are preserved.

Jack of Clubs. Jack of Clubs is receiving a lot of discussion right now in this emergency, almost all-hands meeting called by the IS directorate. Jack of Clubs is the "Ape Rapture" card. Sure, below "Penalty Fine," the "pedigree kind," brush strokes suggest several kids playing a chalked sidewalk game while skipping to the chant "napkin, feminine, masculine, jock." Sure, rowing over to join them, long oars from its *o*'s, comes a Viking "lootool," and sure, from a stage in the corner, a smiling tap dancer with cane and hat sings, "Horrrr-i-fide, I'm absolutely positively horrrr-i-fide" while his only audience is some "laughterslaughter" in a duck blind, shooting up at a flock of "poopoop," each "poopoop" bent at the center "p" in various freeze-frames of wing flight. Sure, there is a variety of discussion on the card, but the angry "Ape Rapture" near the center of the card is clearly there to tag the Aperture program.

At least that's what the IS analyst at the podium is arguing. And there are plenty of heads nodding agreement. Indeed, the Bigloo exposure of Plainview is small potatoes now that the online sleuths have turned to rototilling up the secrets of Aperture. It hasn't helped that a crackpot preacher with a huge online audience has incorporated into his sermons his musing on whether these, these Ape men—these soldiers grown in a vat like sea monkeys—whether they have a soul, finding himself still really unsure and encouraging his followers to keep digging up more of the design specs so they can decide. The fact that the whole wide world now knows Aperture exists is a very big problem for IS, especially Cornbread. Plainview was built as the secret communication system to serve Aperture. But what was Aperture built to serve? Why from the partial documents being reconstructed does it appear to be so mindbogglingly huge? So mindbogglingly well funded? So secretly funded. A massive project. With requisition orders suggesting services and infrastructure that will carry into future decades. What is the mindbogglingly big secret behind Aperture? Inquiring minds want to know and are very busy working this out.

Most of the employees attending this meeting must, as a matter of national security, understand that the details of Aperture are highly restricted. Most of these employees don't themselves know these details. But unlike others in the public sphere, they should not surf at work to find out. Or maybe even at home. When federal employees are told to remain ignorant about something, they have to take this very seriously and carefully avoid educating themselves. This is part of the employment contract they signed.

"We don't know how GAIA is creating these links between Bigloos and secret data," says the analyst. "They have to find not just the sites where the pieces of data are hidden, but also the sites where the pieces for the extraction key are located. Plainview sort of promised that would be impossible. Of course, now, I hear, you can type in a Bigloo and the search engine will give you a page with links to all the pieces you need. But that's pretty much only for the secrets that are already exposed. Basically, just a result of the traffic. What we can't figure out is how it starts. Something may be self-assembling here. Maybe the Bigloos are just being used as sort of a super hashtag, and then the secrets glom on. But it's sort of chicken and egg. No way of really figuring out which came first."

One in the audience objects. Not Bobby Bannister, but he might as well be, at least as far as Gary's impatience is concerned. Yes, of course the search-engine companies have already been questioned. No, of course they can't necessarily determine how the links are formed. A neural net is a nonlinear mapping without a unique inverse. What? Sure, that applies for a PCA ranking but we're talking about... The analyst at the podium wants the questioner to eventually understand that no, not even under arrest and torture can the search-algorithm engineers clarify how the Bigloos and secrets became linked.

"It seems that whoever or whatever made these links is exploiting the inherent instability in the unusual word sequences of the Bigloos. Every time you type in keywords, you are altering the results of all word searches to come. But if you type in 'remove dog ticks' you are probably not going to alter very much, because that sequence has been entered many times before, and the links are now pretty well established. Type in the Bigloo 'beetle mite sarrish in soft reek salmon,' on the other hand, and the search engine isn't sure what to do. It's waiting to be trained. By the whole world."

The upshot of all this is, as Gary surmises despite his late arrival, that there is no evidence that Anita Fray deliberately created the leaks. There is no evidence that she is even now hiding from GIB. Perhaps she is simply hiking the Pacific Crest Trail.

Nesbitt. Evidence of his involvement is also lacking, technically. But he has been showing up in some pretty weird situations, and jumping out your third-story apartment window to avoid answering questions seems excessive.

"IS's priority..." Associate Director Cornbread has taken the podium now. "IS's priority right now is Nesbitt. Fray too, but especially Nesbitt."

Gary thinks about this. Of course, Jimmy Pea, not Nesbitt or Fray, must be the most urgently wanted by Aperture. In one of his recent sermons, the reverend held up the Ape Rapture card and went through it like a children's book for his listeners. Showing even the least internet savvy how they can type in keyword combinations from the card and be delivered to a trove of partially assembled documents describing the secret Aperture program. Showing, also, how easy it is to link anything new you find. Contribute.

Reverend Pea is almost certainly the one Director Cornbread most wants to apprehend. If Director Cornbread is not right here in this meeting admitting this, it must be because the reverend is already on the Ape's hit list. If you already know you are going to assassinate somebody, you don't declare you hate of them first.

Associate Director Cornbread is up there in front of a nearly all-hands meeting to demand that any information on these fugitives be immediately brought to him. But because he's up there, he is also brought into answering some embarrassing questions. Seems that over the first couple days following the Bigloo breach each of these two prime fugitives escaped from him multiple times. Just disappeared. Seems his Aperture boa-down thing don't work so good.

Finally, a young analyst, new and immature in his understanding of all-hands etiquette, just has to ask a question while everybody is gathered here: "Hey, can I ask, has anybody been able to find anything on that guy, Tom Guy? Or did the preacher just completely make that up?"

NO REVERSE

Eve is thrilled with the upholstery. Slick white vinyl. This isn't the original upholstery, but it's sure nice. The waxy material is pulled smoothly over the seats and shows less of the constraints that usually connect fabric to seat. There is something pimpish about it. Over the passenger windshield of the 1964 Plymouth Valiant, written in neon pink, remain the characters: "$400—- No Reverse." The car also has some triangular flags on its radio antenna that they got to keep.

Nicolas holds his foot against the meaty pedal and watches through the upright windshield as the Valiant pulls the world toward him. He has never had such a driving experience. He likes the unusual engagement of the column shift: the "three on the tree" that brings his right arm up like a communist bicep as he brings the car into gear. The posture is pleasant and empowering—unlike the usual floor show, which looks like cane support. Nicolas likes the hard, cool feel of the corrugated steering wheel—not soft and Nerfy like modern ones. He likes the green tinge in the glass—so elegant and earned. The Valiant's windows are, in a real sense, photographic plates. Long-exposure images of decades of light.

"I want to go with you," he announces.

"I know," Eve responds.

A unique piece of artwork. Unlike modern cars that are snapped together from pressed pieces of plastic, the Valiant is built from hunks of metal. Hunks of metal hammered and forged together into a rolling sculpture. A baroque progression from the hungry grill to the spacey taillights, the car is art. Imaginative and thoughtfully pretentious.

"You'll be staying with a deaf mute while I'm gone." Eve then nods upward, as if irritated with a neighbor. "Do you want to keep the car?"

No-nonsense wind vents—simple and effective. A weighty Batman buckle clips the seat belt around Nicolas's waist while his head and neck continue, with some disbelief, to roll in their freedom. The Valiant's bench seat has absolutely no head restraints.

"Yes, very, very much."

"Then we need to stop and get some spray paint."

Origami Clutch

Martini and Muumuu

Martini in hand, Mrs. Nesbitt opens her front door. Heavy-metal music plays very loudly from her backyard, her muumuu is wet, unpleasantly see-through, and covered with paint. She is drunk and quite uninterested in the federal man at her door. "No, he's not here," she says, and pushes the door closed. The Gibbon loosens again his tie, turns to look back at the motorcycle on the lawn, and then slowly returns to the security guard and golf cart that has taxied him here from the gate.

Gary stops this clip. He returns to the clip of Nesbitt's truck parked at his apartment. Yes, he remembered right. The tailgate is down. And he notices this time that straps hang over the side walls.

Gary then searches for the keyword intersection of "motorcycle" and "diaper" in the California highway cam database. And then in the database of social media posts. In the satellite imagery data. He soon assembles—huh, they even went off-road for a bit—a whole illustrated story of Nicolas's motorcycle ride to his mother's house in the desert. There are plenty of photos posted of the man in diapers riding bitch, but who is that driving? Soon, Gary has the answer.

The satellite images confirm that, technically, what Mrs. Nesbitt said was correct. Her son was not there when the GIB officer came by. Seems she and Anita Fray had sent Nicolas off to buy more paint. The two women were busy painting the walls of the backyard swimming pool from air mattresses as the water drained out.

Gary notices the time—his session is done—and shifts over to complete the required questionnaire.

…Yes, he too found the loud music and the motorcycle on the lawn to be a little freaky.

…Yes, Mrs. Nesbitt did seem drunk.

…No, she did not seem like she was lying or hiding anything.

Quorum Sensing

"We like to pretend that the world is full of smooth transitions, but it's really full of discontinuities. Why do you think that is? Why do you think we prefer continuities over discontinuities? Who would like to answer?"

Big words aside, the seminar speaker sounds like he is speaking to children. He has an overlooking enthusiasm, and his expression is so stripped of all but the most ebullient markers that he looks like the face on a Mr. Bubbles bottle. And now he holds his finger fluttering in front of him like he is selecting Willie Wonka's successor from a crowd of kids stabbing their arms into the air. This is all that Gary can see as he opens the door. But Gary doesn't need to see the audience to know that Mr. Bubbles is out of his context. Probably a junior professor swimming for tenure somewhere and teaching such a large load of freshman classes that he now addresses everything in the world as though the transaction will appear on an instructor-evaluation sheet. He probably caught an early morning flight from—where did the announcement say he was from? Harvard? And underneath all that *yippee!* He is probably so exhausted that he hasn't noticed that people in *this* audience take themselves very seriously—very important analysts working on very important issues of national security. Enthusiasm is, for them, a put-off. Gary sneaks around the podium as the speaker grows ready to provide a hint.

"Think of calculus."

Gary looks for a seat—while thinking of calculus. He also wonders why the fucking podium was erected on the entry-door end of the seminar room. Did some designer, insulated in a cubicle of a private universe somewhere, envision seminar rooms where people always arrive on time? Or is the decision a result of a self-fluffing committee who, in the process of their pillow fight, discovered they had the power to coerce people to come on time by making them very visible if they don't? Did they hit high squeals when they realized this would also make it hard for people to duck out of boring lectures early?

"What it comes down to is that we just don't like it when an x has more than one y. This makes calculus and our other easy methods break down. Even the formulation of General Relativity---" Gary winds up in a chair behind Bobby Bannister and immediately wishes him ill. "--- requires that a sufficiently local patch of space-time appear Minkowskian." Bobby is big and blocks the view. Evidently competent in his tiny niche but dumb as a board in every other way. "Which are just big words to say the same thing."

The speaker says something about how he will come back to his point—about discontinuities or General Relativity, presumably—later. He has squid up on the screen now.

Bobby leans over to a Fly seated next to him. This temporarily improves the view for Gary, but on the downside, it also causes Bobby to speak, to imitate a Jethro Clampett accent while claiming he has always knewd calculus had something to do with squid. Bobby Bannister is pretending to be someone stupid—Gary must acknowledge the fractal that had just blossomed in the seat in front of him. Then he tries to return his attention to the speaker.

"The light you're seeing coming from the squid is generated by a symbiotic bioluminescing bacteria, *Vibrio Fischeri...*"

Gary searches around his chair until he spots a seminar flyer in a lap. Steven Attwater, Harvard. Understanding Threat Using Quorum Sensing Models. Coffee and Cookies.

And squid. Huh.

"These bacteria don't normally light up—when they're living off on their own, that is. Most of the time these single-celled organisms are just plankton *flooaating* around in the big ocean." Mr. Bubbles moves his arm to suggest how plankton float around in the big ocean. "It costs these bacteria an awful lot to light up...and that would anyway probably only get them gobbled up! So why do they do it? Why do they come together to light up inside of a squid?

"Well, you see these bacteria have established a relationship with the squid, a symbiosis. And some of you may remember from your biology classes that there are different types of symbioses. Most people think of parasitism, but this is not really the most common symbiosis. With parasitism, one partner is taking resources from the other and not giving much back. Much more common and efficient are relationships where they each bring something to give each other. Parasitism is usually just a temporary stage—either the partners work out something of mutual benefit or else they eventually both go bust. It's like a basketball team: it doesn't matter how good the players are; if they don't cooperate with one another then they'll probably be edged out of the playoffs by a team that does.

"Now the type of symbiosis that the squid and *V. Fischeri* have together is a communalism. This means that both benefit. In this case the squid gives these bacteria food and lodging. But what does the bacteria give the squid?" Mr. Bubbles flutters his index finger, hoping, if only briefly this time, to find a raised hand.

"Light!" It's a Borderline in the back of the room who answers.

"Brilliant!" Bobby Bannister whispers to his Fly neighbor.

"Yes, that's right! There are situations where the squid benefit from the light that the bacteria provide. At nighttime, for example, some of the bacteria in the underside of the squid light up. And what's really amazing is that they know how to do this *just* right to make the squid's underside look like moonlight coming down from the sea surface! It's really amazing when you think about it: all those little single-celled creatures come together and coordinate themselves somehow to produce a pattern and intensity of light that makes the squid's shadow disappear! Any hungry fish looking up at the squid just sees the moonlight coming down. There's no shadow—the squid is invisible. I'd say that's a pretty nifty service these bacteria provide for the squid!"

Gary nods. Okay that's kind of cool. The bacteria provide the squid a cloaking service.

"Now this leads us to the topic I wanted to talk to you about, which has to do with how systems in nature are *full* of discontinuities—nature is *full* of things suddenly *lighting up,* suddenly jumping to a level of coordinated behavior that you would have never been able to extrapolate to by studying just the individual components.

"But first, how is it that all these little creatures know how to coordinate? Remember, they're usually just plankton *flooaating* around in the big ocean." Mr. Bubbles' arm illustrates floating in the big ocean again. "How is it that they know how to come together and coordinate?

"The answer is that they have ways of communicating among themselves—probably many ways, but one way uses chemical signals—pheromones. These little plankton know how to both give off and read pheromones from their environment. So you see pheromones are what allow these single-celled bacteria to come together and coordinate themselves into a multicellular organism. And an interesting thing is that individually they are really in communication with their environment rather than with one another. It's essentially the collective that they exchange information with. How many of you have watched *Star Trek*? The newer ones, I mean. Do you remember the Borg? Now of course on *Star Trek* the Borg are unnatural and evil, but I bet if the producers had been Buddhists..."

Click. Gary understands what the talk is about. It is an enormous insight into how nature organizes itself, and by reference it describes the enigmatic control structure of the GAIA network, which most of the analysts in the room are, one way or another, assigned to investigate. The insight arrives but can only stick around if it becomes properly unpacked—an option partially closed by Bobby Bannister's stupid-ass interruptions; or, perhaps more accurately, Gary's susceptibility to these interruptions. Bobby represents most of the room when he pretends to not know anything about such television shows, Buddhism and whatnot, and pushes Mr. Bubbles to return to his point. Feigning frustration, Bobby asks, "But where is the control center regulating this behavior?"

Bobby suspects that these bacteria are working for the squid—in the same way other bacteria have become enslaved to help digestion in the human gut. The speaker claims that this is not an accurate statement. That it is more fair to say that they work for each other. But only the squid has a brain, Bobby insists. Well, collectively the bacteria also have a brain. What? That makes no sense. Bobby rolls his eyes to indicate this. That it makes no sense. Even if there's a billion of them, not a one of them has a brain. A billion times nothing is still nothing. The speaker points out that the same could be said of the human brain. If you landed inside a head, you'd see just a bunch of neurons. Whatever one would regard as the brain is obviously not the neurons themselves but the pattern of communications they've develop as an ensemble. Gary's insight on how this relates to GAIA's organizational structure is now fully washed away by his irritation with Bobby. Gary would like to see someone in the audience rip off Bobby's head, skull fuck it, then return it to its neck with half-mast eyes and a misaligned lower jaw. He also senses that this wish may be incommensurate with any hatred due Bobby, and this gives him another internal layer of distracting thought, which he ultimately assigns as Bobby's fault.

"But getting back to whether the bacteria work for the squid..." The speaker is retreating to Bobby's initial question in attempt to sequentially disengage himself from his questioner. "...quorum sensing is quite pervasive; there are all kinds of examples, and plenty of them with no squid involved..."

"Okay," Bobby interrupts, impatient, "it doesn't have to be the squid, but..."

"The bacteria *don't need*..." (Mr. Bubbles has now interrupted Bobby.)

"But if it's not the squid, then..." (Bobby re-interrupts.)

"The bacteria..."

"If it's not the squid..."

"The bacteria..."

"All I'm saying is that..."

"The bacteria..."

The seminar has reached its climax. The sum of attentiveness in the room is at its peak. The rate at which information is being recorded in brains is higher now than it has been before or will be after. Paradoxically, this peak in the rate of information being received by the audience is reached precisely when the rate of information leaving the seminar speaker's mouth has vanished.

As the two notch their chins upward, Bobby becomes louder. But Mr. Bubbles isn't backing off. He knows he has the podium, and that all he has to do to keep it is to continue saying, "The bacteria..." until Bobby gives up. The course of action is simple and clear, but it cost Mr. Bubbles some of his ebullience: the Fischer-Price colors that surrounded his speech disappear, and the smoothly waving arm that once floated like plankton in the big ocean now move in a discontinuous, Hitleresque fashion.

"The bacteria *don't need* a boss to organize their collective behavior. The intelligence behind the instructions come from the collective itself. Bacteria are not the simple slime you think. They have rich social lives; they develop a collective memory and common knowledge. They form groups and can identify their own group and others. They learn from experience. They improve themselves and engage in group decision making. The bacteria in your mouth are engaged in a level of quorum sensing that dwarfs all human communication."

Mr. Bubbles takes a breath now only because he absolutely needs to. While holding an evil eye on Bobby. Then he continues: "The name 'quorum sensing' is maybe a little misleading. It was created when it was noticed that many pathogens use quorum sensing to assess their numbers before attacking a host. These pathogens can be bacteria, viruses, or other types of microbes. But they need to wait until they have sufficient numbers before attacking. Otherwise they won't be able to overcome the host's immune system. But by now we have started to realize that the communication systems of microbes are the most extensive and sophisticated on the planet. Maybe one can simply say that they *are* the communication system of the planet."

These are good counterpoints to Bobby's argument, Gary decides. Whatever Bobby's argument was. The point stands: some type of intelligence has to be assigned to the collective of these microbes. Locating a brain or some other type of command post is not a requirement. Microbes are capable of coming together and coordinating very sophisticated responses to their environment that no *one* of the microbes would do or even could do on its own. Microbe collectives are intelligent.

Mr. Bubbles has plenty more to say, but he is now behind schedule and starts skipping slides. The patience in his presentation has declined. But what he wants to say is that the microbial communication network (quorum sensing) that allows single-celled organisms to come together and act as a multicellular organism is not an exotic phenomenon but instead rather the norm. He describes examples of quorum sensing acting *between* species; he describes how even the human immune system can be regarded as a collective of cells engaged in quorum sensing. He describes how the planet is mostly a planet of microbes, microbes engaged in quorum sensing; how microbes outnumber any other cells, how recent observations from hydrothermal vents indicate that four fifths of the earth's biomass isn't even at the surface but rather far below the surface and in the form of microbes! He describes how microbes readily exchange genes, how even the concept of species becomes vague in their case. He describes how the planet Earth is essentially one giant gene pool of microbes. And then he is interrupted by Bobby Bannister again.

"Can you prove that mathematically? That they're the same, I mean?"

It is true that Mr. Bubbles is presently pointing to an equation; it is true that Mr. Bubbles has previously ascribed a variety of sameness to quorum sensing, immune systems, and intelligence; and it is true that most of the audience has now passed their peak in attention and are too drowsy to realize that Bobby Bannister's question is contextless and fucking stupid.

Mr. Bubbles looks desperate. He has allowed his enthusiasm to slightly build again, and this descent back into the idiot pit with Bobby is too much for him. His mouth simply shivers.

"No, you can't," someone in the audience replies for him.

The audience turns.

Orly Kimms, the Borderline in the back of the seminar room.

"We can't what?" says Bobby.

"You can't prove it mathematically."

"Prove what mathematically?" Bobby says, suddenly estranged from his stupid question.

"That anything and anything else are the same thing," the Borderline replies as he begins to stand up. He is wearing some sort of toga.

Bobby snorts; what the Borderline in the man-dress has just claimed is clearly weird and senseless. Right? He looks around the room. Several young Flies snort too. Bobby folds his arms and looks pleased.

Bobby is a Fly, and therefore when the man in the toga leaves the room, Bobby sees the man fleeing. Gary, on the other hand, is not a Fly and can see that the attitude of the Borderline is more of someone who came to take a picture—but the light changed, so now he is leaving.

Gary gets up to follow the Borderline. But by the time he has squeezed by the podium and reached the hall, the Borderline has vanished. Gary decides to get coffee.

He admires the Borderlines; there is an unplaceable elegance about them. And although he also doesn't understand what they say much of the time, he figures that this is because of his own shortcomings; indeed, the more consideration he gives to what they say, the more he tends to understand. This, for example—that you can't mathematically prove that anything and anything else are the same thing. What was that about? He thinks about this as he walks.

The Borderline, Orly Kimms, made the statement and left the room. It is as if he left it behind on his empty chair—like a koan for anyone who wishes to consider it as more than senseless chatter from a malfunctioning unit, and perhaps also beyond a dopey New-Age interpretation where everything's an illusion, and nothing can be done about that.

Gary presses an elevator button. Of course, by merely the semantics "else" would seem to immediately defy "same," but Gary assumes the Borderline's claim was not simply this trivially based. Gary allows that "anything" is pretty arbitrary. And that "anything else" is almost just as arbitrary. If you can't mathematically prove that "anything" is the same as "anything else" then the problem must be with the "is the same as" part of the statement. The elevator opens.

"Well, of course," Gary says. A woman coming out of the elevator is worried he is talking to her. The Borderline was simply saying that sameness can't be discussed mathematically. There's not even a symbol for it. The equal sign can only be used to state that two things are mathematically indistinguishable. It can't be used to state other things, like whether they are two things or one thing. Math can't be used to determine whether two things are the *same* thing.

Gary gets out of the elevator at the small food court and walks toward the coffee kiosk. The more he thinks about what the Borderline said, the closer he comes to being convinced that math can't be the complete language of God. Or even the physical universe. It simply lacks too many symbols. To say that two people make the same wage usually means that their wages are equal. The two numbers on their payroll stubs are equal. But that's not what "same" should really mean. To say that two people drive the same car should mean that the two people share one car. A head-cocked Fly greets Gary, but Gary doesn't notice. It shouldn't mean two cars. Because two cars will always be two different cars, and if they're two different cars then they can't be the same car.

So why is there no word in math—or science, more generally—for "same"? Math allows two different people to drive two different cars that are "equal"—meaning quantitatively indistinguishable in every and all quantitative comparisons that can be made. Not just make and model, paint wear and things like that, but other things like probably even the physical location. And if one could have two such identical cars, co-located in their one parking space, would there be any way of getting into just one of them and driving that one away? How would you grab on to just one of the stick shifts? The only way two things can be the same is if they're really only one thing. Math and science don't distinguish such differences, and therefore are inadequate for discussing some of the most important questions that matter to Gary.

Somebody is in Gary's way. It's the HR weasel wishing to suggest that there may have possibly been a problem with Gary's completion of one of the training modules that is already overdue. Gary understands the HR people to be the agency's defense against its own employees.

"What do you mean?" Gary asks, irritated. His interesting internal discussion has been interrupted.

"Ap*pare*ntly..." the man starts, seeming to upload his people skills, "apparently you walked out of a title-9 training session this morning, Gary. You were requested to—"

"Yeah, after two hours. Fuck that."

Gary walks away, thinking maybe he has been rude. He didn't really say "fuck that" but he started to say it, certainly implied it. Sort of 'fah...thah.' On the other hand, the response was very honest and concise. It is curious, as Gary considers it further, that the middle word 'fuck' can remain so highly charged despite its generic versatility. Indeed, it is probably the most versatile word in the English language: it can be used as just about any part of speech, and it can even replace punctuation marks like the comma, exclamation mark, or semicolon; with change of intonation, its meaning can polarize; squired by the right preposition, it can battle as just about any action word, or just sit home as a lowly noun. It can not only substitute for just about any other word, but it can do so valiantly. It is surprising then, that English dictionaries are so slow to acknowledge what is almost certainly the most important word in the English language. Gary arrives at the food-court kiosk and states his order.

The cashier takes Gary's order then turns her back to press him a short americano. "Three seventy-five," she says over her shoulder.

Three bangs to dump the previous grinds are accompanied by three drops that drip from a faucet in the corner. And, at about the same time, Gary notices three missing teeth in her skirt zipper. A quick analysis leads to the provisional conclusion that although the first two triads are causally related the third probably is not. Or is he just not thinking widely enough?

Gary loads sugar into his coffee while his hungry eyes scan the familiar tray of condiments. Lids, straws, sugar. Seven non-dairy creamer packets.

While these meager scraps of interest arrive at a boring bit rate, his mind wanders back to several annoyances he has been experiencing. Such thoughts are fitting a default process—perhaps increasing with coffee consumption? A default use for the snippets of downtime. The waits in lines, for example. It has become the default to donate such snippets toward fattening his latest bitch. The fragments of time he can find here and there can always be strung together to find her a few more pounds. And because she can eat just about anything, calories hang

68

freely in just about any context. The little fragments can always be chained together to develop impressive prosecutions against the tiny things that piss him off.

Initially, Gary considered this practice to be a slight improvement over wasted time. He viewed it to be sort of like teething. Using the little time shards to sculpt his analytical abilities. Better than doing nothing with them. But then he started to notice that every bitch he ever fattened sooner or later came slinking out in swimwear. Even the ones that he fed until they were obese and preposterously unnatural. All complaints sufficiently well fed will eventually climb out and seek an audience.

Gary plans to put the lid on his coffee as he walks. It will save time. But as he turns from the condiment counter—"What the frig!"—he almost bumps into a cagey contraption that is suddenly behind him.

It's Henry Walker. Henry Walker is hanging on to his walker, fingers clasped around the custom bicycle-grip handles, looking down for a moment to watch a wad of Gary's coffee splatter on the floor between his walker legs. And then he looks up to ask, "Why do you say 'frig'? Don't you mean 'fuck'?"

Henry is a man who looks older than he probably is, maybe even on purpose. He stands with a thoughtful expression reaffirming his question.

Gary isn't sure how to respond. Henry Walker is the head of the Borderlines Division. An Associate Director of GIB. "Ah, I guess because it's more polite?"

The old man considers the response he has heard. "No. I don't agree. I think when people say 'frig' what they're really meaning to say is 'fuck.' They just don't want to leave behind any proof that they said it." Henry is smiling, as if he is discussing an aspect of his religion. "You meant 'fuck,' right?"

Gary smiles. "Yes, sir. I meant 'fuck.'"

Both men seem happy they have established this.

"You're Gary, Saar, yes?"

"Yes."

"Someone told me you're a good multimedia analyst. Told me you're good at seeing GAIA." Henry scoots over to the condiment counter beside Gary. He sets his coffee onto the counter and then leaves his walker to stand squarely in front of his cup. A hot expresso. He keeps his trigger finger through the tiny cup hole. "Could you look at something for me?"

"Yeah. Sure. What?"

Henry takes a thumb drive from his pocket and hands it to Gary. "There's an app on here. Called 'Smutty.'"

"Smutty? I've not heard of it."

"I'm not surprised. Seems the developer, a GIB contractor in fact, but on a different project, he was killed right before he---" Walker makes a senile gesture. "---whatever you call it when they release it, launch it. He was going to distribute it."

"Killed? Someone didn't want it released?"

"Uh huh. Some kind of monkey business there."

"Who else has it?"

"We don't know. Maybe GAIA. That's why I want you to look at it. Could you try it out and tell me if you think GAIA would stoop to use it?"

"Yeah. Sure...Stoop to...?"

"Oh, you'll see what I mean. Smutty's weapon is disinformation and, well, you know that's kind of at odds with GAIA's mission statement."

"But if they do use it, they could benefit."

"Exactly."

"..."

Gary watches the man attend to his little drink. The business between them has been accomplished strangely early in the encounter, and Gary isn't sure if the conversation is over, and they will now just stand together and silently drink their coffees.

The old man drinks his expresso. Sips, really. Maybe Gary has underestimated the little drink. He has always dismissed the drink because of its small proportions, but Director Walker seems to be finding a giant experience inside the tiny cup.

Gary is reluctant to interrupt but finally comments on the ceremony he is observing. Henry asks Gary to not think of it as drinking a tiny coffee, but more like applying lipstick. Gary isn't sure at first what Henry means. Henry lowers his lips into the brown foam, just to frolic there without going any deeper. Just to apply the brown foam to his lips, like lipstick. To rub the foamy lips together. And then suck them clean and start again.

"You don't really *drink* an expresso...at least not the same way you would a cup of coffee," he explains. "But your mouth figures out pretty quickly what to do with it...as soon as your brain stops thinking it already knows."

SMUTTY

As with any monumental bastard, Smutty was conceived amid bedroom blue light and a sexual discussion that could be located with very few coordinates. A new contribution to the conscious experiment on this planet landed wet and immediately unattended, as loud music looped too long to have legitimate listeners and fondled lubricant lay forlorn on the nightstand. The spiritual compression in this arrival provided the thrust behind the explosive freedom that followed. Smutty was blessed to be born with so little to live up to.

While some folks quickly cement their own harsh judgments against Smutty, it should be noted that such people have tiny provincial minds, R-complex associations and limbic leanings that do not really constitute a higher thought process. People with a neocortical layer not like beefsteak but more like expensive butter spread over big bread. Not exploratory in their thoughts at all and therefore fervent in their convictions.

Even a slightly pulpier brain would find alarm in any quick judgment of Smutty. For obviously any judgment of Smutty should begin by distinguishing which choices were made by Smutty and which by his father. But separating what was truly Smutty from what was simply his dad was no easy task. Mostly because Smutty was conceptually designed and raised to be, at least during the formative years, exactly like his dad. In fact, indistinguishable. It was fully intended that Smutty should begin life with exactly every one of his father's vices, and only from there spread his wings and soar into worse habits.

By puberty, Smutty still surfed porn but only because it remained on his list of habitual chores. Honestly, even having mastered the behavior he still didn't really get the point. But he learned where to go, where to pause, the right proportion of videos and pics, meat-and-potatoes versus the exotica. He learned to fast-forward the dingy door-opening scenes, the naughtily stupid premises. He learned to micro sample the sucky-dog and licky-beaver parts, avoid—-even with desperate lunge—mid-intercourse conversation, and finally fall into steady viewing once there was plain and simple fucking going on. If a crescendo seems imminent and the female tailbone begins to rise commensurately with the excitement, then the progress bar should be noted for a potential rewind. If, however, during this incipient climax the dude pulls his wet schooner out of her and cruises it up to her eyebrows, and if she yummy-moans in pretended excitement about this while her eyes in fact turret defensively, if her tongue stud seems suddenly uneager to cuckoo, then by all means Smutty should stop this show, abort, and start with new keywords and categories.

Initially, Smutty followed the abrupt end to the browsing session where, after patience and leisure in surfing through so many colors and shapes and sizes and postures, after such an open mind and world appetite, after such close ups…sudden stop. All open windows closed in seconds. History cache emptied. Full reboot.

At least that was the previous rule. Then Smutty began to alter his father's surfing habits. Not directly—as in his father himself adopting new porn surfing behaviors from Smutty—-but rather as in Smutty adopting surfing behaviors that sort of taxed what it meant to mimic his father. Smutty was developing his own browsing interests. Puberty is very personal.

And besides, there were just some really stupid and easily disguisable practices his father followed. The abrupt termination of a surfing session was one of them. Any miner would have no problem determining from the site connection log what really did it for dad. No problem generating a thick and endearing album, a chronology really, of exactly the naked image frames—-from all of the billions and billions in the world—exactly the naked images that had helped Smutty's father strangle up his own yogurt. A coffee table item to thumb through. To take with to the retirement home. These are the ladies who used to do the trick for me sonny, yup. Or perhaps it would come more as a 'Grandpops, found out this stuff about you. Be a shame if the rest of the family got hold. Wanna talk about the will?' It took a slow-witted generation to see through the various levels of sanction and finally see that data miners are primarily in the service of extortion. Smutty was born as a response.

His father did not plan for Smutty to become a golden goose, although that almost happened. Smutty's dad was simply competent in both programming and locating porn, and also a member of the first generation to suspect that every interaction with a computer is either permanently recorded or recoverable by digital marauders in the future. The first generation to understand that their grandchildren would become able, if they so wished, to instantly command up the complete record of their grandparent's porn-surfing history.

But what if they couldn't really be sure it was me? The father asked himself one night. What if there was a second me? What if he wrote a simple, self-learning program that would watch his surfing behaviors and mimic them? But ultimately with extravagance and exaggeration such that nobody could be sure where he ended and it started. Let "Smutty," as he baptized it, wake at random hours and visit every kind of sleazy site his father could be interested in. And more.

His father did not plan for Smutty to become a golden goose. He lacked vision. A young Smutty has so much more potential than just its use as a smoke screen to hide a porn habit. Smutty is your assistant, your scapegoat, your best friend. Your personal A.I. Smutty gives you deniability in cyber court. Smutty sponges up your guilt. Smutty has global destiny.

But that destiny was stalled by two humorless men who broke into

72

the father's apartment and strangled him at his console before bagging his computers and hard drives.

MOBILE IN WIND

With the built-in furniture and the requirement that it fit on a highway, the prefabricated home is automatically crowded. But a small patch of floor space—or, for some poses, the countertop—is all that is required for what the small brown man has in mind. The man does not speak, but he does know how to rip, rotate, and readjust the way meat hangs on a skeleton. The way a body stacks up. The way flesh bounces. The eigenmodes describing the combination of body motion intrinsic to an individual's gait.

Nicolas was dropped off. Eve stayed only for tea, and then she was gone. Through the window of the travel trailer, he watched her drive down the long dirt road that leads from the patch of permanently parked mobile homes and travel trailers, out into the desert. Through the expanse he saw the brake lights of the Valiant not once. Yes, this is how Eve would drive. She brakes for nothing.

As Nicolas watched her go, he felt an immediate loss, a longing to be with her. Not here. With her. He wants to *be* with her. But this feeling so parallels that of a homesick kid at summer camp that he quickly pushes it away. He has been reborn not to retrace the steps of the unadventurous pussy he once was. He turns to the brown man, looks him in the eyes for the first time since arriving, and asks for more tea.

* * *

By the beginning of the third day, Nicolas recognizes the sequence of postures. They are cycling endlessly through the same sequence of fifty-four different positions. Sort of nonstop. He has learned to get his rest during the positions that are the least painful. Pose five of Clubs isn't one of these.

Nicolas places his hands on the range. His fingers grip the grates above the two front burners. He places the top of one foot on the sink counter. And then his second foot comes up alongside the first. From his elevated push-up position, he begins to hump the kitchen air between the sink and range.

Pose Twelve of Clubs is exhausting. The stove grates are kept from sliding by nothing more than an alignment of dimples and it takes furious focus, a precisely calibrated chord of muscles, to keep the grate dimples pressed straight down the dimple pits in the stove top.

Nicolas falls. And hits his chin on the way down. He lost focus, the grates skated away from him…and then he loses consciousness.

When he awakes, he feels the cool kitchen floor below him. He can't breathe through his nose, and he hears loud, intermittent donkey sounds arriving from very close to his face. But he doesn't panic. Nicolas isn't the type to panic. He has only recently learned this about himself. In any case, it takes him only a moment to identify the situation: this is pose Seven of Spades.

Nicolas sits up and his vision begins to clear. He feels the plastic clip on his nose. And the elastic strap on the back of his neck that holds the harmonica tightly in his mouth like a bridle bit. Nicolas's breath is thereby amplified and easy to monitor. Different tones resonate in his body at different locations. The harmonic amplification of his breath also gives sonic focus to body points in a strangely massaging sort of way. The harmonica's reeds are set to A harmonic minor, and it seems the brown man knew this would suit Nicolas.

Several times, the man brings Nicolas over to the window and points at a wind chime hanging on the other side. The chime is made from shells and desert animal parts, and the man points at it vigorously when it makes noise. What Nicolas comes to understand, with the help of the man's pointing, is that every wind chime in the trailer park can be uniquely identified by its unique combination of tones. Each wind gust causes clanky transients that are different with each gust. But more than that, the wind also sounds the tones of resonances unique to each mobile construction. Any mobile constructed out of any material holds a signature chord of tones that can be used to specifically identify the mobile…unless the string lengths of the mobile's hanging parts are occasionally altered—as the brown man does each time Nicolas achieves a new yogic state of deformation. Once Nicolas understands that he is training his gait, teaching his body to swing in different ways, changing his eigenmodes, his tolerance for the brown man sitting on top of him improves.

PARLIN'S PUSSYTOES

Below an April sky, Minnesota wildflowers bloom beautifully and sparsely over a field behind a middle school. Below an April sky, parents and their children stroll between a few makeshift concessions stands supporting the larger track meet. Below an April sky, dogs stop in Escher geometries and halt their wagging tails while they inspect one another. Below an April sky, concern over this being March is magically absent.

The Reverend Jimmy Pea is among these celebrations, darting and stopping, darting and stopping, one index finger holding a place in a botanical field guide, the other one turreting excitedly as it points through rapidly changing swaths that appear to be very inclusive in their indication. "There a pussytoe! There a pussytoe! Another! Pussy! Pussy!

Pussy! My god, the pussies are everywhere!" Heads turn. Children are pulled closer to their parents. "Now I know. I know what all you folks are thinking about. Worrying about. I know it's way too early for all these pussies to be out. But I just thank the baby Jesus they are. Otherwise I'd have missed them!"

The reverend reaches crude bleachers welded together from recycled plumbing. The stand is full of cheering parents. Jimmy pushes his way in, up and toward the middle, his sermon continuing, and forces his butt down into a bench. "Now, while I'm so tickled to death that I got to show you all that pussytoe, what we're really in church for today isn't that. Today I want to talk you about cooperation."

Jimmy pulls a Bigloo deck from his pocket. "Just got to, first, find the right Bigloo to talk about it." He bends over his lap as he sorts through the cards. "Folks, real sorry I'm not prepared. Shouldn't open my church doors before I have my sermon together. Real sorry, folks. Used to have a whole staff helping me."

"Maybe this one? What y'all think?" The reverend looks at the card for a moment, the four of diamonds, and then sets it back down. "Ah, hey by the way…before I forget. Did y'all see the new Ape secrets that got pulled out today? If you haven't, be sure and take a look-see. Seems if you know how to smack the Ape in the head *juust* right…you can reboot him. Reset him. Get him to imprint on you instead. Have your very own Ape. At least that's what some are saying about some specs they uncovered. We might have some souls to save yet!"

Images collected as Jimmy's phone camera moves around suggest that as he sits crowded among parents. Simultaneous track events are occurring, the most visible of which is currently an amateurishly low high jump. He picks up the card again. Examines it further. He stands up in the bleachers. Then paints sex and anguish on his face to mimic the expression of the woman on the card.

As with most of the Bigloos, the accompanying image is carried entirely by only a few brush strokes. This leaves ambiguity, but some claim to see in this image a woman beside a kitchen stove, in a long, black cocktail dress and tired make-up, slow dancing despondently with a wall phone that trails a cord up her neck and down her arm like a fluffy boa. Jimmy stands up and sings/dances it as a tango:

Dar-ling, will youuuu…du du du, du du du
Honey-be late for dinnerrrr…din din din, din din din
Dear, we're having your liverrrr…du du du, du du du
And the crust you like pie…

Jimmy looks displeased. Sits down. "Nah. Nah nah. Don't think that's the right one." The light around him disappears for a moment as parents leap up to cheer a good jump. Jimmy has to speak loudly for the moment: "See, I'm...SEE I'M LOOKING FOR A DIFFERENT ONE. I'M LOOKING FOR A BIGLOO TO TALK ABOUT COOPERATION WITH. COOPERATION!"

He thumbs through the deck.

Jimmy then has another card—the one he was really looking for, the one he wants to talk about: "Folks, I think this is it. This Bigloo will do. Do nicely. Ah, but hey, first, I need to show you...I need a...maybe down there." Jimmy sinks his face between his knees. He is kicking at a long section of pipe in the bleacher supports below the bench. His kicks get more forceful and his face is almost angry for a minute. "Dang thing's on there pretty good."

The welds of the pipe finally break, and Jimmy gets the pipe loose. He then brings the six-foot pipe section up to the surface, awkwardly, bumping heads as he stretches it out to look through like a telescope trained on the pre-teen athletes. "Darwin---OH! Damned that poor sweet little girl SHOULD HAVE HAD IT!" He yells. The RULES ARE RACIST, YOU ASK ME! SHE CLEARED IT! Just barely brushed the bar with her bottom. Her big bottom. Not her fault she's got all that extra butt back there. WHOLE THING'S RIGGED IN FAVOR OF THAT FLAT-BUTT WHITE GIRL! My lord, haven't we seen just exactly this before?"

Jimmy's only open eye receives photons through a six-foot pipe. "Darwin. See Darwin had his self a pipe just like this one here. Scientific Method and all, he knew that when you got a whole lot of confusing business in front of you---can't make sense of any of it---helps if you get yourself a pipe like this one."

"Hey. Dude. Dude. Hey dude, you just, like, hit my wife in the head with your pole."

"Yessir, a very important survey going on here. Very important. Darwin, see Darwin when he got to the Galapagos and first set foot down in the hot iguana sand, think he wasn't just a little overwhelmed? Like landing on a new planet." Jimmy laughs, still maintaining his pipe-view monitoring of the track meet.

"Dude! Again? Seriously?"

"I mean folks, have you SEEN an IGUANA? Never have to imagine dragons again."

"DUDE! Stop it, man!"

"Not like Charles ever had glossy Nat Geos to go through. Only had those...those lithograph drawings or whatever they were. Where all the animals, no matter what kind, wound up looking like dandy bird people. For whatever the reason.

"See, Charles, at first, he didn't even really set foot on the island. Had his men turn his little rowboat around before he even reached the beach of that dragon planet."

"MAN! Like, one more time and I'm calling security!"

"Yup, rowboat got close and Charlie crapped his britches. Too overwhelming. Saw those iguanas and rowed back to the ship and got his pipe." Jimmy stands up to train his long scope on a putter in the fore field. "See, when you bite off just a little bit at a time, a tiny bite to look at---"

"Sir, could you sit down please, my daughter can't---"

"---well, then even a Komodo Dragon doesn't look so terrifying. OH! See that? That little, skinny-armed kid really threw that thing! Wow!" Jimmy lowers his pipe and holds it now like a shepherd's staff. "Wasn't only Charles doing this. Whole societies were getting pipes like his. In fact, we've been carrying them ever since."

Jimmy begins slowly to walk forward, down the bleacher seats. There is very little room to do so and complaints arise. "Idea was, you collect little stamp pictures with your pipe. Until you got the whole picture. Until you know what an iguana is. Until you know the whole iguana planet. Just keep building up your little pictures and you can eventually explain it all." In his descent over the seats, he reaches ground in front of the bleachers, Jimmy stops. His face is steady in the camera now as he continues to explain this complicated subject of Reductionism. Behind him havoc and panic are starting. The disturbance he caused walking down the seats, together with the recent removal of a supporting strut, has led to the slow-motion, backward collapse of this whole section of bleachers. "Point is, you think you can ever understand everything about an iguana planet by just pasting together tiny postage-stamp pictures? I'm sure it's easy to think you might. Hell, we've all seen paint-by-numbers. Just paint all the pieces and you're certain to wind up with the whole picture."

Jimmy continues his sermon, adding a slow sideways stroll to remove the distracting background. "Problem is. Problem is, there's things about an iguana you will almost certainly miss if all you got is postage-stamp pictures. Sometimes, you gotta see the whole thing. All at once."

"Which brings me to what I want to talk about today. Cooperation. See, Darwin got back to England to tell everybody about the iguana planet he had visited. But he was telling them about a planet he'd only looked at through a pipe. No wonder everything looked like competition to him." Jimmy points his staff toward the contests before him. If you asked me what I saw, what I saw today here at this track meet through my pipe, well, I'm going to say I saw a whole lot of competition going on. That girl there is trying as hard as she can to get her big butt over the rail. This skinny-armed kid is trying to throw that tiny canon ball as far as he can. I can look through the pipe and see competition competition competition!"

"But what I'd be missing is the whole sea of cooperation going on here. Think of it. How come there's someone selling soft pretzels right HERE? Right NOW? Right when so many people want one? Who set up the playground today for extra parking? Who took down all those tetherball poles so nobody messes up their car door getting out? How is it that all these little kids have agreed to play by the same rules? How is it that all these parents have agreed to evaluate their children by the same rules? When you think about it, this track meet is 99 percent cooperation and only a 1 percent competition. Sure, competition is often where all the action is at. Fun to look at." The reverend stomps his shepherd's staff. "My recommendation to you is just don't forget all the cooperation it took for us to have any of this tiddy-biddy competition here today."

Jimmy returns to his cards. The Bigloos in his lap. "See this one. Message totally right. But the gift-store, the retards, they cut it off at the wrong spot. I have to use both the eight of spades and the two of clubs to put it together: "*Dog Eat Dog.*" What does that spell? I mean acronymically. DED. If dog eat dog is your model for the world, well then you know where you wind up.

"Anyways, that would've been a good choice, but I don't like the message spread over two cards. How about this one instead?

    pathyapathy
    pathyempathy
    pathysympathy
        as
        hu
      man

"Now who can tell me that doesn't look just like Bob Marley?" Jimmy seems moved by this art.

The word stack is rotated, turned slightly toward a lone brush stroke rising smokily up from the lower left. Although there is only one brushstroke to accompany the text, it is enough to suggest that the text is dim light reflecting off the nose and forehead of a smoking Rastafarian sitting in a dimmer room, and this is how Jimmy decides to read it. His eyes cast down the stack, "A em sym as hu, man," he whispers.

"Next time. Don't want to miss next time, folks. We're going to be talking about how to have a female orgasm. Even if you're not a woman."

SINGLE SERVING

The Seattle GIB building was built with efficiency in mind. The layout of the building was designed by the analysts themselves. From the space-time metric of past transactions between various employees. Analyses of past transactions led to an algorithm that calculated the best distribution of offices. The metric gave an optimal design for reducing the average distance required for transactions. The most snuggled arrangement possible. And it was thought that this would be a good thing.

"Hello…is someone there?" the old man asks.

Gary is running an errand and has just entered an unfamiliar bathroom. He sees the walker in front of the stall.

"Uh. Yes. Yes, it's me, sir—Gary Saar."

"Oh Gary! I'm glad you're here. Say, could you go down to another restroom and get me some paper?" Henry laughs. "I'm afraid I climbed in here and started my business without looking to see if I had everything I need first!"

Gary says yes…that he will. He will go get some toilette paper. He will be right back.

He hurries down halls, scanning the doors. Because the GIB Analyses building has been designed by the analysts themselves—by way of an algorithm that has sought the most snuggled arrangement—the locations of the bathrooms are largely unpredictable. The algorithm has not been given anything to represent the value of expectancy, the experience a man acquires in his life of looking for men's rooms that he distills into an anticipation, an expectancy for typical places a men's room might appear—near the stairwell, at the end of a hall, beside the elevator, or at least in general proximity to the fucking women's would be nice!

After finding two women's restrooms but no men's, Gary finally climbs the stairs down to a floor he is familiar with. A bathroom he is familiar with.

He enters. Someone is using the stall. He listens a moment. It sounds like the person is finishing.

Paul in the Hall, baby Big Fly, unclips the door and swings it open. He isn't out of the stall before his head cocks and the vacant expression in his eyes reflect that he is accessing the company roster. "Gary! What's up?" Paul in the Hall comes out of the stall using his thumbs to raise his belt and thereby straighten his sagging zipper.

What's up? Gary understands Paul's question to be rhetorical. The inflection and expression of the question mark indicate that Paul's question abandoned all interest in the answer even before it left Paul's mouth. In any case, if it was ever attracted to an answer, if once after conception but before leaving Paul it was ever a real question with a hard question mark, then the question had to do with Paul rather than Gary. It is either a rhetorical question or a self-query, but in either case it has little to do with Gary, who is anyway busy trying to squelch images from forming in his head, images initiated from the sounds a moment earlier. The hasty and aggressive sounds of Fly Paul wiping himself.

Gary waits and watches as Fly Paul first squirts some water on his hands and then wrenches a tall stack of paper towels out of the dispenser. The Fly pats his hands and then throws the still folded stack into the trash.

Once Paul has left, Gary goes into the stall.

This toilet doesn't have rolls. Just a stainless-steel box with a stack of individual paper squares, a dispenser of the same design as that for the paper towels, but smaller; a stack of little wipes, each sheet having some kind of origami clutch on the next one up such that when one sheet leaves the box another peeks out to see it off. An ingenious design that guarantees the toilet-goer a perpetually presented wipe, except in two cases: if the box becomes empty (that is, if the caboose wipe is reached); or if some fucker like Fly Paul tries to reach inside and grab a pile of sheets all at once, as he did with the paper towels.

The second is the case with which Gary is presented. Fly Paul has somehow managed to slip his shitty little fingers up through the tiny slot. Invade the protected space of the stack. But because of the more delicate nature of the operation, he hasn't been as successful as he had with the paper towels. Instead of a crisp single sheet hanging from the lips of the dispenser, a mop of tissue, ripped and raped, vomits from the bottom of the box.

The thoughtful design of the paper dispenser, with its origami clutching train of wipes, is intended not only to decrease waste but to provide assurance of hygiene. It is very clever in this regard. Gary has attended public toilets before where, ready to wipe his ass, he found the toilet-paper spool at large in the stall; a free-range roll, which on closer inspection showed a curious bloating on one end, suggesting that the paper became wet at one time in the past. Had the roll fallen down to a toilet-overflown floor? Or had some fuck pissed on the spool?

While the bare-roll dispenser is prone to waste and hygiene issues, the thoughtful design of the origami dispenser is directed at fixing exactly these problems. And it usually does. But it underestimates the resolution of the opposing forces. Had Fly Paul used a coat hanger or some other tool? How had he managed to pull so much of the inside stack partially through the slot? And clog it so very tightly?

Gary takes a pen from his shirt pocket. Not a good one, but a cheap, disposable one. He pries into the slot and after much effort and shredded paper, he restores the train system Fly Paul derailed. A few dozen more sheets are wasted before the flow of paper looks again crisp and unfondled. Gary leaves the enormous pile of waste on the floor for the janitor, who will hopefully have specialized tools for dealing with it. Now how many sheets should he bring to Associate Director Walker?

How many sheets does someone typically use to wipe his ass? What about old men? Do they use more? Less? One sheet of *paper towel* is justifiably an individual serving. Spartan but sufficient. But one sheet of toilet paper? Is that an individual serving? Is this what most people need—one sheet? Gary doubts that most people get by with just one sheet—he sure doesn't. But how can he know how it is for others? Even records of paper purchases could not provide information about how many sheets are used per session. If studies of primitive cultures are a guide, people should be taking a dump about twenty minutes after every meal. That means several sessions per day. Gary is sure that he doesn't average even one session per day, and he doesn't know what to think about this. He recently read that John Wayne died with forty pounds of shit inside of him. And that everybody—except maybe the primitive people who shit after every meal—carries a discernible fraction of their body weight in the form of crusted-on crap.

Gary realizes that he has little more to go by than his own consumption. He knows how much paper *he* would typically need for a typical session. But still, for some reason that is probably related to the norms of his culture, he is left with almost no ability to estimate how much paper someone else will need. This is important because if Director Walker wipes his ass the way Paul in the Hall dries his hands, then Gary will be pulling tiny sheets from the dispenser all afternoon.

Gary figures that he should err on the side of waste. Not quite a stack in the spirit of Fly Paul, but probably on the high side of what could go down in one flush. He brings the stack he assembled out of the bathroom and quickly into the elevator. He would have liked to wad it up to conceal it from the others in the elevator. But he didn't want the stack looking too fondled.

Gary returns to the bathroom to find Henry beside the sink, washing his hands.

Gary stands, his err-on-the-side-of-waste toilette paper stack silently demanding an explanation.

"Oh, you're back. Thanks, Gary. That was sweet of you. But I made do. Say, did you take a look at that Smutty app?"

Gary sets the stack of toilet tissues on a dry spot of the countertop. "Yes, sir. I mean I took a look at it…"

"Yes, that's what I asked."

"Well, I mean, I don't know."

"…"

"I mean, I don't know if GAIA would use it. Kind of depends on what for and when and stuff like that."

Henry smiles. He leans into the mirror for a minute and straightens his thin hair. "Yea-uh, that's kind of what I thought, too."

DEFINITELY BANGS

MEDUSA

From very close up, say through a mail slot positioned in front of his eyes, it is already clear that there are many lunchers here in the GIB cafeteria who Gary hates. Watching his angry eyes dart furtively, it is unclear if there are even any for which he holds ambivalence. Perhaps there are, and his eyes simply never stop on them.

Back up slightly from the mail-slot view and watch his chew. The manner in which his mouth greets and admits the food is erratic, unattended. He chews too hard and long on some bites, while just swallowing others. His lips are not really closed while he eats. When he sucks from the top of a straw, it is very unusual that there is absolutely nothing endearing gained in his upper lip; the hatred he broadcasts defeats even the sweet suggestion of breast-feeding.

Backing further, Gary's new hair comes into view. It is really spectacular. Both techno and dread, and surely worthy of ridicule.

"Casual Friday? Huh huh huh."

"Mop head. Huh huh huh."

"Medusa. Huh huh huh."

Gary hears the fuckers around him whisper and laugh.

Just filling out stupid questionnaires was not enough. It seems that the Algs are not learning how to detect GAIA as quickly as Cornbread hoped. Sure, the Algs seem to be learning from Gary, but they also seem to be getting very confused, especially recently, sometimes shooting off in weird directions and returning bizarre conclusions. Hogging cluster CPU at a rate affecting the air-conditioning bill and yet still sometimes flopping stupidly over obvious GAIA links. It is hard to be certain, but this is an impression forming with Cornbread and his Algs development team. Sucking Gary's brain has only been partial successful with the questionnaires. This approach requires Gary's cooperation and a can-do spirit that has been very unreliable with him.

And then the idea of just hard-sucking Gary's brain directly through his cranium came up. The analyst who suggested it to Director Cornbread got good praise. Yes, Gary is not really a team player. And he is so unpleasant to work with. How about they just hook him up to an electrode skull cap to measure his brain waves directly? Feed all that to the Algs and let their neural nets decide what's what.

They need simply hook Gary up and watch his brain as he watches data clips all day. Because it takes nearly an hour to get all the electrodes placed on his skull, he can't take them off at lunch time. This comes as an order from his high boss Cornbread and, contrary to what Gary thought, such is permitted in one interpretation of his employment contract.

This is as low as it gets. Not just the humiliation. Not just the lack of any recognition. The lack of promotions. But the whole collapse of his reason for being here. His reason for having joined GIB. GIB has become its own lower-case definition: *merely a bolt, wedge, or pin for holding part of a machine or structure in place*. He is not fighting crime. He is not helping the world. He is a cog supporting a machine that serves the special interests of powerful money grubbers that lurk somewhere in the shadows and only show their faces to those servants willing to seal their kissy lips to powerful money-grubbing buttholes. All the kiss-up, kick-down ambitious Big Flies that have risen through the ranks despite their being intellectually mediocre and entirely lacking in self-reflection and existential worth.

Gary realizes, chest now rising in his chair, hands preparing to rip electrodes from his head, what he must do. He will leave GIB. Quit. Tell Cornbread and all his butt-sniffing Big Flies, all those fuckers, to go fucking fuck themselves. And then he'll grow his hair out into a fat ponytail, and still hang out at the Faraday Cage so all the Flies that come by can see his new freedom, and his carefree, go-fuck-yourself face, and—

"Ahoy!"

Gary turns to see Henry Walker. Arriving slowly, like he will next throw a docking rope from his walker.

* * *

Gary discovers that he will be eating lunch again. The two take trays off a counter-weighted dispenser. Henry sets the tray across his walker bars and points at the tray dispenser. "These things remind me of those Pez things. Don't they you?"

Gary doesn't respond.

Henry turns and looks at Gary. "Pez...you know Pez, don't you?"

Gary looks confused.

"You know, Pez with the candy that pops up?" Henry studies Gary's face. "You never had a Pez when you were a boy? Maybe a Bozo the Clown? Or a Bugs Bunny?"

Gary shakes his head.

"How about Daffy Duck? Did you have a Daffy Duck?"

Gary shakes his head again and diverts his eyes.

"Snow White?...Dopey?...Batman?...Big Bird?...Droopy Dog? Did you have a Droopy Dog?" Henry sets his tray back down in the dispenser and then reaches his arm over the top of his head and pulls his forehead far back to illustrate the manner in which a tiny candy brick would be raised and offered from his open trachea, if he were a Pez dispenser.

"All right!" Gary chuckles. "I had a Pooh Bear!"

"A Pooh Bear." Henry smiles. "You mean that fat little bear with no pants?"

"And a Wilma for a short while before that."

"You mean Wilma Flintstone?"

"Yes, sir. Wilma Flintstone."

One of Henry's eyes becomes small as he looks up at Gary. "How did you wind up with Wilma? I never heard of a boy getting a Wilma before."

"She fell out of a kid's birthday piñata."

"Aah!" This makes sense to Henry. "So you were down on the floor, grabbing whatever you could get. And that's how you wound up with Wilma?"

"Yes, sir."

"But then you got rid of her…once you got your Pooh, I mean?"

Gary raises his tray in front of him a bit. "Yes. I mean no. I'm not sure."

Henry seems pleased that they understand each other now. He picks up his tray again. He slides it down the counter, following incrementally with his walker, and then he stops and turns to the employee on the other side of the casseroles.

"Berries and milk?" the employee asks.

"Yes, Samuel. Please," Henry responds.

"Berries and milk?" Gary asks Henry.

"Yes, berries and milk…Thanks, Sam…I always get the same thing." Henry sets the bowl of berries and milk down on the tray.

"That was…that was pretty quick."

"Yes." Henry slides his bowl and then his walker toward the corn flakes. He describes the recipe to Gary in the same tone as he would if it were complicated. "They put some frozen blueberries in the bottom of the bowl." He points into the bottom of the bowl. "And then they pour in some milk, about—" He shows with his finger. "---halfway, sixty percent, of the way up. They know to leave me room for my cornflakes." He gestures toward a shelf of breakfast cereal coming up along the tray track. "Samuel is pretty good at seeing when I arrive, and he gets the bowl going so the berries will start de-thawing."

Gary pulls a plate of lasagna down.

"But it's got to be soymilk. I can't handle cow's milk," Henry adds as he slides his tray a little further.

They arrive at the cashier. The cashier has to wait because Henry has returned to his earlier description: he has the little cereal box partially open now and is pointing down at the occupants. "I sprinkle them in as I go, so they don't get soggy too quick." He pretends to demonstrate sprinkling. "The milk turns blue because of the berries…purple, really."

They move to sit at a cafeteria table, and Henry begins to assemble his meal in the manner he just described. Gary observes that the milk has frozen around Henry's berries. He watches the old man cruise a spoon back and forth across the bowl like an ice breaker clearing a frozen pond. It isn't yet ready for flakes.

Henry sees that Gary is waiting for him. "Oh, please go ahead, Gary. Your lasagna will get cold."

Gary nods and brings a crossed knife and fork down together through the center of his meal.

Henry sprinkles corn flakes—eleven or twelve flakes at a time; never more nor less by what Gary observes. It looks like a very slow process.

"See that one there?" Henry asks, leaning over his bowl and testing the buoyancy of one of the flakes with his spoon tip. "I think it's already taken on too much milk."

Gary is a little confused but leans over the table to look at the floating cornflake too.

"So what do you know about Braid?" Henry whispers.

Gary hesitates. "The person or the pattern?"

Henry laughs in a manner that blows them both back from the bowl. "You mean the software or the hardware?" But he quickly draws Gary back to the floating cornflake with his spoon. "Both, I mean."

Gary looks around the food-court cafeteria. "Are you sure it's safe here?"

Henry looks up. "I take it you mean whether this is a secure enough environment for discussing classified material?"

"Yes."

"You're right, the bathrooms would be safer. But here's pretty safe too."

"The bathrooms? What do you mean?"

Henry laughs. "Surely you remember Elise Horton over in the Procurement Annex."

"I remember something about a spy cam that was found in her bathroom stall."

"You mean you've never seen the footage?" Henry laughs. "It got out on the internet somehow, and I thought everyone in the world had seen it by now."

"Well I guess I wasn't sufficiently interested in seeing an old lady take a dump."

Henry chuckles, and his voice descends to a growl. "Oh, but this is really worth seeing." He lowers his spoon and leans over, grinning. "I guess the camera was fastened somehow to the inside of the toilet bowl, and it was looking up at her. It's really worth seeing."

Gary isn't sure how to respond. Henry continues: "Anyway, she wasn't just an old lady taking a dump. She sat on the sexual harassment committee, and there was quite a bit of policy change after that."

"How so?"

"Well, for example, all the bathrooms are now screened regularly for surveillance equipment. That's not done by GIB but rather by an independent group set up by the employees."

"So what does that mean? Our offices aren't safe?"

"Well, you never know. Surveillance equipment is all over the place these days. And it can be pretty hard to detect if you don't know what to look for. In any case, the bathrooms are safer."

Gary hadn't suspected that the offices might be monitored, even though he knew the technology existed for doing so. It takes him a moment to pull his mind off the subject. He leans over Henry's bowl and points to a cornflake. "I only know the pattern, not the person."

"What kind of pattern?"

"I'm not sure I've ever been good at describing it."

"You mean you aren't sure yourself what it is you recognize?"

Gary laughs. "That's probably correct. I mostly just recognize her pattern as 'freaky,' 'funny,' maybe 'beautiful.'"

"Beautiful?" Henry asks, raising his head and appearing to appreciate the word as a compliment.

"Yeah. There's poetry in the arrangement of contingencies around her."

"Contingencies? Sounds like she has to rely on a whole bunch of little things going right."

"Well, I'm not sure *rely* is the right word. *Rely* sort of assumes she has a particular plan she follows. I think Braid is just channeling the situation around her as she goes along. It seems like the only thing she relies on is that there is always a hatch, or a trap door, or some secret about her surrounding that will pop up when she needs it and take her where she needs to go."

"But there seems to be so much coordination in her actions. Her actions together with GAIA, I mean. She doesn't have to plan that up in advance?"

"No. I don't think so. She just has to pay attention and plans unfold. I think Braid just reads her surroundings—she surfs serendipity. All the GAIAns do, to some extent, but it's extreme in her case."

"So that's where the name comes from? You named her? Braid braids her surroundings together; she surfs serendipity?" Henry looks delighted.

"Yes…I mean I don't know anything about Braid, the person; I don't even know if she's a female or even an individual. I just keep finding this pattern and had to label it somehow."

"You mean sort of like how unknown serial killers are given names according to their individual crime styles." Henry still looks delighted.

"Yeah." Gary pauses, remembering he has also used this metaphor. "But, like I say, I'm talking about a data pattern. That's the Braid I know about. IS is creating a Braid program in the Algs that attempts a digital embodiment of that pattern. Its neural nets are being trained to act like her. So it can recognize her. You put it in a situation, and it's supposed to act like she would. But it's still pretty lousy at being her, from what I've seen. Computer programs aren't very good at surfing serendipity."

"So it was you that gave her her name!" Henry is smiling.

"Yes, I guess. But like I say, I don't know if she's—"

"You were the one who was first to call her a *her*."

"Well, like I say," Gary repeats, "I don't know if she's really a woman. I just started saying 'she' because something in the pattern reminds me of a woman."

Gary notices that Henry's questions are not unlike the ones Cornbread asked. And yet Henry's intention in asking them seems totally different. Gary sees how much his own response depends on his perception of the questioner's intention. And sort of whether he likes them.

There are two dozen or more flakes left in the box. Henry pours them all into the bowl now and begins to expedite his lunch.

"I'd like you to come work with me in the Borderlines," Henry says, before raising the bowl to his lips to drink the remaining purple milk. "And I'd like you to become a GAIAn."

Gary waits for him to lower the bowl. "I beg your pardon?"

"I want you to learn everything about them, until you can think the way they do." Henry wipes his mouth. "Pretend like you're one of them and try to see things the way they do."

"Why?"

"Why? GIB doesn't understand very well how GAIA organizes itself." He laughs. "GAIA doesn't have any command hierarchy we can find. They don't even have an official newsletter. But, as you know, they carry out wonderfully coordinated activities. Some say GAIA isn't an organization at all but instead a level of awareness. You don't join, you become. And that's how they do what they do." Henry gets up and begins to transfer himself to his walker docked alongside the table. "How about you see if you can learn how to surf serendipity, like beautiful Braid does." He gives a Reaganesque waive and pulls away from the table. "I'm sending you a young lady to help out."

ALIVE SINCE CHRIST

Nicolas awakes in a tree. He sits up in his sleeping bag and looks around. This is his first morning.

The tree, a *Sequoia gigantea*, is named Sequitur and has the curious distinction that its age is identical to the calendar date. This has been verified with a core sample. No kidding, the tree has been alive since Christ. Nicolas's task is to learn what this means. Not just intellectually but emotionally. Two thousand years posted on this hillside. Two thousand years watching that valley. It is such an expansive amount of time that "this hillside" and "that valley" are of little meaning without the tree. In that much time, the tree's branches have probably dropped tons of leaves—or "scales" as they are called. Its roots have probably jack-hammered apart boulders of hillside rock that have mixed with the tons of scales to create rivers of yolk that have washed down into the valley below to await the seeds that helicopter down after a forest fire triggers the opening of the tree's pine cones. Rather than being a rare cataclysm, forest fires are a reliable part of Sequitur's reproductive cycle.

At first glance, the tree seems merely added to the environment, like a birthday candle stuck in a cake. But even a birthday candle, if left to burn for two thousand years, will surely transform the cake with its wax and the air with its breath.

Nicolas stretches an arm out of his sleeping bag to fetch a bag of granola. He pulls the breakfast back and worms across the platform so he can use the tree trunk for back support. The tree house was built a generation earlier by hippies. To save the tree from loggers, they occupied it continuously for over four years.

Four years, probably a whole saga for these hippies, was just a moment in the long history of this tree that remembers the Little Ice Age of the Middle Ages as a chilly midlife event. During its life it has felt distant earthquakes and smelled every major volcanic eruption on the globe. It regards fires, droughts, and El Niño mayhem as frequent. Nicolas's task is to grasp the depth and wisdom of this two-thousand-year-old living being. What does being alive for so long feel like? He will never be able to understand this expansive perspective in all its details, but he might come to appreciate the central aspects. He can come down then.

Neutering Maypoles

Why am I here? Gary Saar asks himself. The question has become the campaign slogan of his rolling identity crisis. It sits in a dark chair at every meal and meeting. It's in his dreams and nightmares. Though the meeting with Walker has indeed shuffled some of his existential thoughts, it is still there—why am I here?

So it is a very pleasant morning when the heart holds curiosity. For then the existential crisis is at bay. Usurped by a wonderful wonder over what oh what's gonna happen today.

Gary has discovered that the aide Henry is sending him is Patricia Concept. That woman from Travel with the perfect hair part. Gary totally wants to see how this thing with the new aide is going to work out. He's never been a boss before.

This is derailed immediately when they meet. Patricia Concept does not accept his thanks for her aid. Because she is not an aide.

There is some feigned confusion over who meant what, but she smelled it out right: Gary is confused. She is not his aide. They are colleagues Henry has set to work together on a task. Patricia read the transfer assignment papers. Gary should have too. To make things worse for him, she claims she can understand how he could make such a mistake.

"Do you want to start this in my cubicle, or yours?" she asks.

"Ahm. Well, we're in mine already. Maybe we can start here? And yours next time, if that's convenient for you. Maybe alternate, if you want, like that and—"

"It's okay about the mix-up," she says. "Stuff like that happens more often than you would think. Maybe I could have gotten out of Travel faster otherwise."

Gary thinks about this. "So did Walker recruit you too?"

"More like rescue. I joined GIB to analyze data. Not to do people's travel admin. I didn't go to college for eight years for that."

"You went to college for eight years?"

"Yes."

"Then why were you put in Travel?"

"Because I wasn't sexually interested in one of my bosses."

"I think I can see how something like that could happen," Gary says, with sudden sincerity and not meaning that stuff like that happening at all is at all good or should ever happen again. "Do you know our assignment then? Because you read the papers?"

"Yes. I collected the files we're supposed to go through."

"..."

"On the Reverend Pea. I already went through them once myself. We're supposed to go through his broadcasts and decide if when he says 'GAIA' he means the terrorist network or the Earth goddess."

"You think GAIA is a terrorist network?"

Patricia turns. Toward Gary. She appears to really appreciate this question from him. She takes his mouse. "That is the classification IS uses."

"But we're in Borderlines now."

She nods, clicks down to one of the files she collected, and presses play.

I heard the story so I just had to come to Sweden and check it for myself. Let me get right to the point: did you know we've been castrating our maypoles?

Patricia explains that Jimmy is at a celebration in Sweden. He is participating in the maypole dance and the camera is probably a smartphone in his shirt pocket. She fast-forwards. The camera hops around the pole a few times and shows colorful ribbons and blond children. And then a few more times but with the lens pointed up at the top of the pole. Patricia narrates quickly to keep up with the fast-forwarded images: "Here he's suggesting that we try to guess what the two big rings up at the top of the pole are. What could they be? Our maypoles back home don't have them. What could they be? We have two laps around the pole to try to guess.

Testicles. That's right. Balls. *Cajones.* He then asks us why a pagan ritual would want to use such symbolism. We have one lap to guess." On fast forward, the lap is quick. "Fertility. The loops at the top are the balls, and the pole is sticking into the Earth." Patricia returns the video to play and lets the reverend speak for himself:

You see the people, here in this land, once upon a time regularly communed with Nature. Their crops sprung from Ma Nature's fertility...and so this kind of festival made a lot of sense to them. They wouldn't want the mother to go into menopause any time soon, so it's just plain prudent to show their appreciation for all she's done for them so far.

Fast forward. "Here he describes how in his home state, at least, they've always had maypoles. But because the testicles have been cut off the poles the symbolism is strangely that of humping Ma Nature while withholding seed."

"Does he say 'humping'?"

"Yes. He recites a biblical description of a shepherd pulling his penis out of a woman's vagina and ejaculating on the ground. He claims this is usually the citation used to support the Christian contention that masturbation is bad. He discusses the implications of an attitude that withholds seed to Mother Earth while zealously promoting our own fertility. He wonders how that's supposed to work out."

"What's he doing now?" Gary asks, pointing at the screen.

"He's eating items he picked up at the smorgasbord."

"And he's talking?"

"Yes, sir."

"Is he still talking about the infertile maypoles?"

Patricia hesitates. "No." She returns the video back to play.

...never thought I needed any self-help, so I'd never ever been in such a section before. But I got to say...there's self-help for just about every kind of self and help you can imagine. I was expecting something like Dale Carnegie describing how to use spiritual transcendence to get ahead of others in the business world. But I was astonished at just how much is offered now. I myself was drawn to a package with a CD and a pamphlet that claims it can teach me to have a female orgasm. Even though I'm not a woman.

They had the pamphlet and CD closed up in some kind of plastic that took me a while to chew through...but soon enough I got it open. And there it was—the steps toward cultivating my very own wrong-sex orgasm.

The language inside the package isn't as strongly worded as it is on the outside. I wasn't sure whether they were still claiming I could be taught to go into that peculiar state I've seen on women—where their eyes roll to the back of their head, and they start spitting and breaking furniture. That's what I was curious about trying. But I decided I was anyway going to keep an open mind and start trying to cultivate my opposite-sex sensitivity. What I've learned so far is already pretty interesting, so I thought I'd share it with you all.

Now I had to listen to the CD six times to understand what they were saying, so expect the same effort from yourself if you're seriously curious about this. Really a small price to pay, when you think about what you're getting.

Orgasms take place in the brain. That's one of the first points the tape makes...I guess it's a CD, really. The second part is that the brain isn't just in your head. You got brain in your gut, in your immune system—brain everywhere. Now they say that this brain equipment is about the same in either a man or a woman. So if you each got the same brain equipment, and it's in the brain where the orgasm occurs, then maybe it's possible to have whichever orgasm you want. That is if you can figure out how to trigger it with the right input. But the next question

I had was whether I needed a vagina...or clitoris...or some of that kind of special equipment in order to produce the right triggering sequence in the brain. Tape says I don't.

First off, two types of female orgasms—vaginal and clitoral. Tape says the clitoral one isn't that different than the one I already know about...so I skipped to the section on the vaginal ones. That's the kind of female orgasm I was most curious about, anyway.

Gary unconsciously rolls in his chair. A little further away from Patricia. Almost as far as he can in his little cubicle.

How does a man learn to have a vaginal orgasm? The tape gives instructions.

When the right combination of buttons is pressed in my brain, I'm supposed to be able to enter a vaginal orgasm state—just like a woman. But do I have the right kind and number of fingers for pressing these chords all together and at the same time? That's what I wondered. Tape says I do. Tape says as far as the genitals are concerned"—Jimmy kind of points with his paper plate at his own groin— *"as far as the genitals are concerned, they're just bundles of nerve endings. Nerve endings that send the same kind of signals to the brain when they get vibrated in a certain way.*

Hard part, tape says, is to get all the signals being sent to your brain that are coming from all the other parts of your body—including even your brain. This is where all the work is. You gotta learn to feel and think like a woman before you can induce a female orgasm state in your own male brain—that's what I understood. Tape suggests spending time closely observing the opposite sex...if you haven't already. If you haven't already done at least this, you probably aren't yet ready for the course, tape says.

Patricia fast-forwards a bit more. Stops. Play.

Let's say you've learned to put yourself in a state where you feel and think like a woman. What then?

She fast-forwards further while summarizing, unavoidably including some of the preacher's southern accent in her speech: "In the rest, he's describing differences between men and women that affect their relationships with their orgasm. In sex, females show great dedication to their precious egg and spend enormous time caring for it and coaching it for the track meets to come. Men produce cheap and abundant sperm, which they generously offer to just about anybody that might make use of it. This inherent disparity in logistics affects the attitudes men and women have toward the orgasm state..." Fast forward. Stop. Play.

Both male and female orgasms listen primarily to the downstroke rather than the upstroke," Pause. Patricia's eyes fix on the screen following Jimmy's rapidly moving but silent mouth. "By 'downstroke' he means when the penetration of the penis is…"

"Yeah, I got it," Gary interrupts.

Play.

But the visualization for the mindset as well as body posturing associated with the downstroke is different for men and women. The curvature of the torso is opposite, for example. A man's chest is pushed out in a jabbing, giving posture, while women's posture is more like receiving; she's a receptacle.

Gary can't help noticing that Concept's posture illustrates these points as she views the reverend. She notices he notices this, and presses play to let Jimmy take over:

Now a man is probably not going to be comfortable holding an image of himself as a receptacle. So how in hell is he going to put himself in a female mind-set? Concept presses fast forward again for a moment. And then play again:

…chord triggering your orgasm has not just your genitals as notes but your whole mind set. So if you are a man wanting to have a woman's orgasm, tape says you gotta be ready to adopt a mind-set where you're ready to spread your legs and scream, 'Give it to me! Give it to me! Give it to…'

Concept presses stop. "I think that's most of it."

There is silence as Gary and Patricia stare at the frozen image of the Reverend on the screen. Jimmy Pea with his shoulders back, his knees raised and parted, and his arms forward like they are holding onto a big steering wheel. A slobbery and excited expression on his face.

"Should we break for lunch?"

"Yeah. Sure."

There's a Cactus

"Nicolas, am I mistaken or is that your second family-size bag of Cheetos today?"

Nicolas's eyes are at half-mast, and he holds a Cheeto in his lips like a lazy cigarette. "Don't worry about it."

Eve wears vintage driving gloves—the leather is delicate and elegantly tattered—continuously since she found them in a yard sale held in the parking lot of a church in a town they passed through the day before. Her British accent continues: "Should I assume then that you will be unable to take a shift at the wheel until we stop to wash your grubby little paws?"

Nicolas sits low on the passenger side of the bench and stares angrily at the glove compartment in front of him. And then he aborts this posture

94

and sits up to choose a different configuration. He turns to Eve and holds up his hands. His fingers, splayed in the air and strangely orange, are reminiscent of a Dr. Seuss creature.

Eve considers his visual comment. She runs her gloved fingers down the hard corrugations that ripple the hood side of the steering wheel. "You make a good point."

"I mean the, the steewing wheel---" Nicolas gestures, his hands moving closer to her. "---is the pwimary pwoint of ewecticul contact bwetween dwiver and dwiven." He sputters a bit as he speaks.

"I said you made a good point." Eve's British accent stops, and now it is something else. She looks impressively irritated. He continues:

"The ownwee contact pwoint---" He licks his fingers. "---where you can gwab it hawd and fweel that knuckled webbing on the underside of it."

Eve laughs like an applause.

"Sweaty hands hwolding it like one of dose dubba-handed, antiaircraft, da-da-da-da guns. A couple fingas always weady to stwetch over to the horn bar in case—oh, look!" Nicolas presses his orange finger on the glass. "There's a cactus!"

Eve is silent and uncertain for exactly a second while her mood boils over like a pot of milk. She laughs. She continues to laugh. Her laugh resonates in her and increases to make more laughs. She laughs hard. Harder. Harderer. Attempting to repeat the "oh look, there's a cactus!" but getting progressively less far through it with each new attempt. She has to pull over.

Nicolas watches and waits a minute.

"Eve? Are you all right?"

Eve is all right; she just needs a minute. She comes off the carousel teary-eyed, some pistons in her chest still dieseling.

Through the passenger window, a breeze tosses a thin clump of Nicolas's hair. Eve stares at him. Her eyes are teary, her mouth looks like "eat" and otherwise her expression is neutral.

After a moment, she shifts her eyes slowly toward the open window. Her pupils adjust, her posture animates suddenly, her British voice returns, and she says with the glee and genuine surprise that only a British tourist could possibly have: "Oh look, there's a cactus!" In a delighted fashion, she hops out of the car to run across the desert. Nicolas moves to follow her. On the car floor he finds a plastic baggy— no, a paper bag—and covers his hand with it before pulling the door latch to run after her.

ILIAC SPINES

Patricia Concept's cubicle is small. So is she. These two facts help Gary with some awareness concerning his cowardice in describing how he feels about her. His inability to even call her Patricia.

She stands on a chair to reach the top of the cabinet; she needs the schematic of the car Jimmy Pea rented. Her white blouse has come loose from her navy-blue skirt. Not excessively, just slightly.

Gary sits only three feet away. Under her. And is transfixed…by two bones. Two protruding bones. The ones casting parentheses around her womb. Two bones still mostly covered by blouse and skirt. The valley, the shallow gulch on each side of her naval is bracketed by her beautiful anterior superior iliac spines…the rim of the Jiffy Pop pan…the part that will stay put when she becomes pregnant.

A reverberation bangs around in Gary's body and delivers the message: how can he compliment her at all—on her extreme competence, her professionalism, her punctuality, her organizational abilities, or her new glasses, which are so nicely smaller than the last ones—when he hides what he feels about this, this in front of him, these two bones?

"Gary?"

"YES!"

"Gary? Can…" Patricia is trying to hand a file down to Gary. But she sees Gary is distracted. She notices the direction of his eyes. "Oh Jesus! Spaghetti sauce?"

"YES!"

"Dammit!" She drops the file onto her desk. She bends and pulls the front of her blouse completely out of the skirt and stretches it forward to examine it. "I just bought this. I can't believe it. I'm like a little girl that needs a bib."

"NO!"

Patricia looks toward Gary. Confused.

"No. No spaghetti sauce."

"No spaghetti sauce?"

"No, sorry. I was…I was looking at something else."

This seems to worry Patricia even more than spaghetti sauce. She pulls her blouse forward again for inspection. "A hundred and thirty dollars. Did I already catch it on my car door?"

"No no. No. Your shirt is fine."

Patricia steps down from the chair. She looks now a little self-conscious. "Then what were you staring at?" Her fingers land defensively on the soft, slightly untoned, center of her stomach.

Gary's eyes are now evasive. He's trying to reply. Maybe vocally soon, but for now he can hold his hands in the shape of little parenthesis as he starts and immediately aborts sentences.

Patricia laughs, a little shortly and maybe aggressively. "You caught a fish how big?"

"No. No, I mean---" By way of clarification, Gary makes reference to Jiffy Pop. There's a part of the pan that puffs out. And there's a rim part of the pan that doesn't. Doesn't puff out.

Yes. Patricia knows this. About Jiffy Pop pans.

"No. No, I mean...your...your superior anterior iliac spines."

"My what?" Patricia immediately raises her blouse up to the brassiere cups and begins a more careful examination of herself.

The whole Jiffy Pop pan is now in plain view for Gary one office chair away. Her beautiful anterior superior iliac spines casting parentheses around her womb. But Gary's butane gaze has shifted now to the small underside section of her undergarment that has appeared. The cloth is black, sheeny, and wrapped tightly on the thick underwire that forms a gentle sinusoid supporting her large breasts. From the bottom of the wire, the cloth stretches across the center bridge as would a solution to Laplace's Equation. This part of the brassiere has zero net curvature, a result of the fabric being needed more urgently elsewhere. Here it obeys a boundary-value equation that seeks the least fabric needed to span the support wires.

Very little of the brassiere above the underwire is visible, but it is clear that this section is governed by the Poisson, not Laplace, Equation. Net curvature is maintained by an inexorable outward pushing force. Stretching the fabric from the underwire outward and upward, bilateral symmetry arrives ultimately in twin zeniths, each of which is technically called the 'point of burst' of the brassiere.

"The schematic of the car that Jimmy Pea rented."

"..."

Patricia has lowered her blouse. "I was showing you the position of the drink caddy, which I believe Jimmy used to support the camera he used to record the Florida episode we've been watching."

Patricia waits for signs of comprehension in Gary. "The one where he counts the orientations of dead frogs in the highway, sir. Where he claims to have found support for a systematic shift in their wetlands...Gary?"

"Yes, of course. Wetlands."

UNIVERSAL EXPANSION

Nicolas engages Eve with an erectness in posture that he has not held over most of his life. She has it too, and since longer. So they both have erect postures. And this is how they are engaged.

The erectness in posture refers not to a stiffness but rather to a high degree of attentiveness—attentiveness toward each other as well as toward their surroundings. And of a sort that is equally distant from ambivalence and attachment. It is as if the two of them are together on rafters above a stage, legs crossed and sipping champagne, observing the porcelain-faced versions of themselves tap feet on the stage below.

Nicolas observes himself in a round glass door.

"Do you think I would be better with a haircut?"

Eve turns and pretends to form a deliberated opinion. She scans the top of his head, the squirrely hair that thins more like a rarefication with altitude then a pattern baldness.

"Hmm...perhaps bangs...bangs might be nice...I think you should have bangs. Yes, bangs would suit you quite nicely."

"Bangs? Are you really sure?"

"Yes, I'm quite sure, Darling. Definitely bangs." Eve gets up from the wall of plastic chairs and hops clumsily in her sleeping bag toward the wall of dryers.

Bangs. Nicolas considers this.

Nicolas considers bangs, and regards Eve—the elegance with which she holds clothes with her teeth as she checks the dampness of the few garments they have aboard this road trip.

Bangs. Is it the pervasive expansion of the universe, or just its grossly flat shape? Which allows this laundromat to be right now as good as its center.

KOALA BEAR FILTER

Fantasies have approached Gary Saar in various ways. This one is sponsored by a tiny sliver of Gary's visual memory of today. As Patricia Concept lifted her blouse up to the brassiere cups, in pursuit of Gary's reference to her iliac spines, Gary's observational sampling rate went into burst mode. Collected a lot of data in a short amount of time. Gary is cycling through it all just now. As he lies on his bed below the short stucco ceiling, sirens, beautifully singing sirens, lead his factual memory astray. Patricia is up on that chair, blouse up to the brassiere cups, just as before...but now she laughs.

"I'm just shitting with you." She smiles and stares down at him. "I *wanted* you to see my belly."

And Gary hears then his own voice, "Belly? That's no belly. That's almost a six-pack, Mamma. You're tight, honey."

"Tight? Who you saying is tight?"

"You're tight, I'm telling you."

"I'm not tight, Honeybee, look at this."

"That's just your little pudge, Pumpkin. That's the whipped cream. Best part."

As much as fantasies allow, and as much as can be projected onto the stucco ceiling and still be seen through Gary's closed eyelids from the dark bed below, Gary's recollection has left work. This Gary and this Patricia have been transported from her cubicle in a federal intelligence agency to a playful garden where Gary and Patricia have been deeply in love since they were children. A playful garden where the emotional commitment is long and solidly understood and there remains only this new, exuberant, exploration of their body parts.

WAEHHHH...WAEHHHH.

His phone. Landline. The fucking thing rings so few times in a year that each time it does it freaks him out. Gary stumbles out to his kitchenette counter, "What?"

There's a short silence. And then, "Please hold for Mr. Trevor McGregor."

Gary sets the phone on the counter. Thinking. He steps, finally, his missing leg into his boxer brief. He adopts a larger stance over the phone on the countertop.

"..."

"Hey.

"..."

"Hey!...Hey! You called me!

"..."

"Hellowuh? Hey, I'm going to hang up now."

"..."

"Hey, mother fuckers! YOU woke ME up and you aren't even ready to take the call? I mean what kind of fucking shit is that?"

"I'm sorry, Mr. Saar, what kind of what?"

"Hello?"

"Yes."

"..."

"Hello?...Hellowuh?""

"Yes, Mr Saar. I am here for you. I will stay on the line until you are connected."

"Connected? What? Why are you calling me?"

"..."

"Hello!"

"Yes, Mr. Saar, I am here for you."

"Well then---"

"Please hold for Mr. Trevor McGregor."

"What? Who the fuck is Trevor McGregor? Hey! I'm kind of ready to blow up now!"

"Mr. Saar?"

"Who is this NOW? And can you talk finally some STRAIGHT SHIT? Who the fuck ARE you?"

"Mr. Saar?"

"YES! What?"

"Tell me. Tell me what you mean by 'STRAIGHT SHIT'?"

"Huh? What? Who the fuck!"

"My friend. You have asked for STRAIGHT SHIT. I've been tasked with delivering that to you. I'm at your service."

Gary is confused. He earlier left an eighth of the bottle of wine to avoid having drunk a whole bottle this evening. It's here on the counter and he uncorks it and nurses it below the kitchen chandelier. "STRAIGHT SHIT? OKAY. So tell me WHO the fuck you are and WHY the fuck you are calling me like this at this Fucking Hour?"

"Yes, Mr. Saar. Okay, STRAIGHT SHIT, I'm Sonny, and I lead the crisis customer management department. You've actually reached a pretty high level in this conference. I'm sort of here to interface between two species who might not, you know, see eye to eye. Like the panther that must come to understand the cheetah."

"CHEETAH? What the fuck! WHY ARE YOU CALLING ME!"

"Hello, Mr. Saar. We are calling you because Mr. Trevor McGregor would like to speak with you. I am here to expedite this call."

"Expedite! WHO the FUCK is Trevor McGregor!."

"Just one minute, please."

"Mr Saar? Chee chee chee. I am so sorry, Mr Saar. You are waiting long time. Chee chee chee. Very sorry. I am here and very happy to help you now.

"What? Help me? Help me with what? Put McGregor on the phone right now or I'm hanging up!"

"Yes, sir. So sorry. Chee chee chee. This is Mr. Trevor McGregor."

"What? Isn't that a man's name?"

"Yes, chee chee chee, you are right Mr Saar. I am a man."

"A man? What? You sound like some kind of cross between a Japanese schoolgirl and a koala bear. What the fuck is going on?"

"Schoolgirl? Koala bear? OH! Sheeut. You are abso-lutely right! My apologies, partner. Didn't see I was getting piped through that filter. Well it's off now, so we can talk. How can I help?"

"Filter? What?"

"Yes, very sorry about that, partner. I guess your high-decibel level automatically triggered it. The Sweet Girl filter. Supposed to help calm customers down."

"What? I'M responsible for YOU sounding like a fucking koala bear?"

"OH! You mean to tell me the filter is still on? I thought I---hold on, let me check again."

"No, you're not a koala bear NOW. You're a fucking Texas oil man or something."

"OK! Well alrighty then, we're good to start. How can I help?"

"ME? How the fuck should I know? YOU CALLE---"

"Would you like me to review the setup configuration categories we need to go through?"

"Setup config---setup what?"

"Earlier this week, you agreed to receive a setup call from me, Mr. Trevor McGregor."

"I did?"

"Yes, you checked the 'I agree' box."

"I agreed to set up something?"

"Yes, partner. You sure did."

"Set up? What THE FUCK! SET UP WHAT?"

"Chee chee chee. So sorry, Mr. Saar. Chee chee chee. I am here to help you. Your business is very important to---"

"TURN OFF YOUR FUCKING KOALA BEAR FILTER!!!"

"Already on it, partner. Sorry about that. I'm afraid I'll need your help though to keep it from coming back on. See it triggers automatically. Sort of an issue of your loudness, if you know what I mean."

Gary's teeth become very tight in his mouth. He grabs the wine bottle and steps away from the phone. Over to the recycling bin. As far away in the kitchenette that he can get from the phone. The bottle is now empty, he discovers. He grabs it like a toilet plunger and starts forcefully mashing it down into the recycling bin. Crushing aluminum. Breaking glass. Reducing trapped air and lowering the whole center of gravity of his recyclables.

"Mr. Saar, looks like your Smutty already took care of most the preconfig steps." Gary drops the bottle into the recycling bin. Turns sort of in shock toward the phone. McGregor continues, "Sorry it's taken a few days, but Smutty found out what it could about you on your hard drive, as well as anywhere else it could reach through your contact lists. We just need now to complete the final configuration."

"Smutty! FyeNull ConFiguration!" Gary yells inside his closed mouth.

"Your Smutty needs to know what philosophy you want it to start with. Underneath everything, partner, your Smutty needs to understand what you really want it to accomplish."

Gary. Breath. Breath. "I dowunt Have Nor do I Want a Smutty!."

"Ooowh. Hmm. I'm afraid the cow's already out of the barn on that one, partner. I'm looking at your 'Agree' boxes right here. And the time stamps. Look at that. Looks like you just kind of pressed all of the boxes at the same time."

"So. Fucking. What. I don't. Want. A Smutty!"

"Yeah. Don't want. Hmm. Describes right here box three. I'll recite: 'Your Smutty is a distributed intelligence. Once activated, your Smutty cannot be recalled or retired.'"

"What the Fuck? Just Kill it! I DON'T WANT A SMUTTY!"

"Chee chee chee. Hello Mr. Saar, very sorry, I am here to---"

"TURN OFF YOUR---"

"Got it. Sorry that keeps flipping on. Maybe we should try to keep it down?"

"Wait. Holy mutherfuckingshit. YOU're an AI. You aren't fucking Trevor McGregor, you're an AI!"

"Sure thing, partner. You can call me that if you want. I think of myself more as an installation helper agent, but you can---"

"You're a fucking AI!"

"Well, now, I don't know if you should be calling me a fucking AI. Technically,---"

"You. Are. A. Fucking A I. I can't fucking believe it. Why all the Please Hold, and You are There for me Bullshit?"

"Well, as you know, partner, this is a beta version of the software and so as a beta customer you are helping us sort out some kinks. That was Agree Box nine. Our Smutty installation package is still working out the best approach. We have modeled our customer support side using information retrieved from the customer transactions of highly successful and prestigious businesses."

"What? You had me on hold and dicked me around for twenty minutes just so my user experience would seem authentic?"

"Yes sir. We work very hard to try to make the experience feel as human as possible. Now back to config. Seems, from the messages coming out of your neighbor's apartment, that you aren't really concerned about whether people know that you watch porn. Masturbate. So---"

"What?!" Gary looks through his bedroom toward the window. "Which neighbor? The fucking Applebaums?"

" So tell me then, partner, what is it? If you're not trying to hide your porn, what is it you want your Smutty to accomplish for you?"

MARAVILLAS

FERNANDO'S LEGEND

Jimmy Pea weighs the open lunch box in his hands, but his eyes are on the cliff face, the cliff face of interesting stratiform thingies. The cliff face under construction in front of him.

"Over here. Dis way, Jimmy." Jimmy's new friend Fernando has a lunch box too. He points with the leg of a cooked chicken as he walks toward the base of the rock wall. At the base of the scaffolding. "We going take deh estairs. Okay wid dju?"

"Sure, I think I can walk and eat at the same time," Jimmy says, somewhat distracted as he looks down into his lunch box. "Why's this chicken yellow, Fernando?"

"Maravillas!" Fernando's mouth is full so the reply is short, and he is leading the way, so his face is also turned away. "Dju say marigold."

Jimmy doesn't understand Fernando's reply and searches the context for meaning. "You said *marigolds*?"

"Um-hu." Fernando points, again with his chicken leg, toward the entrance of the temporary stair structure. "In dere." He wants Jimmy to go first.

Jimmy lowers his head and takes the first step. "You mean they feed the chickens marigolds?"

"Djes, marigolds." Fernando's eyes are on the giant wall. "*Flor de muerto*...dat's whad is called."

"Flor dee mwerdo? Doesn't that mean dead flower?"

"Flower of death," Fernando corrects.

"Oh, right—because of the 'dee' in the middle. But how come you think it's 'flower of death'? Wouldn't 'flower of the dead' make a little more sense—sort of flowers you take to the graveyard, or something like that?"

"No, Jimmy, dat would be *flor del muerto*. Or maybe *de los muertos* is better. Espanish is real careful."

"And these flowers of death make the chickens turn yellow?"

"Djah, the chicken turns deh esame color as deh flower."

The two stop. Fernando's chicken leg hoovers over a scaffolding rail, eager to begin pointing out the stratiform thingies. But the preacher is still looking into his lunch box.

"You're saying the chickens turn yellow because they were fed yellow flowers?" Jimmy can't get over this.

"Djes, marigolds."

The Reverend slowly raises a wing from his box and regards it in the sunlight. Fernando takes this as permission to begin, and he begins—at the bottom of the massive wall, pointing first to the wispy layers representing the planet's debut from space debris, a crunchy layer above this describing the geological moment three and a half billion years ago when the planet first cooled to a solid, and then boom! Life forms. Layers and layers of single-celled life forms looking out from the stacked sediments like dense inhabitants of a Tokyo apartment building.

"Dju see dose? Dose dju ancestor, Jimmy."

Jimmy is looking toward the wall now but still isn't paying close attention; he has pulled some of the wing apart and is looking to see if it is the same color all the way through.

"I still don't get it, Fernando—why should a chicken turn yellow just because it eats a yellow flower?"

Fernando looks at his pointer and shrugs. "For a chicken and a flower, I doan know." He points back toward the wall. "But for dese guys, totally normal." Fernando wants to talk about the wall but now includes the marigold and chicken strategically. He explains that if the chicken and marigold were microbes meeting in the microbe world, they'd meet up and after they were done the chicken might go away knowing how to smell like a flower, and the flower might go away knowing how to grow feathers. Microbes actually swap genes!

"You mean like neighbors swapping gardening tips, or something?"

"Djah. Except instead of jess tips dey eswap genes."

"You mean their genome?"

"Djah, dey trade genes."

"Their blueprints."

"Djah. Blue prince." Fernando explains that the concept of species doesn't even always make too much sense with them, the *microbos*. The whole planet is just one big gene pool for the microbes. It's like they all make up one big living thing that's trying to improve and develop itself. You can't really consider them as merely individual organisms.

Jimmy watches and listens. He has some of the meat in his mouth now—he is trying to decide whether it *tastes* yellow—and nods at the features in the wall Fernando points to: the planet's earliest life, our ancestors, all of them frozen in still-life poses.

"But where are the sand crabs, Fernando? Shouldn't there be some kind of sand-crab creatures in there?"

"Oh!" Fernando understands exactly what Jimmy means. "Dey nod really called esand crabs, Jimmy, but I know wha dju mean; esand crabs are coming. Doan worry, my friend." Fernando points upward but realizes the scaffold is too close to the wall for him to point out the location. "De esand crabs don't come till up dere. Almost de whole time on Earth it was jess dese guys." He points back to the wall in front of them. "*Microbos.*"

"*Microbos*, huh?" Jimmy looks more closely to make sure he isn't missing something. "Aren't *microbos* supposed to be *chiquito*?"

Fernando explains that his wall isn't really to scale. He means it more like a legend, more like a diagram the elderly tourists coming off the cruise ships can read. And beside the stairs he's going to build a little elevator too. Because some of those tourists can't walk very good.

Fernando points toward one of the pancake-size microbes, toward the inside of it where fine etchings have been included to suggest the massive complexity contained in even the simplest single cell. He wants Jimmy to understand that there's more coordination going on inside one of these cells than there is in his entire nation's public works. Even if he were to expand one of these cells to the size of the whole wall, there still wouldn't be enough room to do it justice. But he thinks this gives an idea, anyway.

Jimmy nods. "Oh sure, it gives an idea."

The simple life forms are not really that simple. Most of the obstacles that life ever sorted out were already sorted out right here by these microbes. Fernando points roundly at the community of oversize microbes pressed into the wall. "At dis poin, dju already most of de way to a chimpanzee."

Jimmy sucks on his wing and considers what he heard. "But what about the hair and the tail and the teeth...and the brain? Microbes don't have any of that. Don't you still have quite a ways to go to get from here to even a little rodent?"

"No, uh-uh. Most of de work, it is already done. De *microbos* already invented de wheel and de engine and de..." Fernando looks up the wall. "...from here on dju jess making wagons and lawn mowers out of wad dju got from de *microbos*."

Fernando skips up a flight of stairs and stops to point with excitement at a blob in the wall. "Righ dere," he says, stretching his chicken leg out proudly. "Look ah dat. De one little *microbobo*, he started living inside de other little *microbo*. Dju esee dat? Dat called endosymbiosis."

Jimmy looks thoughtfully at the blob. "Endo what?"

"Endosymbiosis." Fernando explains that endosymbiosis is one of the kinds of mergers microbes can make with each other.

"Looks like one ate the other."

"Esort of like dat. Djah." He points back to the microbes. Explains that this is more like a business deal. Like the one you have with the bacteria in your gut: they help you digest your food and you give them room and board. Fernando points again with his chicken leg. Explains that that one inside there, that *microbo*, he is a chloroplast. He knows how to convert sunlight into chemical energy. And that one there is a mitochondria, powerhouse for the cell. He was probably separate once too, but now this *microbo*, he has entered into this codependent relationship with the cell he's sitting in. Now neither can live without the other.

Fernando and Jimmy continue to climb stairs.

"So, Fernando, according to the tourist attraction you're getting together here, life starts---" Jimmy peers over the rail. "---down there with a bunch of simple *microbos*. And then the *microbos* start teaming up...and that's how we get to---" His hand rises to flutter above him. "---palm trees and zebras?"

Fernando stops to prepare his response. He explains that the *microbos,* they have probably always been teamed up. Jimmy should think of them like cells in a giant body. A whole globe body. Most of life on the planet—whether in terms of the number of cells or in terms of total weight—has always been microbes. The palm trees, zebras, you and me—we're more like specialized skin cells on the surface of the living globe. We're big and complicated, but we're not much more sophisticated than a microbe. In fact, we're probably *less* sophisticated than the microbes when you consider what they're capable of when they work together. And they're constantly exchanging ideas and services and genes...and information about the environment. Doesn't make sense to call a microbe just an *organism*; it's more like a cell in a superorganism.

"You're saying microbes come together to act like a multicellular organism? I think I heard that somewhere before."

Fernando and the reverend climb more stairs. Many stairs. Most of it microbes. A cursory description of the sagas that have gone on through the earth's expansive history. The merging, mating, feeding, fighting—all the tiny dramas perpetrated over the expanse of the globe, reaching from miles below the rocky surface and all the way up into the clouds. From frozen substrate to boiling vents. From pole to pole. Through the planet's long history. All highlighted on this artificial cliff face.

"So you kind of got a story here?" Jimmy says, pulling up his second chicken wing.

"Djes—maybe two. Dat's de big question."

Jimmy leans back on the scaffolding like he wants to take a picture but is too close.

Fernando continues. One story describes the creatures. The other storyline is about the evolution of the substrate, the surroundings. Now he points to the whole wall in a manner that is strangely specific. "De second one is mostly aboud cooperation. Symbiosis." The little single-celled thingies organizing themselves in communities to behave like multicellular thingies. Pulling together to work out their wants and wastes. Doing it all in step with the evolution of their background. "Dju esee, little guys righ dere…" Fernando speaks with love. Explains that these little guys are kind of buried in their own quarry dust. The dust of their dead ancestors.

Jimmy turns. "You telling me they got overeager and choked themselves in their own mines?"

"No." Fernando sounds protective. That's probably the wrong way of thinking about it. They're more like Pharaohs. His eyes glisten as he looks toward the wall. Pharaohs buried in their own pyramids that they built out of desert nothing.

"Hum." Jimmy picks his teeth while nodding at the wall. "Cause I would have thought they just died, fell down in the dirt and more dirt fell on top of them…that's how they got to be in the wall like that."

"Ah, but de dirt!" Fernando says, raising his eyebrows. "Where dju think de dirt came from, Jimmy?"

Jimmy sucks the tooth he just picked. "Well golly, Fernando. I don't know. Never thought about it. I guess I just always kind of took dirt for granted."

Fernando looks at Jimmy. He recognizes some ignorance but is polite about it. "Is de *microbobos* dat make de dirt, Jimmy." It's sort of their condensed bath water. But maybe that sounds too accidental. Fernando climbs up to the next landing and Jimmy follows. He then wants Jimmy to think about what would happen if every Spring he backhoed the bottom-most section of the wall out from under it, ground it up, cooked it, and sprinkled it way up on the top, up in the jungle soil—and did that for billions of years?

Jimmy looks intensely at Fernando, because Fernando looks like he is thinking about actually doing this.

But then Jimmy turns toward the wall and starts to nod. "Yeah. Okay, I see what you're getting at. The microbes and the background are really the same thing. The background's just a bunch of dead microbes that have been through the loop you just talked about."

"Exactly." Fernando explains that this history is really about symbiosis…symbioses with each other and symbioses with the background, which is kind of the same thing but looped over big time and space scales. Fernando looks back up at the wall—a slow, long arm motion, like he is bowing before majesty. "De *microbos* dey mostly aboud cooperation. Only little bid aboud competition."

"You're saying Mr. Darwin got it wrong?"

"Oh no, nod wrong. Jess more to Nature, Jimmy." Everybody thinks that 'survival of the fittest' means trying to bite and claw and whatever it takes to get ahead of all the others. And maybe sometimes that's even a good description of what's going on—especially when you're only looking at one tiny part. But when you think of that—trying to get ahead of *all* the others—how can that make sense? The *fittest* ones must be the ones that also contribute to the health of the environment they leave their children. The ones that form the best symbioses with their environment.

"So what kind of backhoe does Nature have? To do that digging and sprinkling you talked about to make the quarry dust and all?"

"Plate tectonics, Jimmy. And de heedrological cycle." Fernando leaves Jimmy and climbs up to another landing.

"Plate tectonics...and the hydrological cycle. How does that go again, Fernando?"

Wind and rain erode the rocks and make the substrate—the dirt, as Jimmy probably calls it. And the dirt, she gives life that eventually dies, and the dirt and dead life—

"Dead life? Think you maybe got an oxymoron there, Fernando?"

"Dju know whad I mean, Jimmy. Okay, biomass. De dirt and de biomass, dey get mixed together and dey wash down into de rivers." This mix eventually drops onto the bottom of the ocean where it forms layers that can be kilometers and kilometers thick.

"That's why the stuff on the top is the youngest and the stuff on the bottom is the oldest?"

Well, it depends on what part of the mix Jimmy means; the dirt part can be pretty old everywhere. You see those layers don't stay at the bottom of the sea. The plates are moving and eventually those layers get pushed down into the earth, compressed into rock, and pushed up into the continents where they erode, make dirt and life, and eventually wash back into the sea again. And this happens over and over until you get something like Fernando's wall here.

"Where you got a bunch of recently dead critters looking out at you from a background of dirt made up of the crushed-up remains of generations and generations of their ancestors. Kind of stewing in the waste of their ancestors."

"Dad's righ," says Fernando.

"Okay, but it's like you said; if you started hoeing out the bottom of the wall and sprinkling it in the soil up top, you'd go through cycles and cycles until all the background was a ground-up history of ancestors. So the critters don't just affect the environment of their children, you're saying they *are* the environment."

"Djes." And since most life is and always has been microbes, the conditions of earth's surface—the dirt and the air and the water—are mostly a living legacy of microbes.

"At least until man came along."

"*Exactamente*! De man he is messing wid de backhoeing and de esprinkling."

Fernando explains that the microbes living on the rocks control how fast the rock comes apart when the wind and water run over it. There are even some ways in which they might influence *how much* wind and rain there is running over it."

That *is* an interesting thought. Almost as much as the marigolds. Jimmy looks at the splotches in the wall with new respect. "You're saying not only do they control their background on a local level—like with their wastes and whatnot—but they also control it in the bigger picture—what kind of background their kids are going to get, and how fast they're going to get it?"

"Djah. Dju not taking care of dju kids if dju not taking care of de environment."

"Look! There they are." Jimmy spots the sand crabs he has been waiting for.

Fernando and Jimmy climb stairs, the sand crabs and other multicell blotches appearing suddenly in the wall like a tree line they have just climbed through. Fernando explains the various explosions and extinctions, the unrememberable names of the various layers in which they occurred, and Jimmy follows as they climb ever higher—having decided to rely on Fernando's initial summary that all of this is just increasingly complicated combinations of the stuff he has already learned about below.

"And dat...dju esee dat, Jimmy?"

"What? The black line?"

It's a layer rich in iridium. Fernando wants to know if Jimmy notices anything around it.

Jimmy scans up and down the wall. "Ahm, tell me."

"De *dinosaurios*...dju esee? Dead *dinosaurios*, dead *dinosaurios*, dead *dinosaurios*...but den, ride here, no more dead *dinosaurios*. Extinction, Jimmy."

"Hold on...extinct because there's no more dead...oh, okay, I see. When you stop having dead *dinosaurios* it's because you stop having live *dinsaurios*. Okay, I'm with you now."

"Djah, dey disappear ride here. Ride here at the iridium layer. A lot does."

"Owuuh...Yeah. I even read about that. Big asteroid, or something. Landed not far from here, I think."

"Djes." Fernando arrives to manually turn the preacher's head to look out, over the mangroves, past the docks of cruise ships, out over the Gulf of Mexico. That's where the iridium came from. From the asteroid. When it landed out there somewhere. Exploded and showered the whole earth in iridium.

Even with the huge exaggeration of scale, the full history of humanity is represented in less than one flight of scaffolding. With the effects of agriculture, and then the industrial age, on the composition of the substrate...and with the hand axes, arrowheads, hula-hoops, and such things marking important technological transitions...the topmost part of Fernando's wall is intricate. A general increase in shininess starting with bronze sculptures and reaching up to the bisected and half-surfaced Cadillac Esplanade with the jungle plants growing through its broken windows. But somehow this upper crust is less convoluted and complex than the lower wall. Up here it is easy to understand. It is mostly just the waste products of one species.

"What's that little blue layer there? With some white. Looks like squished plastic, or something."

Fernando laughs. "Dat's de dog doo doo layer."

Jimmy leans over the rail, intrigue high. "The what?"

Fernando explains that geologists always love to find some thin, crisp layer that they can use as a temporal marker—like the iridium layer. But they're hard to find. So he includes this to help future geologists. They'll probably arrive from another planet and be real happy to find Fernando's legend—so they'll know what they're looking at when they dig through our rubble. When they backhoe through the strata of our compressed landfills. The extinction of the Homo sapiens is reliably marked by a thin, sharply defined layer of compressed dog shit sealed in plastic. Such a layer is certainly distinct from anything lower on the wall.

Fernando is very glad Jimmy understands Fernando's project. He is worried it will be too abstract for most of the tourists. Especially the older ones. He is also worried about two men in suits he sees arriving in his construction lot below. "Hey...Jimmy. Dju want we go to lunch? I know we jess ade but dju know maybe we getting hungry again. I know a restaurant down dere in de port," he points. "Dey god good mariachis."

INVISIBLE MARIACHI

The Apes did their job. Despite the added difficulty on foreign soil, they got their perimeter together quickly. The Algs found Pea in a tourist port on Isla Mujeres in the Yucatan of Mexico. The Apes flew to Cancun and had their perimeter set up only a few hours later. In that time, the Algs could tell that Pea had not really gone anywhere. Still in the port. Hanging out over by a weird tourist attraction still under construction. Some geology thingy.

The Cancun Ape team waited for another team to arrive from Merida. The Algs and Apes have now a solid surveillance perimeter around Pea. They are ready to boa down on the preacher.

But they lose him. The Apes. Pea. Gary knows how this story works out. He is reviewing the Ape footage because he has been asked to determine if GAIA is involved. Is it GAIA freaky? How did the preacher simply disappear?

Gary shakes his head. Well, he didn't. Pea didn't just disappear. The Apes didn't do their job; he was right there and they let him go. This will be hugely embarrassing for Cornbread. Again. Employee satisfaction is quite high with Gary today. He copies a frame from the Apecam footage and sets it in his report file. Of the preacher's shoes.

The Algs found some social media posts from a retired couple on a tour of the Yucatan. In the background of the frames, one sees the preacher zip-lining down from the top level of the tall geology tourist-attraction thingy. He is with another man who escorts him then down a street to the waterfront. The Algs have their eyes all over this area. Pea winds up going down a side street. Now there's only a restaurant, a T-shirt shop, and a moped rental place inside the perimeter. Pea is in one of these.

Because he's been in there now for almost an hour, the Algs think he's in the restaurant. Doesn't take that long to buy a T-shirt. But two Apes search that restaurant up and down. All the patrons, the kitchen, even look in the oven. Don't find him.

The Apes are very thorough. They go through the tables and staff, even manually turning chins up to make sure their Apecams get a good look at everyone in there. The Algs then confirm that none of these faces could possibly be the preacher. The restaurant is designated clean.

Gary watched the footage, and he, too, was almost convinced the restaurant was clean. The Apecams got extremely good coverage, even looked in the oven, and Pea was not in there.

And yet something caught Gary's eye. Right before he was going to move on to a different clip. Something wrong with this picture. The shoes. One of the mariachis doesn't have the right shoes. Gary plays the clip several times over to be sure. Yup, wrong shoes.

It is only after he has repeated the clip, trying to find the face that goes with these shoes, that he realizes that the Apes didn't do a good job at all. In fact, Gary realizes that he didn't do a good job either. He finds it now extremely interesting that nobody noticed that the Apes didn't record any of the mariachi faces. Even though the mariachis are seen to be always very close, little boots eagerly closing around the Apecam like spermatozoa around an egg.

Gary thinks about this but then thinks he has a theory to explain this. First, he takes it as understood that an ordinary healthy adult human being cannot look a mariachi directly in the eyes. Or even glance anywhere toward a mariachi's face. To do so would be a deliberate request to be injured. A form of self-mutilation. It would be someone accidently falling over a rail at the zoo…and then going over to poke the sleeping lion. The Apecam sees what the Ape sees, and if the Ape was an ordinary healthy adult human being, it would be understandable why his footage is missing any front-on shots of the mariachis singing at full bore and close range. The footage showing only the mariachi boots closing in by little steps as the Ape tries to avoid them would make sense.

But the Apes are not normal healthy adult human beings. They are designed to never feel uncomfortable, no matter what the situation. They could slice a blue-eyed toddler's throat with a box razor as perfunctorily as they could shoot a face-tattooed criminal with a sniper rifle. When an Ape is born from the vat, the donor brain he is given has been first washed clean. No memories retained.

Ah, but there is body memory. The body has been trained to add to the repertoire of pain-avoiding reflexes. Even if an Ape has no cerebral memory of the experience of its skin being burned, the Ape need not wait to discover this experience if it sees its pants on fire. Body memory from the past life will take over, and the Ape will pat out the fire. Avoiding eye contact with a mariachi is clearly in this category of pain-avoiding reflexes a body learns. And retains evidently when recycled.

As the Ape in the dining area goes through the tables of patrons, turning up chins, ten little feet are not far behind, nearly closing a circle of paralyzing music around the Ape before the Ape dodges and escapes. Within this footage, Gary finds the clearest frame showing that one of the buttoned and embroidered *pantalones de charros* ends not in boots, like the others, but instead in a pair of Parham slip-ons. And in another frame the holding posture of the guitarron also seems a little low and droopy for a professional musician. This is aside from the fact that the audio indicates bass strings being plucked vigorously but also sort of independently of any harmony or song going on. Gary moves a copy of this frame to the report file too.

He plops the file in a message and headers it "Attention: Pea may be wearing mariachi pants!" His finger then hovers over the send button. He is reluctant to send this information to Cornbread. He reviews in his head the explicit instructions he has been given. Even his new boss, Walker, reaffirmed that they are to follow the all-hands order and immediately submit any relevant information they uncover concerning GIB's top list of fugitives, one of which is the reverend. Gary presses send.

Once the Algs learn that Pea might be wearing mariachi pants, and thereby a sombrero, they easily pick up his trail once more. The Algs determine that the mariachi band hit two more restaurants and then boarded a cruise ship that left port two hours ago. Two Apes have already helicoptered aboard.

SHOWERING EARPIE

The reverend fondles the ball cage.

"I want to tell you all a story…a story tonight…I want to tell you a story tonight because today's a special day…the anniversary of the death of my closest friend."

The audience waits behind its score sheets.

"When I was about eight years old, a new family moved in next door, and the family had a boy…Earpie…boy's name was Earpie.

"Earpie and I became best friends. We were real close."

The audience listens closely.

"Almost every day after school, we'd sit together out back—up on his daddy's sit-down mower. B 11."

The audience consults its sheets.

Jimmy cranks the ball cage.

"The seat was like a saddle with indentations to show us where to sit our butt cheeks…because the folks selling the mowers know the people buying them don't like to figure stuff like that out on their own. And there was a little ridge down part of the middle of the seat to help out. A little ridge separating the two cheek holders. A little ridge to keep us from sitting in the seat the wrong way. Probably the first bonding experience Earpie and I had was when we realized we could stop fighting with one another over who got the seat and simply join together to trick the chair into letting us both sit down on it. We figured this out together.

"You see, the chair expected two, and only two, butt cheeks. We both agreed on that. But after looking over it closely, we could see that Earpie's daddy's double-cheek sit-down lawn-mower seat had absolutely no way of knowing whether the two cheeks sitting down on it were from the same butt. Q 21.

"So Earpie and I would get together just about every afternoon after school. Each with a butt cheek on his daddy's mower, we'd talk about the world and everything else. The whole growing up thing was pretty perplexing, and we liked to get together to compare lab notes. I often wish he was still around. G 17."

Reverend Pea looks around at the hall of old folks seated and facing him. He explains that what he really wants to tell them is that they are all easily brainwashed. Controlled. And he is going to prove this. Demonstrate this by showing that he can control them. Change forever something most of them have been doing their whole life. They'll never be able to do it again. But before he can get to that, they need to hear first about Earpie.

"You see I told Earpie about my discovery with the shower wand, and we sat together and tried to sort out what that was that had happened to me. At that point we couldn't determine if I was the only one on the planet who had experienced such an abduction. We decided that if anybody else had experienced it before...well then we'd have heard about it. From our parents and probably our teachers too. I mean, compared to all the piddly dangers they *did* warn us about...Earpie and I decided that I must be the only one so far to ever have experienced such a thing. He thought we should tell our parents about it. Get their advice. Make sure I wasn't sick.

"I disagreed with Earpie there. You see, even though we were in the same class I was almost a full year older than Earpie—on account of my mama having filled out some paperwork late—and I'd already begun to learn that there were a lot of things our folks just really didn't want to know about us. There wasn't much rhyme or reason for us to be able to predict which things these would be, but I found as a pretty good rule that if it was real *real* important to me, then it was probably one of those things.

"Earpie was a friend of the best kind. He wasn't going to tell our parents or anybody else about my freaky experience if I didn't want that. And anyway something like this was so big that we couldn't believe our parents could know something about it and never have said anything to us. They worried about us eating paint off the walls...made us keep our sharp pencils in our lunch box—things like that. So they can't have seen this thing with the household shower wand coming.

"Earpie wasn't going to tell our parents, ask them for help. But he also wasn't going to leave me stuck with this, alone and wondering if I was still a normal kid after having had a freaky seizure thing like that happen to me in the shower stall—a thing that evidently nobody else knew anything about. Earpie decided to back me up in the only way he knew how: he decided to try it out himself. But he admitted to me that he was a little scared after hearing my description. P 5.

"Since our tract houses were built in the same batch, our lab equipment—in particular the fixtures in our family bathrooms—was almost identical, and Earpie reproduced my result—A 16—pretty quickly."

Jimmy drinks from a glass—a big maroon tumbler that is transparent enough to show that the color of the contents are no different than that of the air.

"But there's hungry evil in the world!" Jimmy's expression suddenly shows anger and sadness. He pauses a moment before continuing. "Earpie came running out of the bathroom with his butterfly discovery, in the midst of completing the most honest moment of his life and also ready to share that moment with the people closest to him, the people he loved, his family.

"And do you know what they did? His family, I mean? R 11. They assaulted him! Assaulted him with shock. After all, he was blocking the television.

"The family, the people closest to him, the very people he loved, ripped into Earpie and then sent him to his room where he consoled himself through the night by humping a stuffed panda bear, all leading to a latent sexual identity crisis that caused or led up to Earpie's suicide as a late teen! I'm so angry!" Jimmy looks downward. His lower lip opens and closes like a mail drop a few times. It is a technique he has learned to buy some time to think of his next lines.

"But to take control, as GAIA, we have to all be like Earpie!"

Gary Saar, seated beside his task colleague Patricia Concept, straightens up. "Whoa, whoa, whoa. Back that up."

Patricia operates the remote.

"...take control, as GAIA, we have to all be like Earpie! Stop letting the situation make us cynical and less trusting. The only way the world deserves more trust is if we start to have more trust! Q 12."

"Why's that like GAIA?" Gary asks. "Or Earpie?"

"He doesn't explain."

"You see, Earpie was a sunny child. Always gleeful. Until he started being told about the sinful character of his own inner nature that was unfolding. This surprised him, because up until then the boy had received little indication that he was so rotten. R 8.

"And I still remember the day I told him. I was over his house. We were out back, sitting on his daddy's mower, a cheek apiece. I was staying for dinner because it was his grandma's birthday. 'So, tell me! Tell me!' he said. Earpie wanted to know real bad what it was all about. So I told him about my experience with the shower wand.

"Well, as soon as the extended family dinner rolled into extended TV, Earpie excused himself to go take a shower—what? Yes, N 5.

"Well Earpie instantly repeated my experiment and went even beyond that. I guess he had entered with a lot more momentum; whereas I'd stumbled upon the experience one day while lathering my head and looking for a place I could put the shower wand without opening my eyes, Earpie had a date with the idea a whole evening first. At that age, being afraid and being excited were kind of the same thing. Earpie told me my experience sounded something like the epileptic seizure he'd seen a kid go through in his homeroom the year before. And Earpie had to sit through Grandma's cake and song before he could get his hands on trying the seizure out for his own.

"G 12. He came running out. He ran right by me. There weren't any chairs left around the TV, so I was sitting on the floor; I was leaned up against the wall. Earpie's eyes were rolled to the back of his head and he ran up the hall and by me, naked and dripping. Into the family room, he ran back and forth in the TV light, vigorously shaking up his fruit at the bottom. His mouth in the shape of a Cheerio.

"'Ahll Bee,' said Earpie's Uncle Frank. Uncle Frank was really Earpie's grand uncle. I guess Uncle Frank had never seen anything like that before."

After some somber silence Jimmy looks like he is about to cry. He reaches into the drum cage and grabs another ball. "I sure miss him. K 12."

Jimmy straightens, brings his hands together in front of him and addresses the camera more properly. "Later, in our late teens, Earpie asked me to hold his ice cream cone and then he stood and raised his arms up above his head. He had decided to end it all. He was ready to spring from the roller coaster. H 13.

"Well there I am holding the two ice-cream cones, and before I even have a chance to think about what to do, I feel cooool air on the back of my neck. The cool air grabs my attention because I know what it means: I've read about it, I've seen it, I've smelled it, I've felt it's strong clutch on my bones before: Our coaster cart was falling…Falling…FALLING INTO THE LUCIFER PIT!"

Jimmy's audience leans forward expectantly.

"S 21. Our cart fell. We entered the pit and Earpie was gone. I sat there, my hands holding our cones and my elbows on the safety bar that Earpie had squirmed out of. It took me a moment to understand. To understand that Earpie was gone. Gone from our coaster cart. Plastered against the Mons Veneris of the Alabama Fair's most popular ride. Six people in the carts behind us got neck injuries as Earpie's body raked over the top of them. Q 9.

"Earpie clogged the tunnel entrance, and seeing him missing from my roller-coaster cart, I went through almost—well almost an angry flash. An angry flash that was there to block the unbearable compassion and misery I was feeling. You couldn't stand up on the roller coaster! R 22. It wasn't allowed! There were signs all over! What was he thinking?"

"Bingo!" says an old man.

The man's wife adjusts his chips. "No, look Walter, you got Mega-Bingo."

"Oh, hey, I got bingo too."

"Me too. I got a mega and a regular."

"I got a regular too."

Jimmy listens with satisfaction. Pats the side embroidery of his mariachi pants. "New game." He draws a bingo ball. "C 5. As our cart rolled without Earpie, I got off at the next peak in the track—where the cart slowed down enough to get out. I sought and found the secret passageway along the track. Used by the repair personnel. Scuttling down that dark catwalk with our two ice-cream cones, I went back to look for Earpie. V 7.

"I found him. Earpie lay on the tracks below the Mons. He was in great pain, but at that point he was still alive. I didn't know what to say, so I told him I had his ice-cream cone for him. Hadn't even eaten any.

"You could see Earpie raise his head up as he looked toward me, then at his ice-cream cone, and then at the next cart coming down the track at him."

Patricia stops the clip. She and Gary are quiet for a moment.

"What do you think the point of all this is?" Gary asks.

"I don't know."

"Any guesses?"

"Perhaps the reverend has decided that he needs to completely alienate himself from his remaining parish before he can form a new kind of congregation."

"Do you mean as chaplain for GAIA?"

"Perhaps. Or perhaps this is simply an expression of his remorse for not having included such important discussions in his previous sermons."

"How do you know he didn't?"

"I checked."

"What about what he said near the beginning—how he was going to show everybody how easily their minds are to control? He was going to demonstrate."

"Yes, that's why he was telling us about Earpie, first."

"…"

"Yes, he gave a demonstration."

"Well, what was it?"

"Yeah. You don't want to see that part. I sure wish I hadn't."

Gary looks at Patricia. "I don't want to see it?"

"No, sir. You'll never get it out of your head if you do. It will change you."

Gary remains looking at Patricia.

SATURN IN THE CENTER

Henry sits like Saturn in the center of his belt. And on top of the table at the front of the room. His legs dangle like sunny laundry, and his torso sinks down into his trousers somewhere, leaving his gray head poked up and looking around like a little bird in a nest. He has a bag of circus balloons in his lap. A remote control in his hand.

"I thought that because we have a couple new people here this meeting," he presses 'play,' "I thought we could start by playing, I know the rest of you've seen it before, the Plankton and Tuna talk. Oh, look there, see? See how young I look? I wanted to start with this because the talk sort of explains the philosophy underneath our division. How we started. What makes us different."

Henry dims the lights with his controller. The talk begins. An only slightly younger Henry is speaking.

Gary has seen the Plankton and Tuna talk before. It's sort of famous. Henry Walker gave this talk to a congressional committee and the response was the Borderlines Division. Independently funded. A division within GIB but with autonomy. Henry was made head.

Henry's reasoning, his reasoning for the need of a new GIB division, was based on Goedel's Incompleteness Theorem. In the interpretation of Younger Henry, Goedel proved that there are always important questions about a system that cannot be answered from within the system. Computationally, it's like you have the can opener, but it's inside the tuna can with you.

Henry claimed that an agency is a system. So he could also apply the theorem to an agency. The Global Information Bureau, for example. An effective agency is a well-tuned agency, and a well-tuned agency is self-reflective, it knows itself. Has studied itself. Continues to study itself.

But you can only go so far. On account of Goedel's Theorem. There are always some important things about itself that the tuna wants to know but can't answer from inside the can. What an agency, GIB, say, should get is a team to go beyond the tuna can. Explorers. Aquanauts. Retrieve the answers to those important questions.

Younger Henry then makes a very compelling case for independent funding. And also a case for the exemption of Borderlines from many of the inside-the-tuna-can GIB-employee restrictions and requirements.

Like drug tests.

Henry's enormous success in birthing a whole new intelligence division could have been due to his approach. One can think of many alternative ways for requesting a fringe division of freaks that would have been less successful.

Another theory is that this surprising endorsement from congress was really a response to the consolidation of intelligence agencies. They had all been dumped into one. The reason for that was supposed to be about increasing the efficiency of data sharing. Because each in the previous collection of agencies had had fuckups due to bad sharing. Agencies in competition are not motivated to share information. So dump all the agencies into one: GIB.

But a suspicion was that this centralization of intelligence was pushed for by lobbyists. Special interests. Representing the interests of groups that make their money on controlling information. Consolidating the information agencies into GIB would make the information easier to control. Even if from the outside of GIB. Maybe the members of the congressional committee Henry addressed had had this suspicion. And the idea of an independent, deeply reflective, division of GIB made sense to them.

Younger Henry is by now describing, to the congressional committee, the surface to volume ratio of a body---more immediately, the balloon he has blown up. "I told the guards when I came in here that I was going to blow something up." Laughter. Henry has the congressmen clapping like pinnipeds. "And here I am. See this one. Just a normal balloon. A normal one you blow it up and PFFFFT---" Henry inflates a balloon in, it seems like, one breath. "---it wants to assume a spherical shape. See that?"

"Why? Because a sphere is the shape you can get the most amount of volume inside the least amount of surface area. This shape is what happens when the rubber says it doesn't want to be stretched any more than absolutely necessary. Henry raises the balloon and shoves it off toward the committee members."

"But you see this one," he pulls a new balloon from his lap, "this one here is a circus balloon. This is a special kind of balloon. The rubber distribution is not equal, and that creates forces. When you blow it up— PFFFFT----see there? Sort of wiener shaped, this one. Not a sphere. That's because special interests have embedded themselves inside the rubber. The stretchiness of the rubber now varies. So when you blow a couple of them up---PFFFT PFFFT PFFt---you can--- wrewro wrewro wrewro---make a little balloon dog, like this one." Henry sets this balloon similarly in sailing motion toward the committee members. The buoyancy of these launched dirigibles is unexplainably neutral.

"The most efficient balloon for storing air would be a sphere. So, when you have special interests creating inequalities in the rubber, you always get something less than most efficient. But, in exchange for the efficiency, you could get something real interesting. PFFFT. PFFF FFFT. PFFFT. Wrewro wrewro wruwro wre wre wrewro. Like this walrus. Couldn't make that out of spheres. Without those special interests creating disparities in the rubber, we wouldn't have been able to build this."

Gary has not noticed this until now, but while he has been watching the video of the talk projected on the wall at the front of the room, watching Younger Henry make balloon animals for a congressional committee, Older Henry has also been making balloon animals. Pffft. Pffft. Pffff ffft. Right up there at the front of the room in which Gary sits. When Henry finishes an animal, he similarly launches it off, this time to his audience of employees. With the help of hands, each animal is delivered to a specific recipient. Gary isn't sure what's going on in this meeting.

"A balloon, a regular one anyway---not one twisted up by special interests---a regular balloon wants to minimize its surface-to-volume ratio. But there are other bodies that want to do the opposite. Plankton. Everything they get to eat depends literally on how much skin they have in the game. The rate at which they take in what they need from the surrounding water depends on how much surface area they have. You got a certain amount of volume you have to feed through whatever surface area you have. So a plankton takes on really complex geometries to get enough surface area to support its volume."

The point Henry concludes with, from applying this surface-to-volume physics to an agency, GIB, for example, is that even if an agency has found the perfect surface-to-volume ratio, the perfect amount of surface area they need to support their volume, that ratio is going to change if the agency grows. When you blow up a balloon, a normal balloon, the surface area increases with the square of radius, while the volume increases with the cube of radius. Two times as much radius means four times as much surface area. But eight times as much volume. The point Henry is embedding is that the Borderlines are GIB's nutrient supplying surface area and IS is the fat volume that has to be watched as the agency grows.

Gary watches Henry. Henry up at the front of the room. Older Henry. He's on his seventeenth balloon animal. He still blows the balloons up like he's got a secret compressed air cannister in his mouth. Their neutral buoyance is still unexplained. Gary's animal arrived by hands just a moment ago. A lama maybe.

* * *

Gary isn't sure what has been decided in the meeting, nor exactly what instructions have been given to him. Patricia got out of the room faster than Gary could and she is probably already gone from the halls. At least these parts of the experience are familiar.

Henry ended the meeting by saying, 'You all have your assignments now.' And everybody got up." What assignments? Gary enters the hall, walking slowly just to make sure he doesn't outrun any opportunities for further understanding.

"Your fly is down." The passing man says this as though he is referring to a coffee cup left on a car roof.

Gary looks down and sees that his fly is indeed unzipped. He looks up and sees the back of the man disappear into the men's toilet. A toga. It is Orly Kimms. Gary follows him, zipping up his fly along the way.

Inside the bathroom, the man hoists his toga in front of the urinal and begins to pee. And speak, seemingly to himself. And yet the words splatter off the close ceramic and fill the bathroom. "In metaphors, the Bigloo describes what's over us, a global environmental crisis, and how it got there." Gary looks around for a suitable place to stand as audience. "The Bigloo mixes the overlapping ideas in Gaia Theory, Deep Ecology, and Ecofeminism, and describes a dangerous destabilization underway in the Earth System, in Gaia, the living planet. But this is only the condition, not the cause. Most of the dialog in the Bigloo is directed at discussing the true nature of the problem, the processes and parties that have been invested in blocking awareness—-cultural inertia, reductionism, the special egos and interest groups that have priorities other than finding truth. Disinformation."

Gary lands, still listening, in front of the sink and mirror.

"Henry finds humor in the fact that some of the same groups that previously invested heavily in casting doubt on global warming are now making bribes to get first peaks at the climate predictions Aperture is quarantining in our vaults..."

"Henry said he gave us assignments," Gary interrupts. Vocally. He sort of lobs this over the small screen that hides Orly Kim's urinating dick.

"Yes." The steady sound of the mid-puddle trickle stops. "Didn't you get yours? He gave one to each of us."

"He did?"

"Pretty sure." The mid-puddle continues.

Gary looks down at the balloon lama in his hands. "The only thing he gave me was a---"

121

"Here, let me take a look." An open hand appears from the other side of the urinal divider.

Gary hands his balloon over to the hand. It quickly disappears.

"Oh, yes," Orly says. "Well that sounds fun. Want to trade balloons with me? My assignment sucks."

"What does it mean? My lama?"

"Your assignment?"

"Yes."

The hand returns the balloon animal to Gary. "Says Henry wants you to examine the Bigloos as a collection. He knows you're really good at seeing what's wrong with a picture." Squirt. "But not so good at seeing what's right." Squirt. "He wants Patricia to help you with that." A final squirt marks the end of the man's report. "When you go to Patricia's house tonight, you're supposed to bring swimming shorts if you don't like being naked in front of other people." Orly is finished. He pulls down his toga, turns and gives the room a disoriented expression. He steps around Gary and leaves the men's toilet.

UMBRELLA ORGANIZATION

The elevator door opens on the third floor of the apartment building. It waits appropriately and then starts to close. Gary brings his hand into the door and lightly backhands the door bumper. It coughs and opens again.

He walks slowly down the hallway and watches the numbers on the doors. He finds her door—311. He guesses the width of her apartment from the spacing between the neighboring doors—about twenty-five feet. The depth of her apartment—also about twenty-five feet—he has inferred from the outside of the building. Her apartment is small. A studio.

He is nervous. He rings the doorbell and then wishes he had knocked instead; her bell is too loud for the size of her apartment.

Patricia opens the door. Her blouse is untucked from her navy-blue skirt and her nylons end in fluffy house slippers. Other than that, she looks like she did at work.

"Please come in..." Patricia goes into the bathroom to turn off water. " You found it okay?"

"Yes," Gary replies.

Patricia comes back from the bathroom. "Well, you would have been the first to have a problem; it's pretty easy to find."

Gary's swimsuit is stuffed into one of the pockets of his jacket and he is glad to see that this isn't overly apparent—because she carries the jacket away from him and hangs it on a rack where it is now on display.

Most of the walls are bookshelves. There is a short ladder. Patricia walks back and forth in her fluffy slippers and untucked blouse. In front of the window is a double bed with some throw pillows arranged in a way that seem to invite reading more than sleeping. Gary looks toward Patricia, and then he sets her dimensions in the bed in six different configurations that reduce to just one once he notices the position of a head pillow. Once he notices the head pillow, the stripe of tucked sheet under it soon follows and the *bedness* of the counterfeit couch, thinly disguised in its throw pillows, becomes apparent. The bed...that thing right there. Just a few feet away from him. Every night Patricia Concept stretches across it, and sleeps on it, and reads on it, and dreams on it, and maybe even kicks her panties out the bottom of it during full moons in her window. Would a full moon cross her window? Yes. Gary can calculate such things.

Patricia picks up a small pad of paper from the kitchenette counter and consults with it. Gary sits in the wooden rocking chair. As he doesn't have a book or knitting needles in his hand, it feels a little too stately. But he chose it over the kitchenette stool, which is too hard, and the edge of her bed, which is probably too soft.

She reviews her list. "I think I have noted all the steps here. I got very specific instructions---" She nods toward a partially deflated balloon turtle beside her purse at the end of the counter. "---to show you exactly how I read the Bigloos. We can start any time you like."

Gary looks over at the bulge in his jacket pocket. He wishes she would offer him something to drink.

"Would you like some green tea? I don't have alcohol."

"Yes, please."

She turns the stove on under the kettle. "Are you ready to start?"

Gary doesn't usually drink tea and is reminded that it doesn't require much preparation.

"Yes." Gary's response is meek. He wishes he could try again.

Patricia opens the packets and hoists the little bags out by their strings.

"The first step is for you to remove your clothes and go get in the tub."

Remove clothes and get in tub. Gary considers what he has heard. Her instructions are clear, articulate, conceptually straightforward, not at all hard to understand. He holds the rocker arms and leans forward to suggest motion, which is otherwise absent. Meanwhile, the shelves of books, and the little book ladder, and the double bed with its throw pillows, and the stretch of floor where panties might fall under full moons in her window, it all pulses in a manner that distorts the dimensions of the small studio apartment.

The light in the bathroom is on. It is a bright light, certainly much brighter than the stove light in the kitchenette, or the narrow spot beams pointed at book spines on the shelves. He stands up from the rocking chair and walks toward the bright light. He arrives in the bathroom and then cannot decide whether to shut the door. Closing it would give him privacy, but perhaps he should have stayed at home if he wants that much privacy. He turns around a couple of times. He'd have been luckier if the bathroom were arranged differently—a nook or turn in the floor plan, some place where he could stand and hide his bare ass from kitchenette view. But there isn't that. Gary unbuttons his shirt, slowly and inefficiently, and removes it. He folds it...and then unfolds it and stuffs it in the towel rack the way a man would.

"Honey? I don't have sugar."

Gary extends his head from the bathroom door. His eyes track immediately toward the floor at the foot of the bed. "Just black is fine...or green, I guess I should say—ha, ha, ha," he chortles softly and stupidly as he turns to see if she is watching. She isn't; she is banging the bottle head of a little bear against the countertop.

He pulls his stomach in to undo his belt buckle and consummate a posture that started when he removed his shoes. In the kitchenette, Patricia squeezes the little bear with both hands. Gary bends over and pulls his underwear down to his feet.

Gary's feet are cold on the tile floor, and under bright bathroom light his butt is on display for the kitchenette. He shuffles quickly over to the tub and gets in.

The water is ice cold. She has probably not used the hot water at all. As he lowers himself into the freezing bath, he doesn't complain but instead embraces the sensible opportunity to be tough and silent.

Lying in the cold water, his concern with the Bigloo poems is distant. His thoughts are more in the present, more on the tunic cords hoisting his scrotum up into his body, his nuts trying to keep warm like a self-aware egg under a penguin. The little that remains above surface is not something he wants his colleague to see, and he pulls a knee over the other leg in a centerfold Marilyn Monroe posture. Because he might be brought tea.

"I have to go down to the basement to take out my laundry. When the kettle whistles, you can dry yourself off with the orange towel and then put on the bathrobe hanging on the door. Turn off the kettle, pour water into the cups and then do some yoga—you'll have to push the rocking chair aside for floor space." She picks up her laundry basket.

"I don't know...yoga," Gary says from the bathtub.

"Well then you can substitute that part with ten push-ups, twenty sit-ups; repeat three times." She pulls a laundry basket up to her hip and leaves the apartment.

After she shuts the door, the tea kettle whispers, whistles, and screams—all before Gary can get up from the tub. He frantically towels himself off; his heart pounds as he tries not to drip on the floor. He grabs the bathrobe off the door, scurries out of the bathroom, through the living room, and into the kitchenette where he lunges for the stove dial as if it were a red abort button.

Except for his heart, it is quiet again.

Gary begins the sequence she has described, hoping to finish before she gets back. He doesn't want her to see him trying to keep her little bathrobe over his nuts while doing sit-ups on her floor.

Patricia Concept finds Gary Saar panting in her rocking chair when she returns. She sets the basket of clean laundry on the bed and goes over to the kitchenette. She brings Gary his tea and takes hers over to her bed and starts folding laundry while they drink.

"So how long have you lived here?" Sitting in her little bathrobe, his body having somehow produced the quota of push-ups and sit-ups she requested, Gary's screaming bewilderment over the situation has produced just this stupid question.

"About four years," she replies. "But I lived in a unit on the other end of the building for a year before that."

"Why'd you move? Was the first place too small?" He laughs, or snickers maybe. In any case, he feels a small sign of his usual self come back and wishes it hadn't.

Patricia finishes geometric folds in a T-shirt and then picks up lace panties, which she then inspects for lint. There is hardly any fabric to the garment and Gary does not recognize what it is at first.

It is a long moment before she responds, but then she folds the fabric shard, with an excellence Gary would not have guessed possible for such a garment, and sets it down on the bed beside the T-shirt.

"No, it was actually a little bigger, but I like the view better on this side of the building. So I moved into this unit when it became available." She picks up a brassiere and folds one breast cup into the other. Patricia has quite large breasts for her size. "I couldn't see the moon from the last place."

Gary coughs tea back into his cup. It makes a plopping sound that distinguishes Gary from others who have learned how to drink out of a cup. Gary says he hadn't expected it to be hot—so hot, still hot...still hot, he meant—and excuses himself for the plopping sound he made.

Patricia seems to remember something. "How much tea do you have left?"

Gary leans his cup over so she can see, suddenly knowing that what he is showing her has just been in his mouth.

"You have about half. Then I should start the water." She gets up and goes into the bathroom. The sound of running water returns but Concept does not. She stays in the bathroom. The bright light goes out and is replaced by dim flickers that describe her lighting the many candles he saw around the tub during his polar visit. Does this mean he is going to take another bath? Gary wonders. Or is it her turn? Will she need her robe back?

Gary sees steam coming from the door—now she is filling the tub with hot water. And the bright light is gone. He leans back in the rocking chair.

Patricia comes out of the bathroom with something sticking out of her mouth. It looks like a cigarette. It isn't lit. She goes over to the kitchenette counter to retrieve her list. "Okay, next you're going to—are you done with your tea?" Gary gulps the rest of his cup as if following an order and nods. Consulting the list again, she wanders over to him and hands him the joint from her lips. "This is marijuana—oh, and we need the umbrella too." She goes to the closet beside the front door and comes back with a big beach umbrella. She asks him to follow her into the bathroom. He follows her into the bathroom.

Concept looks at her list.

"I sit on the toilet," she says, indicating that he should sit on the toilet, "and I put my right foot in the tub, and I smoke while the water's filling."

Gary looks around the bathroom. He has been here before, but it is beautiful now. A dozen different candles flicker light on the walls and ceilings, and steam from the aromatic bubble bath wafts into the air. The warmth in the tub calls to him and he goes and sits on the toilet as instructed. But he puts the lid down first so he will feel less vulnerable.

Patricia hands him a lighter and then she climbs up onto the tub edge to fasten the tip of the umbrella to the shower rod.

Gary lights the joint as he would a cigarette and takes a drag. He coughs and takes another. There are ducks on the walls. All over the walls. He didn't notice this earlier under the bright light.

"What do I do now?" he asks. "Why's my foot in the tub?"

"So you'll pee in the toilet instead of the tub."

It is true. He has to pee now. She is expecting him to pee. She is right there, right beside him, fuzzy slippers on the tub wall and her thigh in his face—expecting him to pee.

He waits until she steps down and leaves the bathroom. He carefully lifts the seat cover below him, sits down, tucks his plumbing through his legs and begins to pee. He aims for the ceramic to reduce noise.

The back end of the rocker slides through the doorway like the arrival of Santa Claus. The chair blocks the exit. Patricia sits back in it and gazes outward at her apartment. Gary makes some dripping sounds. He is done.

Patricia takes her hair out of the bun, the bun from work, and then watches Gary a moment through her rocker. She looks relaxed. Her hand comes through the bars, and her arm stretches toward him dreamily. Candlelight flickers around her.

Gary hesitates. With one foot on cool bathroom tile, one foot in the tub, and his urethra still pointing downward into the toilet hole, he needs more balance to respond. His thoughts on the Sistine Chapel, his elbow on the towel bar, and his dignity stretched over his tremendous nakedness, he leans forward and drifts a shy hand through the bathroom fog to meet hers.

She swats at it before it reaches her. Wrong hand. She wants the other hand, the hand with the joint.

The Sistine Chapel disappears. Gary pulls back the empty hand and jabs the other one toward her. She chuckles and takes the joint from him.

Patricia pulls her legs up into the chair and leans back in the rocker as she takes a deep puff and then slowly lets the smoke out to mingle with the steam. She hands the joint back to Gary.

"Get into the tub," she says, getting up from the rocking chair and leaving the bathroom. Her manner suggested to Gary that she has gone to retrieve something and will soon be back. He quickly moves from the toilet to the tub. His hand agitates the water to make more bubbles.

Patricia comes back and steps onto and over the chair blocking the door. She brings a deck of Bigloo poems with her. She holds the stack of fifty-four cards in one hand and an instruction card describing their placement in the Bigloo in the other. She puts her knees upon a pillow beside the tub and inserts herself under the umbrella, which hoods the tub like the cover of a room-service meal. Consulting the instruction card, she begins to assemble the postcards in the umbrella in the same arrangement as they appeared in the Bigloo—sliding the cards into the umbrella struts while she leans over with her untucked blouse, exposed stomach, and a rising suggestion of the bottom of her poorly illuminated brassiere cups. Gary's lips sink below the bubble line.

One card...and then a second...a third...the postcards appear like stars randomly igniting in the empty space of a celestial half shell. Poems begin looking at him in his tub, from all angles, seemingly as curious about his presence as he is about theirs. Thought vapor rises from him and condenses onto the cool metallic struts of the umbrella, and then falls back down to him as distinct droplets representing items as near as throw pillows. The moonlit floor where panties might fall appears intermittently in this roiling presence like an important ingredient regularly coming to breathe at the surface of boiling soup.

Panties on the floor below the moon in her window...

Panties on the floor, and the moon is in her window...

A simple change to the present makes all the difference. Gary suddenly reaches the present tense of his imagination. And finds his petite colleague already there, in her bed, some kind of elegant sheet spread over her elegantly as she lies among her throw pillows under the moon in her window. Her softly erratic motions under the sheet make her appear as if she is posting on a thin horse through hanging laundry, her body form pressing through a captured sheet and fingers clutching the reigns close to her saddle as she keeps her full attention on the gait.

Panties on the floor below full moon in her window...

A poem is accreting in Gary's head. He isn't used to such a thing. A poem assembling inside of him and claiming a destiny directed toward the woman placing cards above him.

But he can't share it. A poem in him, creating itself entirely for her, entirely because of her...but he doesn't give it to her. A love letter undelivered because of insufficient postage. It just isn't appropriate. They don't know each other that well. They are work colleagues. And he isn't a poet.

Patricia disappears from above him. The fifty-four cards are in place, and she returns to her rocker.

Gary lies in the tub and looks up in wonder at the candlelight inside the umbrella. Soon he isn't concerned about the distribution of bubbles over his naked surface. The life of his own poem has passed. Patricia is gone now. He is under the umbrella alone, alone but in the busy company of the Bigloo poems.

But his thoughts also turn toward asking himself *why* he cannot share the poem with her. The poem is for her...about her, at least...and yet he doesn't share it. It is relevant in the context and would probably be the most interesting thing she could hear from him. And yet he does not tell her.

Fear. A circuit of hard-wired excuses are convincing for a moment, but from where he lies in candle-lit bubbles, the excuses waft away and leave him with the unshakable conclusion that he is a coward. It isn't very much more complicated than that. He is afraid that if he opens the gate to let himself run out she might point and scream at what she sees. Becoming honest with himself, he realizes that if he opens the gate he does not really know himself what would run out. It would be him, but is

128

it bad? Is it good? These questions melt into deeper ones. Bad...good...he realizes that he has never developed much precision in determining the difference. He searches to identify two items—one bad, one good—that could sit adjacent in his head but with a clear line separating them. But such items do not exist. At least not for him. Not for him as of yet. He cannot see any clarity in the boundaries between good and bad as he understands them.

The congress of poems, the candlelight, hot water, the bubbles and pot are drawn into him as a tide of honest breath. He realizes that if he cannot find a clear boundary between good and bad it is because he has not yet created one. It isn't very much more complicated than that. And as he lies with that revelation a moment, he discovers that his sudden feeling of inadequacy is inappropriate. Bad and good...differentiating between the two can easily be done to stupidly arbitrary precision. He hasn't done that. This is an equally valid way of looking at it. And then he realizes that the validity of his last thought remains at a level commensurate with the precision he retains for differentiating bad and good. The line of logic closes on itself and snaps free to roll away from him like a smoke ring. He is free of it.

"So you say you've been here four years?"

She does not respond.

The tub makes a "bork" sound as Gary turns to see if she is still there. She is still there, relaxed and observing him through the rails of her rocking chair. They both laugh.

"Hand me a poem," she says.

Gary reaches up blindly and takes a postcard from its strut. Bork. He stretches to hand it to her.

As she studies it silently, Gary wonders which card it was. That he handed her. There is now a blank space where it had been. He drew the card randomly, or so he thought. As he stares at its space, at least, he cannot remember what was there before. He turns in the tub to see what she is doing and to ask if she is going to read her card.

"No," she replies, realizing she might have misled him. "I just had you draw a card so you would have a place to start. That's the way I do it. A place to participate from."

"Bork. I see," says Gary, relaxing back again to look up into the umbrella above him and assume the perspective of the missing card.

And then he does see. The excitement of his comprehension arrives before the comprehension itself, almost frightening it off. The primary insight falls on him as a droplet from above and he spends the next hour unwrapping the significance of it.

It is even ironic, he thinks. His strength is in fact his ability to look, his ability to see patterns without a pre-described basis for how to look for them. This works well for images and various types of data. But with text, the basis for decoding what the eyes see is prescribed—left to right, top down—and this starts right from the moment the eyes start looking at text at all. This has inhibited his ability to simply look at text. He also wonders how he had ever expected to understand the Bigloo poems reading off letters sequentially through his Rolodex of postcards the way he had. Concept has the right idea. Preserving their half-shell assembly is important. That's where you see what's right with this picture. The conversation going on. The heightening of awareness. The Bigloo poems chatter overhead. Together, they raise a dome of awareness.

Concept turns to look through her rocker bars again. "I know the liberty is overwhelming, but I also know you do this kind of looking all the time. Imagine the umbrella is a surveillance image."

Her suggestion is very helpful. He keeps his appreciation subvocal, because it would otherwise be a squeal.

"Bork." Gary is moving around in the tub quite a bit now as the domain of symmetries he recognizes grows from word to sentence to phrase and finally to the whole chatter in the half shell. As the poems are no longer limited by their words, his mind scrambles excitedly with the fresh approach—rotating, enlarging, bouncing parts off other parts—and finally his mind is free from respecting most conventions enforced on the alphabet. It is then that he understands the Bigloo poems. It is not a book of poems. It is a Scrabble board. Not a Scrabble board, but a place off to the side where things are still unassembled. The Bigloo isn't poems, and it isn't a Scrabble board. It is a coffee table of Scrabble letters and suggestions.

Gary looks down only to turn the hot water on with his big toe. Isn't music like that? Music plays left to right, but you don't really assemble it that way in your head...or wherever it is that music meets the soul. Otherwise why would someone listen to the same song more than once? Rhythm is just symmetries in time. Did the Bigloo have rhythm? He finds himself trying to sing one of the poems above.

"You need to go home now. So I can go to sleep, sir."

It has become late.

Bork. Gary turns to look back at her. She isn't in her rocker. She is standing. Then she leaves the doorway.

Gary is invaded with embarrassment and misery. Dumbass. He dries himself with a towel. Did he want to stay in her tub forever? Why didn't he leave earlier? He begins to dress. As he stuffs his pasty, poorly dried foot into his shoe, he tries to blame his oblivion on the pot she gave him. On her. This makes him feel worse. And his scurrying now to get dressed makes him look stupid.

"So...(hyuck, hyuck)...see you back in the coal mines tomorrow—today! Actually today (hyuck)." He stands in her doorway and laughs stupidly.

"Goodnight, Gary."

"Goodnight."

She shuts the door and he hears the deadbolt slide before his arm has lowered from its dopey-ass bye-bye posture. He slowly turns and tries to remember the way to the elevator.

EGRESSES

Gary has discovered that they don't just *look* like snowmobile seats. They *are* snowmobile seats. Director Cornbread's idea.

Gary has also discovered that some of the analysts down here are not just analysts, they're Ape handlers. In an active-shooter situation like this, a full-time handler is assigned to the Ape to make sure the assassination is carried out correctly. Intel and instructions are quickly changing. The handler seated on his snowmobile seat leans into his console fairing to follow everything the Ape sees, smells, hears, touches. In this exciting moment, the Director rides passenger, leaning over and screaming into the Ape handler's ears. "Get them to the lifeboats! Ape 1, stern, Ape 2, port! We have to control the egresses."

"But sir, we don't have an Ape 3. If 1 and 2 are watching the lifeboats, who's going to go go after Pea?"

Cornbread rises a bit on the back of the seat like they've hit a bump. "Just do what I say! Ape 1, stern, Ape 2, port!"

"Yes, sir."

"We can't boa down if we don't have the egresses covered first." Cornbread stands, still in straddle and with his big fly kissing the back of his employee's head. He yells, "Simon! See how long it will take to get a third Ape on the ship. Greg! Get the ship's layout, schematic, whatever it's called. Find out if there are any egresses we aren't—"

"Sir, isn't, like, the whole perimeter of the ship an egress?"

"I mean *real* egresses, Simon." If the preacher wants to throw himself into the ocean, that'll just save us effort."

Gary watches the head-humped handler relax as Cornbread climbs off him. Gary watches the handler lean into his control fairing and send the Apes new instructions. It seems the Apes can be plenty autonomous, but they desperately aim to please. An Ape needs to understand minute by minute what Master's evolving priorities are, what Master wants Ape to do. And this is accomplished by the director screaming into the handler's ear and the handler relaying this information to the Ape.

Director would like to drive the Ape himself but operating an Ape is not easy, and a handler with the technical know-how is needed. Cornbread can't yet drive the Ski-Doo, but he can ride on the back and command from there.

If Gary were to see the freaky snowmobile command in footage, he would flag it GAIA. Maybe even Braid. But he doesn't think there is a point to pointing this out. Instead he says, "Anybody notice somebody's driving golf balls out of the crow's nest? Up there." He points a finger at the Apecam footage displayed on the front wall. "Up there on the ship's radar tower."

Gary has been summoned again to the Aperture Situation room. This time it's more of a casual visit. For him, at least. He has brought no groceries or office supplies with him. He works now for a different division. He is here only as a favor his new boss wishes to extend to his old boss. He stands with hands in pockets and simply looks up at the Ape feed splashing over the front wall. Night or not, the golfer up there is pretty noticeable and out of place. You can't tell who it is, but the golf swing of a Homo sapiens clearly stands out from the stationary antennae, guide cables, and radar fins of the ship's tower.

Cornbread doesn't hear Gary, but one of his analysts does. The analyst examines the frames and agrees. Somebody's up there. But it could be anybody. This is a cruise ship. Why is Saar pointing this out? Is it GAIA freaky?

The analyst submits the frames back to the Algs to get a new assessment. This request really clogs things up, and he has to cancel it. Aperture has been having more and more problems with the Algs. The Algs' ability to flag GAIA is still there but they have been taking forever to do so, and in the meantime flagging sundry other shit. The once simple request—see anything freaky GAIA in this picture?—now provokes a whole exploration by the Algs of potentially related databases including kinky porn, beheadings, and cat food preferences that seem immediately unlikely. It seems the Algs may have learned too much from Gary. They now get easily side-tracked and misdirected.

The analyst is, even without the Algs, able to enlarge and enhance the image until the identity of the golfer becomes strongly suggested: Pea. Still wearing the mariachi costume.

Cornbread hops back on the Ski-Doo, back on top of the driver: "Ape 2! Send Ape 2 up there. No, don't send him to the ladder. We'll lose sight. Send him up that cable! That cable right there. Ape 1 watch the ladder! Ape 2, up the cable! No, no guns. We can take him with a knife. Keep it quiet. Kill him and then throw him over."

Gary now squats beside the Ape handler. What the Apes see is up on the wall, but this view through the handler's command fairing feels more present tense. Like Gary's right there inside the ape, knife in his teeth as he shinnies up the cable toward the crow's nest. It is a long cable, but the Ape does not tire. He shinnies almost all the way up, pauses, then with a burst of body-memory pirate sounds, his head rises above the rim of the nest, he is ready to spring the rest of the way up and attack when---

The team will ultimately slow the Apecam clip down to see what went wrong. First, the Algs have scanned the frames and found a periodic text—*Titleist...Titleist...Titleist*—associated with the print on the rotating, dimpled white ball as it rockets through the air and into the right eye socket of the Ape. An impact so hard that the Ape is carried by it off the cable, off the ship, and down into the sea. Now offline.

"Ape 1! Ape 1 move in!" Cornbread is screaming orders. "No, not a cable, the ladder! Get him at the ladder!" Cornbread and his team try to fix this situation, get a perimeter back together, but the reverend has taken off his belt and is now using it to zipline down the cable. The Algs will find ship surveillance footage that shows that Pea reaches a promenade deck, grabs two cushions off a love seat, and leaps with them, one under each arm, after the poor man who has fallen overboard.

ZEPPELIN

It took Gary fifteen minutes to call it in, and only ten more minutes for the Apes to arrive. Gary sat at the bar of the Faraday Cage and was very, very surprised at what he saw. And he was very, very drunk, so his novelty response to surprises was, if anything, dull.

Who could have expected Nicolas Nesbitt right here, in Seattle, suddenly squeaking through the Faraday Cage in his rubber boots? That's him, right? Right here and right when Gary sits at the bar, off duty, relaxing and, one would think, temporarily free from such monitoring assignments.

Annoyingly, a patriotic flag rises up to push and then pierce the pool cover of Gary's inebriation. Fuckingshit. I gotta call this in.

Gary was already trying to pay up. But the bartender still makes Gary wait. And he can't call from in here. Inside the Faraday Cage. He waits to pay his bill. He'll call it in once he gets outside.

And maybe Gary didn't even see right. Could have been somebody else in those golf clothes and rubber boots. The man wasn't here in the bar long enough to take a good look at, anyway. He headed straight up to the Gentlemen's Room.

One of the Apes stays at the front door. The other enters the ground floor. Once inside, the link between the Apes breaks. The Ape inside is disconnected from the Ape at the front door. Disconnected from

Aperture. Disconnected from the Algs.

The Ape walks through the bar and climbs the stairs to the Gentlemen's Club. He walks through the scanner and ignores the alarms. He forces the end door open, trots down a hall and busts through the door to a poker parlor. All recorded by his Apecam. His commotion upends a poker table. And that starts a chain reaction that leads to men in suits flat on their stomachs, collecting fallen chips from the floor. The greed, the snapping at each other. The true nature of the men showing so sharply right now.

The Ape sights Nesbitt on the floor of the other side of the side-turned poker table. The Ape is first going to just come around the table at him, and does...but is distracted. Nesbitt has pulled down the pants of one of the men. One of the men who is flat on the floor collecting chips. The face of the man shows concern over his pants being pulled down, but his hands cannot leave the scramble for chips on the floor. The Ape is distracted not solely because Nesbitt looms over a man's naked ass, eyeing it from close proximity like a scientist studying the mouth of an eyeless cave animal. The Ape is distracted because in the commotion a cylindrical projectile farts out of man's ass and collides with Nesbitt's forehead. Nesbitt shakes it off, picks up the cylinder, and skedaddles.

The Ape stumbles around the table and then is right after him. Right after Nesbitt. He chases him down a hall. He makes a wrong guess on a turn and this costs him some time, but soon he has Nesbitt contained. The Ape moves in, searches the hall slowly and thoroughly, and then pauses before a men's room. The hand dryer is on.

The Ape draws his gun, sets his stance low, kicks open the door.

The hand dryer is so loud. The Ape cannot be sure Nesbitt even knows he's here. Nesbitt has his back turned. He's standing on an overturned waste-paper basket. He's having hot hair blown into his groin.

The Ape remains in the doorway, gun still drawn, and...he hears Aperture. Weakly. He suddenly has one bar. The Ape sees that a small window above Nesbitt is open. An unexpected break in the Faraday Cage. He's getting a signal through the window apparently. Here he is, ready and able to shoot Nesbitt...but he's been sent a pause.

The Algs are looking through his live Apecam right now. That condom wrapper. Over there by the sink. And what's that by it. Some kind of capsule? The Algs upload the ape's feed from minutes earlier...say, that's the same butt plug that shot out of the man's ass in the poker room, isn't it?

But the butt plug is open now. It unscrews. Electronics. A memory card seems missing.

The Algs determines in a flash that this butt plug is very likely a recording device. The man has been recording the secret discussions that go on in the Gentlemen's Club. The dealings of the reinsurers and water-rights lawyers and disaster profiteers. The extension just agreed upon to have climate-model results first quarantined by GIB so the profiteers can get a look at it before others do. So that they can profit from that information.

"Hands—!Freez—!" The ape's next moves are conflicted and, so far, still voiced below the sound of the hand dryer. New situational understanding is being processed by Cornbread and the Algs and new instructions are being sent to the Ape. The priority is now not Nesbitt but the memory card. The Ape must, at all costs, retrieve the memory card. The dryer stops. "Hands up!"

Without turning, Nesbit very slowly lifts his hands, rolling them upward in a symmetric blossom. Gently, no quick movement. At zenith, the hands gently release a condom inflated with heated air. The Ape watches, uncertain of so many things right now, as the little zeppelin floats out the high window and into the cool night air.

"Balloon! Balloon! Get the balloon! The memory card is in the balloon! That's Priority One. Get the balloon!" The ape's new orders from Director Cornbread are coming through loud and clear. The ape, relieved by this clarity, turns and runs out of the bathroom.

SILLY UP AND SOMBER DOWN
TWO YEARS LATER

COUGH DROP

Spokane is on fire. The whole city and even some pets and people are being converted into lofting particulates that might, with some irony, seed rain to dowse the embers. Seems these days so much is on fire. Since the global war started.

When the world suddenly realized it was at war, the nature of the war was so clearly different, yet fundamentally the same, that the expected nomenclature "WWIII" dissolved in the confusion. Instead, what stuck was "WWWTF". It seems large populations on a planet become most indignant when they suddenly become irrevocably aware that they have been butt-fucked from behind. Since a long time. And in no good or consensual manner. By leaders they voted for. Leaders who seemed so relatable. Leaders they imagined they could drink a beer with. Without later being forcefully bent over a car hood in the bar parking lot. "World War What The Fuck" arrived when people across the world finally realized that their own denial process, their own hopeful thinking, their own chipper avoidance of glass-half-empty attitudes had been exploited by a very few very greedy people. People saw that they had been mickeyed in the bar then buttfucked in the parking lot. When they woke up, head on a car hood, undies around ankles, they were inconsolably upset. And grabbed pitchforks and such.

The mentality of those few greedy grubbers is not one a reasonable man could have anticipated. In one of his sermons, the Reverend Pea tried to describe this. He asked his followers to imagine some flowers growing in a field along the highway. Some real beautiful flowers. The kind of flowers you take to your mother while she is still alive. He asked his followers to imagine a man, a short man with an unfortunate harelip and a slow-cooked inferiority complex. The man happens to see that when he cuts some of the flowers and puts them in his house, well, neighbors tell him how beautiful that is. How beautiful his house is. How better his house is. Better than theirs.

As is the situation with short, harelipped men, the reverend claimed, the visiting fragrance and compliments in his house are not enough. The man worries that his neighbors could do exactly what he did---go pick some of the flowers and put them in *their* house---and then his own house wouldn't be better than theirs anymore.

Now being short and harelipped does not necessarily make him unclever. The man knows just what to do. Just what to do to win at this game. He goes and picks ALL the flowers. Seeds too. Locks it all in his garage.

Of course, the flowers finally wilt and the seeds mold and decompose in his damp garage. So soon there are no flowers for anybody. Ever again. But the short, harelipped man finds it to be self-evident that he won this game. And for all time.

Yes, such a mentality is almost impossible for a reasonable man to anticipate. Seems little Harelip took winning the game too seriously and forgot what it was supposed to be about. But this surprisingly senseless behavior of short, harelipped men does not alone explain how the world has been brought to slide over a cliff edge.

The reverend took his followers through the math: Forty years ago, do you know who was studying the climate effects of CO_2 pollution the hardest? The big oil companies. They spent a lot of money on it. And when their labs reported that CO_2 from the burning of their fossil fuels was warming the planet, and moreover throwing things completely out of whack, the oil executives believed them. And, in response, fired the scientists. Dissolved the labs. And then spent even more than they had on the climate research to stall awareness over what their scientists had discovered. Spent way more. Massive programs were built with the single goal of emphasizing the uncertainty of this finding. And so successful was their campaign that they magically kept the public thinking climate scientists were uncertain for decades.

The good reverend tried to illustrate the unbelievable success of the butt-fucking money grubbers in another way. Mixing his own beer pint with that of a confused man sitting next to him at the bar in which he provided this sermon, he held up two beer pints for his camera to see. The beer on the right represented all the CO_2 humans had ever put into the atmosphere by the time of those studies. The beer on the left represented the amount of CO_2 put into the atmosphere since those studies. The reverend held the two pints very closely together, though this was not necessary to tell that the left pint had a little more beer than the right. The awareness blocking campaign had been so successful that the oil companies managed to sell more oil after knowing about the dire problem than they had in all the time before that. It was like---the reverend guzzled the right pint---I drink this beer you sold me and find out it has arsenic in it. And yet you somehow manage to get me to buy and drink this second bigger beer? The point the revered wanted to make is that the money-grubbing buttfuckers could only be blamed so much.

Men of god have often learned to choose specific words that will knit together limbic associations between the different topics in their sermon. So when Jimmy Pea reviewed for his listeners the giant secret that Aperture had been hiding, the secret that exploded out over the world and caused people to finally pick up pitchforks, his audience had been preconditioned with the image of objects wrongfully entering a butthole. An image relieved by his description of an object exiting a butthole. A small, audio recording device was snuck into a black meeting between the Ape masters and the negotiators for the greedy profiteers. The recording, presumably obtained as it descended from the sky in an inflated condom, was leaked by an anonymous source. The conversations recorded were enough to point the global community of Bigloo miners toward documents showing the deepest, darkest, buttfuckyist secret of Aperture and the profiteers yet. The exposure of this secret made Aperture and the profiteers so unforgivable that their whole former strategy of controlling awareness became untenable. It was sort of a global "buttfuck me once on a car hood, shame on you; buttfuck me twice on a car hood, shame on me" moment. The world chose instead to pick up pitchforks. Their leader now was GAIA.

The deepest, darkest, buttfuckyist secret that Aperture was supposed to protect concerns tipping points. In the climate system. Jimmy had a pendulum when he described this. A 360 pendulum with a stiff rod. He first pushed it just a little. The weight is moved and immediately wants to come back to where it was. Does some overshooting. A pendulum.

Then Jimmy restarted it. Pushed the weight twice as hard. The result was sort of the same thing but bigger. Maybe twice as big.

He restarted it again, pushing twice as hard as before. The result was twice again as big. But still sort of the same thing.

For Jimmy's final restart, he pushes only a tiny tiny bit harder and…completely different. He had not a pendulum but instead a propeller. Two completely different resulting behaviors despite only a tiny tiny change in the initial push.

Jimmy then told his parish that there will be no going back to the Garden of Eden. We have passed the tipping point. We have become a propeller.

Jimmy asked his followers to not believe him. He asked that they believe the buttfucking money grubbers. Look where they put their money. They accepted the validity of anthropogenic global warming four decades ago. Even before the scientists did. And made bank by keeping people confused on the topic.

And now they're doing this a second time. Look at where they put their money. The Bigloos will point for you. The deepest, darkest, buttfuckyist secret Aperture has been protecting is that the profiteers already accept that our climate has passed the tipping point. Hell, they helped accelerate it. Our climate, our world, has passed a tipping point. If the profiteers can block people's awareness of this, they can make shitloads of money. If a man thinks a field is suffering a drought, while you know it's really suffering a new climate, you can make a huge profit selling it to him. You have control. Information is money. Information is power. Information is the fundamental currency.

Or maybe not. Maybe awareness, not information is the fundamental currency. Information that doesn't get analyzed is sort of just potential information. The war in information has become a war in awareness. Just as before, when the profiteers lost control of the information, they shifted instead toward controlling awareness over it. The deep dark secret that was released like a genie from a buttplug is that the profiteers have been lining up a massive campaign to make people doubt anybody who claims we have passed a tipping point.

But, 'buttfuck me twice on the car hood, shame on me' didn't happen. The fact that the profiteers had accepted as most probable that we have passed a tipping point, and they were planning to make everyone think the opposite, this was an important secret Aperture was supposed to keep safe.

That was two years ago. Aperture and the profiteers had lost their war on awareness. So they reverted to a more conventional approach of force and violence. The tactic of disinformation that had become so carefully honed since the last world war was no longer tenable. If Aperture could no longer control the thought-ways, then they must revert to controlling the highways, airways, the resources. The internet. The ham radios. Crush or control any of the infrastructure GAIA might be using to communicate and organize its actions.

In response, GAIA raised its game. They showed that they could blow shit up and hurt people too. An example of this that is very important to the bounty hunter Cory Petersen is the destruction this morning of a government satellite that was to be launched. Some kind of predator satellite that can jam GPS and communication signals that GAIA might be using. It was being heat tested at a base in Eastern Washington when Nicolas Nesbitt and an accomplice snuck in and, well, turned the heat up too high.

The two were wearing some kind of monkey costumes to confuse the fence surveillance software, but one---one with a peculiar femur to torso length ratio---was almost certainly Nesbitt. And Nesbitt had been cited the day before, nearby in Spokane. That's when Cory got the print-out.

Spokane is on fire. But Cory Petersen doesn't care anything about that right now. Not about the war. Not about the climate, not about the fire. He is sixty miles upwind of the blaze. And besides, he needs to locate the print-out in the back seat of his vintage V-8. Cory Petersen is a bounty hunter. This is a new career for Cory, and he has to make this work.

Some call it the "Transition." Indeed "War" does not sound very hopeful. But for the hundreds of thousands of climate refugees displaced from their now uninhabitable homelands and still roaming with hungry children in search of the "refuge" part of their classification, for the millions living under climate Apartheid, or among the warlord gunships that now rule their streets, for the billions oppressed by a small cabal of climate profiteers, "Transition" seems to withhold much.

"If you can't beat them, join them," is Cory's justification. The short-term incentives are definitely on his side. The profiteers make sure of this.

Cory digs through gas receipts, fast-food wrapping, auto parts. He finally finds the Pee-Chee folder he is looking for. He opens it and flips through the print-outs. There. He found it. Yeah, that looks like him.

He moves back into the afternoon happy hour, back into the bar of a Chinese restaurant in a suburban strip mall. He inserts the sheet he retrieved from his car into a restaurant menu and walks slowly through the restaurant, as if he is composing a complicated take-out order, reading and deciding.

There are only two customers in the restaurant. They are seated at the bar and are laughing as they play hockey with an olive on the counter.

"No, come on! That's not fair; you gotta use the stir-stick," says the man.

The woman squeals as the olive she shoots jumps higher than she expected it would. It is a dingy squeal, and she covers her mouth and lowers her head as she giggles. Her squeal and giggles also make it clear that it is the man's job to find her olive on the floor, a job he takes up eagerly.

"If I make another goal, do I get your phone number?" the man asks.

"Maybe, if they ever restore the service, but you got to get it into my cup for that," she giggles, and flicks the green olive back at him. "And you gotta get my bar tab, too."

Cory passes by again...

"You DEEW NOT have green eyes, let me see!"

...but still doesn't get a good look at the man. The two are moving around and Cory keeps finding his view of the man's face partially blocked by the dingy woman. He turns his menu around to make another pass.

"What would *you* know about my real hair color, anyway? You'll never find out."

Cory and his menu pass by three more times until he finally gets a good look at the man at the bar. He looks down at his menu again, down at the picture of a man in golf clothes and rubber boots. It's Nesbitt, all right. His excited eyes start to spend the big reward printed at the bottom of the page. Nesbitt is known to travel with a woman, some GAIA high operative referenced as 'Braid,' and the bounty on her is even higher. There's not a reliable photo to go by—but this woman here is obviously not her. Cory will settle for Nesbitt. He opens his legs into a wide stance, pulls out his gun, drops his menu, and points his three arms at the back of the man seated on the barstool. "You're coming with me, Nesbitt!"

Nicolas turns to look into the barrel of the firearm. The olive rolls by on the counter behind him. "Sure, I'll go with you." He points his thumb toward the woman. "Can I get her phone number first?"

* * *

The wind direction has changed and smoke from the fires in Eastern Washington are coming over the border into Idaho again. As Cory approaches the checkpoint, he congratulates himself. It was smart to put Nesbitt in the trunk. *Do you know what the first thing a grizzly does after he makes a kill?* Cory was presented with this question in the DVD that came with his bounty-hunter training kit. *They haul it off somewhere away from all the other bears. Somewhere they control. Maybe even bury it for a while.* Cory moves slowly forward in the line of cars. He rolls down the window.

"Where you headed?" the federal officer asks, scanning the back seat of the car, then Cory's bounty-hunter ID.

"Clara Vista," Cory responds, rolling up the window after the officer's nod. Cory's thoughts return to the broiled steak, his wife's pie with the flaky crust just like he likes it, and the apology she will make for the disparaging remarks she has made concerning his career transition.

Twenty minutes later, Cory pulls over onto the shoulder of a desolate highway. The old muscle car sputters and coughs and can't go further, while on the horizon an eerie sunset takes place behind smoke. Spokane is still burning.

Cory leaves the engine in its troubled idle and gets out of the car. He walks around to the front. Bends over, pulls a latch, and using both arms he heaves the heavy hood up into the air where it stays, like a beakish upper jaw, the grill attached to it extending downward like hillbilly teeth. Cory leans forward into the giant mouth of thc car. He twists the fuel valve on the carburetor. The eight cylinders pound into a misfiring whir of explosions that visibly move the giant engine block. When he opens the fuel intake, the misfiring gets worse. Cory doesn't understand this.

He climbs further into the car's maw and begins to unscrew the wing nut on the plate cap of the air filter.

"Do you need any help?"

Cory is startled. He wants to jump. It is the natural reaction of an untrained mind. But Cory has a trained mind. He is a bounty hunter, a certified grizzly, and he stays still while he assesses the situation. Where is the voice coming from? In back of him and to the right—probably standing in front of the left headlamp. Nesbitt. But how is that possible? Cory is leaning far over the many cylinders of his engine, and he would need an extra second to draw his gun from the holster. Only one of his feet is technically on the ground and a fan rips inches below his stomach. Even armed, he is more vulnerable than he would have first guessed.

"How'd you get out of the trunk?" Cory asks, pretending to still work with the wing nut.

"Oh!" Nicolas says with a friendly laugh. "I found a car jack in there...in there in the trunk with me."

The first thought in response that comes to Cory is that the trunk of his car might be damaged. His rational brain fights to deprioritize this thought—what's done is done. But his emotional brain holds on to it with the same fervor as his growing apprehension. There are only two junkyards in the Northwest that have parts for this car. And Bondo repairs can crumble on a trunk when it is slammed shut. Cory can't see Nesbitt—not without turning his head and perhaps altering the dynamics of the situation—so he continues to screw his wing nut and think.

Nesbitt wasn't packing—Cory checked that. What could he have—a tire iron? This doesn't seem too bad at first. But then Cory imagines the back of his head being pounded with the greasy tool as his forehead bounces up and down on the air-filter plate. Or perhaps a sideways swing of the lug-nut socket will capture his ear drum like a donut hole from dough. Cory won't make a move until he has a plan. He tries to estimate how long it will take him to draw his gun from the shoulder holster. He would have to get his feet more securely on the ground before he can take his weight off his hands.

"You get those handcuffs off?" he asks, pleased with the steadiness in his voice.

"Nah. I tried. But it didn't work."

Nesbitt is still handcuffed. Cory is glad. A two-handed tire-iron attack on the back of his head seems less formidable. He'd probably get in just a hit or two...and then Cory will have his gun out. Still, the calmness of Nesbitt's voice confuses Cory.

"I suppose you found that tire iron back there?"

"Uh, yeah. You mean that crooked bar thing? I think I saw

something like that back there. Do you need it?"

Cory's wingnut is reaching the end of its bolt, and he discreetly begins to screw it the other way. He is still trying to assess his predicament. Nesbitt is unarmed, handcuffed, and he isn't making a discernible threat. Cory looks for the shadows. Nesbitt's arms are casually raised up to the hood. Like someone watching a neighbor work on a car. His hands are probably holding onto the grill section that extends down from the hood on this antique...Cory swallows...thinking of the heavy, beakish hood ready with a collapse of Nesbitt's legs to come down and snip Cory's legs off and leave him to fall into the fan to be digested.

The thought of being eaten by his own car, the vintage muscle car he restored himself, is worse than any death Cory can imagine. He screws his wingnut almost imperceptibly now as he imagines the sequence more carefully—the cocked hood springs stretching through their center position before the giant hood accelerates downward with Nesbitt's weight. Cory figures he'll feel the grilled overbite of the hood first; the hood's front teeth will come down and bite into the back of his thighs and nip his legs off. Then, with his legs gone, he'll start to slide, probably feel the fan blades on his scrotum first. The fan is being driven by only the coughing idle of a V-8. But it's a giant V-8 and the fan is the only thing it is pulling at the moment. Shredding Cory's body would probably count as less friction than the engine is already spending to turn its own crankshaft. Everything from his balls up, slowly turning to hash browns as his head, squished between the hot engine block and the hood, slides like an oily olive under a panini iron.

"That problem with the idle...I know what it is," Nicolas says, helpfully. "It's not the air intake. The problem is you got a gooey cough drop in your fuel line."

Cory tries to laugh, but it sounds small and insincere. He is busy thinking about chunky parts of himself being pulled out of him by the fan belt and spun around the alternator below him. And he is remembering the incredible length of the human intestine—like a mile long, or something. His one foot on the ground begins to quiver as he asks with a shrill voice: "Why...why's there a cough drop in my fuel line?"

"I put it there," Nicolas says, and budges. He is just shifting his weight, but Cory squeals and begins to cry.

"I think the cough drops fell down from the back seat. And your fuel line was in there with me too, you know."

Cory lowers his head...so Nicolas does too. He speaks toward Cory's ear. "You were wondering how cough drops got back there in the trunk, I bet?"

Cory shakes his head and makes wet noises.

"Yeah, I was too. But I think I figured it out. Ever been between paychecks and go digging through your car looking for coins?"

Cory is sniveling. He seems to have lost touch with the situation. But he nods.

Nicolas chuckles. "You find plenty of Lincolns, but you're really looking for those silver faces. Even a nickel...you hold it in your hand like it's a gold nugget." He chuckles. "And even though you started off looking for coins, you find all kinds of other things you'd never have expected. You know what I mean?"

The wing nut on its bolt forms a little crucifix that Cory prays to as he slobbers on his engine block.

Nicolas waits. Cory doesn't answer, really, so Nicolas summarizes: "I think the cough drops fell down from the back seat." Still nothing from Cory. Nicolas lowers his head further under the hood to be closer to Cory. He paraphrases part of a poem he once read off a wall he saw in a planetarium dome: *Don't you think it's amazing—all the crap you find in your seat when you're looking for change?*

Cory Petersen nods and with simultaneous sounds from nose, throat, and mouth, he seems to agree.

CAMPAIGN CABOOSE

The Reverend Jimmy Pea waives from the caravan as if it is his campaign caboose. He is going away. Taking a break. Rest and relaxation. Going off to live with the gypsies for a little bit.

It is a well-deserved rest. The Reverend has delivered sermons tirelessly from several continents. He has visited islanders in the South Pacific—asked them what they thought about their land sinking into the ocean. And then he asked the half of the world living in coastal cities a similar question.

He visited the Amazon jungle and brought slides with him to show the locals: slides of the type of savanna they'll be living in by the time their children grow up. He has made sure they understand that the savanna isn't going to recycle water like their jungle did. And he has described to the rest of the world that they too are losing something, and not just opportunities for better aspirin; their planet is losing its parasol. Without the Amazonian clouds, the Earth looks a little different from space. And she's hotter.

Jimmy has visited a farmer in the Sudan—given the man his watch and the money from his wallet. Explained that he, Jimmy, is partially responsible for the man's failed crop; that the man's crop was overrun by cattle looking for plants that are now gone not because of poor land management by his countrymen—as the man has been told—but because Jimmy and others in the rich world spewed a bunch of pollution into the air that changed the climate.

And Jimmy just had to stop at this lake in Cameroon that his friend Fernando told him about. Wanted everyone to know about how it once belched up some carbon dioxide that killed all the villagers nearby. How, by what Fernando told him, this was kind of like a little poem about much bigger ordeals that may have happened already a couple of times in the past. When rising temperatures triggered the release of a bunch of that fart gas, methane, that the planet usually keeps locked up in icy little clathrate cages under the permafrost and the sea floor. And how that greenhouse gas is burping out again now. The other times this happened there were mass extinctions as a result. Jimmy thought it was sort of accurate to say man's been feeding the planet *burrito supremos* since at least the industrial revolution...and because of the formidable length of the planet's intestine, we're just now starting to see how all that went down.

Africa is a special place for Jimmy. Not only is Lucy from here, but this is also where the human population on the globe almost bit the dust. According to the microbiologists, the human population once encountered some big challenge where they almost all went extinct. At one point there were only a couple thousand of them left— "somewhere around here," Jimmy says, gesturing to the Africa behind him in a strangely specific manner. "Only a couple thousand people left in the whole world! What do you all think about that? Was that close or what?"

Then Jimmy passed a swath through the monsoon countries. Told the people there how scientists think the monsoon might go either way— strengthen or weaken. But seeing as how half the world's population is dependent on it being the usual way, there'll probably be a whole lot of hungry folks unhappy with the change no matter which way it winds up.

After generously dedicating so much of his time to help point people toward the adaptation challenges they face, helping the younger ones to understand the really shitty situation they have inherited, Jimmy is now taking a break. A break with some folks that already have their adaptation program up and running. The reverend appears on a bee wagon with Romanian gypsies.

"I bet you're wondering what these three big towers around me are."

The bee wagon from which Jimmy waives sits among three giant radio towers. In the grassy field between the towers, gypsies load the last items onto their wagons. They are breaking camp.

"If these radio towers seem a little bigger than the ones you've seen before, you're probably right. You see, yelling over the top of somebody else's signal always takes more throat than singing your own song." Jimmy's camera moves to survey the three towers more carefully. "It was the Communists built these towers. These towers are left over from the Communists. Built them because they didn't want their people hearing the broadcasts from the West. But it's kind of hard to stop a radio wave at the border, so they had to build big jamming antennas like these to scream over the top. Drown them out. Don't want folks to get all the facts. Might start thinking for themselves, and then who knows what could happen."

After finishing his description of the triad of jamming antennas, Jimmy explains that the gypsies aren't traditional beekeepers. They just moved into the niche because it opened up. The changing climate has been moving around the flowers that the bees depend on for pollen, and the traditional beekeepers aren't yet prepared for the type of uncertain, mobile lifestyle needed to retain their occupation. But the gypsies are.

SURFING SERENDIPITY

"Can I eat the other cucumber slices, or do you have plans?"

Eve laughs, her face blindly skyward and her shoulders bouncing slightly on the lounge-chair cushion. "You can eat these ones, when I'm done."

"Hey, I rode in a car trunk for you. Least you can do is let me have the rest of your cucumber."

Eve laughs. "Toi, tu exaggeres! You only rode in the trunk to get by that checkpoint."

Eve stops. Even through the face cream, her disease shows. "They're getting closer and closer," she whispers.

Nicolas sees this. Her disease. He takes this opportunity to see her while she cannot see him back. He takes this opportunity to admire her body stretched out in a swimsuit. He takes this opportunity to observe the textured dimples pushed up by her nipples.

And then he straightens, his ears suddenly fixed on a sound. "They're not just getting close. I think they're here. Now."

Eve sighs. She sits up, the cucumber slices fall from her eyes. They both stand and pull on their white hotel bathrobes. She slips on her sandals. Nicolas slides a foot into one flip-flop, takes a moment to find the second.

Both make their way around the pool, around the flower garden, over toward the other end of the roof where the glass door is. Nicolas, then Eve too, stop to examine a heavy barbeque. Like they are considering buying one. Or maybe they will just take this one. He hands his magazine and towel to her. He gets behind the barbeque and starts to push it like a shopping cart. Eve holds the door open for him absently while she looks down at a leaf blower resting in one of the flower beds. She picks it up like a gallon jug of milk and follows the barbecue and Nicolas through the door.

"Halt!" shouts an armed man in body armor. He is positioned further down the hall. The barbecue does not listen and accelerates toward him. "Halt!" Shots are fired. There is a commotion with the retreating man's body camera capturing closeups of carpet, baseboard, wallpaper...and then wider-angle roominess as the man crashes backward through the mezzanine railing and falls toward the check-in desk in the lobby below where most of his colleagues have taken up position.

Inside the elevator is a fire evacuation map for the building. Eve decides it is useful and slides it out of its glass case. She is mostly just interested in the lobby, so she folds the map into convenient quarters, which show this part more compactly. Nicolas pulls the start cord of the leaf blower, adjusts the throttle, and experiences the trigger a couple of times. He lifts up the barbecue hood.

As the elevator doors open on the lobby, Nesbitt and the woman pull the tails of their bathrobes over their heads, the woman sets her hands onto the push bar of the barbecue, and Nesbitt holsters the angry nozzle of the leaf blower into the deep ash pan. The sounds of multiple rounds hit metal somewhere under the thick, roiling cloud of soot. The barbecue rolls through the lobby and out the front door. It leaves.

FAUCET HANDLE

Matoo of the Quiet Bellows figures he can field a punch or two from the good reverend—then he'll be inside, close enough to start cutting him up. Matoo's equipment is pretty bad, so it won't be his best work, but it'll have to do.

It's all about visualization. Matoo plans to let the reverend swing—to get him leaning forward—then he'll punch his blade up through the preacher's face. This is the basic plan. And through visualization Matoo is designing the optimal event sequence. He visualizes the blade neatly cleaving the preacher's head in half. Exactly in half. A clean slice following the neutral plane of bilateral symmetry defined by the suture parting the preacher's nuts. A clean slice straight up through the corpus callosum—that abalone connecting the two brain halves. Matoo knows his way around the human brain; he has cut them up before.

The preacher has his dukes up, sort of, though he's still talking about the harmonica clamped in the metal neck rack he's wearing. Keeping his fists up, he blows a note from time to time and wishes to convince Matoo that their instruments—both free-reed, by the way—are remarkably similar.

Matoo lunges forward to provoke the punch he wants from the preacher. Simultaneously, the blade in his hand twirls to a new position (he's holding it now like a little walking stick, whereas before it looked like he was interviewing the preacher with it). The plane of Matoo's swinging arm aligns with the plane of the Reverend's bilateral symmetry, and the bladed fist begins to punch upward. Matoo is purposely moving slower than his top-secret, chemically enhanced capabilities allow; he's waiting for the reverend to throw a punch, to lean forward, so he can spring upward and bring the muscles in his legs and blade arm together against the Reverend's own falling weight. This should also leave him with an intimate view of the preacher's expression while all this is going on.

Of course Matoo doesn't really expect that he can cleave through that much mass and bone—from the preacher's chin all the way through the center of his skull. Not with this poor blade, anyway. But this is the right imagery to use in the visualization. Such imagery is used in all the martial arts. Punching through a stack of bricks, one aims not for the top brick, or even the bottom brick, but rather the air on the other side of the bricks. It's the air on the other side that is offensive. Likewise, Matoo is offended not by the preacher's face but by the center of the preacher's brain, and he focuses his rage on cutting through the man's corpus callosum. He's got all the imagery together. He'll enter the chin and go straight up from there: equal portions of lip and nose on each side of the blade, the nostrils maybe turning to kiss each other because of the entrainment of skin by the rusty blade. The Reverend's eyes crossing to look at each other because they never believed the distance between them would ever change in adulthood. And then once past the hard surface parts, Matoo will keep the blade stable: he'll hold course like a butter knife on its way to an avocado pit, seeking with great attention to produce a fairly halved fruit.

Matoo of the Quiet Bellows visualizes hog heads, band-sawed into precise halves in the controlled laboratory of a butcher shop. With the equipment he has available here in the field, he can't mimic such accuracy, but it's the right imagery. His lunging fist continues to rise, and his hand slightly adjusts the position of the knife he holds like a little walking stick.

This last part—fine adjusting the position of the knife in his hand—is usually an instinctual maneuver. But he's having to think about it today for some reason. Matoo has practiced the motion so many times that it should be first nature. The purpose of the practice has been precisely to provide the opportunity to stop thinking. Thinking, in as much as this involves rational analyses in the left brain, is usually too slow to be helpful in a knife fight. Such thinking is only useful if done as an exercise beforehand. And Matoo has done his exercises. Plenty. Usually, at this point, his hand, fingers, and wrist complex would coordinate in some way that no longer requires Matoo's conscious participation. But as Matoo tries to keep his head empty—except for visualization of halved hog heads—annoying distraction come from his hand area. The hand, fingers, wrist complex that have already been thoroughly trained for this situation.

The problem is probably the knife. More thoroughly, the problem is probably Ivlian, the gypsy teen with whom Matoo had been sharing close living quarters as he infiltrated the gypsy community where Pea was reported to be staying. Or even more thoroughly than that, the problem is the bee-hive racks. They take up too much space—leaving little room for living space at the front of the caravan cart. And because of the opportunity afforded by the close quarters, Ivlian, being a gypsy, took Matoo's expensively balanced switchblade and replaced it with a cooking knife. Hiding things from gypsies isn't very easy. One side of Matoo's new knife is missing its side of the wooden handle. Little rivets stick out as if they don't know this and are confusing Matoo's hand, fingers, wrist complex. This is causing an unexpected request to Matoo's higher brain areas, which are occupied trying to visualize band-sawed pig heads.

The preacher's punch arrives. Matoo was fully expecting it. His plan is to absorb the punch and then launch his counterattack—Operation Corpus Callosum.

But the punch is harder than Matoo expected. Much harder. This needs to be explained. The punch is well centered and remarkably shattering relative to what Matoo would have expected possible from the preacher.

Matoo's tongue sorts through the broken teeth in his mouth. And as the preacher's hand withdraws and returns to the side of its owner, Matoo can see that the hand is decorated with something: *A-ha!*

The discovery of the preacher's hand decoration is of very important parallel relevance. And it is the nature of the *a-ha!* experience to usurp all attention in the brain for at least some tiny amount of time. The discovery of the reverend's hand decoration is capable, quite possibly, of providing a resolution to several direct and indirect mysteries Matoo has been experiencing. It is central to understanding why Matoo still has honey in his hair, and why he stinks. It may also explain why he has not been able to cool the bee stings on his welted hands and face...the welts aggravating the hold of his hand, fingers, wrist complex on the half-handled kitchen knife. Essentially, Matoo of the Quiet Bellows has recently seen many faucets with missing handles, and now he thinks he knows where at least one of the handles went.

Matoo's *a-ha!* experience might also be alluding to iconic evidence for the intrinsic nonlinearity of systems of cultural practice, and maybe even the *Tragedy of the Commons*. For having experienced the frustration of arriving at a rest-stop sink, irrigation spigot, or landscape sprinkler system, with the T-shirt he uses as a towel and a devoted eagerness to rub his bar of soap all over his body...only to find his plans thwarted by his inability to untwist the tightened valve, Matoo discovered an incentive for stealing a fucking faucet handle for his self.

The reverend's faucet handle illuminates the sensitivity of cultural practices to initial conditions. Matoo doesn't dwell on this—now is certainly not the time—but it is in his mind now, nonetheless. From what he has seen, everywhere these gypsies go there are missing faucet handles. Assuming for the moment that these people are not so destitute as to deliberately regard the plumbing fixtures as collectible weapons (although, in consideration of the condition of the knife in his hand, Matoo realizes this may be a poor assumption), the missing faucet handles must be something that just got out of hand: a small initial perturbation—one missing handle, say—leading to a cascade destabilizing a whole system of properly equipped faucets. All it would take is the removal of one faucet handle. And then gypsies arriving at the faucet and not being able to turn the water on would, on their next occasion, steal their own handle to hold for backup. And because each of these preemptive actions catalyzes further preemptive actions, soon even the least thievish of gypsies will have stolen a faucet handle for their toilet kit.

It is the nature of the *a-ha!* experience to spontaneously commandeer all brain functions. The justification is that the *a-ha!* experience requires all resources of awareness for its execution and is incapable of understanding any kind of scheduling. But by agreement it will, without any complaint, give back the processing powers anytime they are needed for other things. If there is something else more important going on it will be glad to finish unpacking its revelation later.

Matoo's *a-ha!* experience about the nature of the reverend's hand hardware has barely arrived, and already it senses a larger urgency in the air—now is not the best time—and graciously begins to relinquish the higher brain functions it has temporarily usurped. It just needs a moment to index the items of parallel relevance so it can get back to them later at a more appropriate time. Let's see, there's the honey in his hair, the uncooled bee welts, the—BOOF! The reverend's reinforced hand strikes again, mashing Matoo's eyebrow this time.

Okay, this is enough. Matoo is awake now. He is now a half step back from his lunge and has jumped into a higher gear of awareness. Some threat-risk code posted in Matoo's head has changed color in a way that would flatter the preacher. Matoo thought slicing up the reverend would be child's play—dessert, really. Matoo has tolerated a lot living with the gypsies—just to get this opportunity. This access to his target. Now the opportunity has arrived.

Matoo of the Quiet Bellows circles the preacher, grinning in a manner that is new to him on account of his missing teeth. Matoo is good with a knife. Very good. So good that a single opponent is no longer challenging. Usually. But the swelling from the bee stings is making him less nimble. And he can no longer see properly out of one eye. And the rusty kitchen knife with the half handle—not ideal. He rotates the shoddy blade to a new position in his hand. He holds it like a bicycle handle now. He'll ride by the Reverend's ribs...up near the armpit. Bring the preacher's reach in. And, while the good Reverend is thinking about that, Matoo will slide the knife back to the walking-stick position and go back to his plan o—KALUREERUREENG!

Matoo's eyes dilate. He is looking up at the sky suddenly. His lower jaw might be broken. And the dilated eyes and the broken jaw...all that goes with the sound of something like a falling piano hitting the ground. Or not necessarily a piano. But some instrument that would make a noise like that.

Yes, Matoo understands now. He's wearing an accordion, and the preacher must have knee-kicked it from below. Yes, this explanation seems quite reasonable. Matoo returns to the knife fight—knife/faucet-handle fight—but never really regains his initial confidence. The half-handle knife feels awkward in his hand, the toothless grin feels awkward in his broken jaw, and the broken jaw awkward in his face. And the latch to hold his accordion closed has broken, leaving one end of the bellows to hang and make a hee-haw sound as Matoo circles the preacher and tries to bounce himself back into a menace.

But most distracting is his rational mind, which is busy estimating whether it is possible that the enhanced reflexes he has received through top-secret experimental drugs...if his super-reflexes might be incomplete in some way...if it is possible that the time required to receive and deprioritize an *a-ha!* experience is no faster than normal; no faster than it is for normal people. Could it perhaps be even slower? Could these enhancements be interacting in an unanticipated manner, in an unanticipated context such as this one here, to actually *diminish* his fitness—at least here in this current situation? If such enhancements as these he has been provided with are universally advantageous, then why has Nature not provided them already?

Two Chewbaccas

"That's when big business swupt in," he tells her.

"You can't say *swupt*. It's *sweeped*."

"Can too. You can say both *swupt* and *sweeped*."

"What's the difference?" she asks.

"*Swupt* is more in the past than *sweeped* is."

"So says you," says Eve. "But I rather think *swupt* is in the future. And that's where we're supposed to keep it." She giggles with delight at her Hepburn imitation. "It'll be centuries before the world needs the word even once."

Nicolas brushes back the hair on his palms and grabs the chain link to follow her up. "That's when Big Business—let's call her 'BB'—swept in." He immediately returns to the ground. His feet are too furry. He can only get one big toe in at a time. "BB swept in and took over." He tries further. "Took over states! National governments!" His full weight rests now in the crotch of a toe and he groans. "Courts. International unions."

"Or is it *swept*?" Eve asks herself aloud. She sounds like she could accept being wrong.

"Control over the whole world." Nicolas now has a second furry toe in the chain link.

"I don't much like how you speak about the future in the past. Get up here," Eve says, now at the top of the fence and laying a rug over the barbed wire. Though it is dark, Nicolas knows the rug to have green paisleys. He also knows Eve's Chewbacca costume to be snug on her ass.

"They nominated an orange masthead for their ship," he continues.

"You know what? I think it is *swept*. Get up here.'"

"And rammed their ship through the last sutures…how do I get my?…the last sutures holding on the last…the last skin grafts of the last opposing authority."

"Will BB be better once she has had a nap? Get up here."

"No. Unfortunately no." Nicolas has returned to the ground. "Power mongers never tire, my dear." In the dark, he sees her up there at the top of the fence. Expectant. He must have her understand that he must work out his clasping technique, down here, before he can climb up there. And first he must comb the hair on his hands. "BB has pulled all the reigns back to the bunker."

"Oh my! But is there really no way to stop the power consolidation?" Eve asks with diffuse sarcasm.

Nicolas powers his way up in response. His voice then lowers to compensate for the distance he has covered. He reaches a furry leg up and over the V-post supporting the coil of barbed wire. "In the end, it will be just one—" He feels her sit her weight on his ankle helpfully and so he reaches his second ankle up for the same. In an aerial sit-up, he brings his torso up and onto the top of the fence. "In the end it will be just one hand left in the bunker stabbing to death the other." He settles in.

Silence.

He feels her light grip on his forearm. He feels her pull his hand to hers. He feels her put the lead of a rope into his hand. "You're the man," she says. Nicolas sighs, sits up, and pulls the heavy packs up and over the fence.

In a moment he has returned to his settled position. At the top of a fence. In an unexpected nest formed from green paisley rug and barbed steel wire. Two Chewbaccas inquisitive under heaven and shouting stars. No moon, of course.

"What do you think they think when they see that? Them." Eve nods skyward with her chin.

Nicolas thinks…about what they think. Them. Tries to remember which ancients had the theory that the stars were just pinholes in a giant sky blanket. A theory that sets man on the unilluminated side. "They see us splitting atoms…but still shitting in our cave."

"That must be confusing for them."

He can tell that she sits leaning on hands behind her. One leg bent at the knee and horizontal in the calf. The other flopping freely downward. She is beautifully comfortable.

"Maybe it's not confusing," she says. "Maybe they just know it to be all too tremendously typical. All the different worlds they can be watching, and they select our channel. Start rooting for the characters…"

"And then in the second season all the main characters suddenly melt in the sun!"

"D'Oh!"

"Typical."

"So they've been watching the Earth channel since we were salamanders, really grow to root for us, and now it looks like we'll succeed in strangling ourselves as a species. They must be getting ready to change the channel."

"Or maybe this is exactly when they tune in to watch. Planet Earth strangles self—tonight on Channel 7."

"It's very hard to strangle yourself."

"Show me."

"In nature, a hand releases its own throat before unconsciousness is achieved."

"Yeah, exactly. Hands like that don't exist in nature. On Earth we had to invent such a hand."

"Ergo the delay in our mass strangulation."

The two are silent a moment.

Above them the stars bleed some sadness. His suit itches him. She begins down the fence. Through the moonless night he observes, best he can, her clasping technique.

* * *

They walk together toward the white light burning the night grass at the top of the hill. The duffel bag swings between them, chaotically at first, until Nicolas adjusts his gait to that of Eve's and the bag glides smoothly between them.

The light bleeds into their moonless night. It is not the patient light from far away stars, the light they just had together, but an urgent industrial light that breaks thoughts and intimacy. Nicolas stops, takes a last moment to enjoy Eve's beauty in the dark, then pulls the strap from her hand and hoists the bag onto his shoulder.

* * *

Under bright lights they dance together on the face of a dam. High and slow, as would underwater octopi in sideways gravity. On their long ropes, their attraction to Earth is in dispute. On their long ropes, they launch aerial cartwheels from front handsprings. On their long ropes, they redefine ballet. Together, symmetrically, and antisymmetrically. Until the silent song is done. With elastic smirks, they collide, sweetly, repeatedly, their ropes intertwining. They double helix down until their separation becomes small and finally their foreheads park together. Her eyebrows sadly sigh, releasing a hope beyond this circle. She smiles.

He smiles. Nodding downward into the cleavage of her Chewbacca suit, he says to her: "I know you're the explosives expert, but aren't your bombs a little small?"

Eve looks down her chest, thinks about this, Chewbacca face paint showing concentration. "What do you mean? My bombs are big enough."

"Pshaw," he says. "Those little bombs will make only pockmarks."

She is first confused by what he said. And then, "hahum. No." She laughs hard. Harder, harderer. "You thought we were going to blow up the dam! The whole dam!" On her rope, she jolts in front of him. His ignorance is hilarious. "No, you idiot! We're just here to take out the jamming antenna. Not blow up the whole...the whole dam!"

Nicolas disengages with her. He shoves the vertical wall of concrete and swings out into a slow, scanning spin. Repeating the sequence. A furry paw against his big brow he is looking hard. Harder. Harderer. And the harderer he looks for the antenna the more she laughs. She zips up her suit, grabs onto him in his next bounce and rides out with him. She brings her lips to the earhole of his monkey costume. "It's built inside the dam, dummy. Just below the surface."

He thinks about this. Nods.

She nods back. "We're just going to break it a little bit," she whispers. "With my little bombs."

KABLOOMISH

Every Ape rig has bolt cutters. The two get through the gate, and they speed out onto the dam, screech to a halt at the ropes. They jump out, leaving car doors open, and then bend over the rail to begin emptying their guns on the two furry marionettes far below.

It's a long range but mostly straight downward, so it's just a matter of aiming straight. Just aim straight at the monkeys. But the Apes are finding themselves to be surprisingly bad in this weird arcade. The monkeys are bouncing around, now agitated by the gunfire and gaining higher valence. Becoming ever harder to aim straight at.

So the Apes shall now try to rappel down the ropes to get at the monkeys. Two ropes, two monkeys, two Apes . Each Ape takes one monkey. But the ropes are quite tangled together at the top where the Apes wish to clip on. They simply clip around both ropes. But soon that's not working, at least below a point where the ropes are periodically diverging. Now that the monkeys below are, in opposite directions, galloping back and forth across the dam, building more momentum each lap in a resonantly forced rock that finally ends with them each reaching escape velocity and launching into the air from opposite ends. Each on a long arc through the high air, until they dock hands at the center and drift inward to complete the giant heart they have traced. The face of the dam explodes.

This is recorded by a drone. One of the frames it takes will become the screensaver of millions—spies and farmers alike. It looks like a poster for a Bollywood action/romance movie. The background is a blast of gold and yellow. Kabloomish. In the center foreground, two Chewbaccas are hurled through the air toward the camera. The bigger one with his hairy chest forward, motorcycle innertube worn as the shoulder belt, legs like a galloping stallion. The smaller one flying by his side, clutching his strong hand. Both with an expression not of fear or surprise, but rugged providence.

* * *

When the dam explodes, the two rappelling Apes go with it. The camera feeds from each Ape stop. The handlers in the Aperture situation room drop these channels off the wall and shift to the eyes they have in the air. A GIB drone. It's a moonless night, so the drone is mostly just a thermal camera right now.

Except at that dam where the lighting is excellent. With the drone's eyes, Gary and the analysts watch as the two Chewbaccas fall through the air and into the frothy river below. Gary watches Cornbread's anxiety during the minutes the drone loses the couple. As he switches back to the thermal camera. They're lost in the froth. The drone can't see them. But then, boop. They're back; two sets of hot heads floating downriver.

Cornbread makes a call. To one of his Ape captains. Even hearing just this side, it's clear what's going on. This has to do with what certainty-number the director wants dialed into the perimeter that's being established. Cornbread says he wants a high number. Wants to be real certain the targets are inside it. Such a high certainty-number is possible, but it makes the perimeter very large.

A pivotal section of the perimeter is a coastal-highway bridge six miles downstream. The Apes have rolled generators onto the bridge and now have floodlights showering the river and banks below. Two Ape sharpshooters are posted at their rifle tripods. An attack helicopter is arriving to provide further support. Accordingly, traffic on the coastal highway has slowed to the crawl of spectators. Their cameras collectively provide continuous and near-live coverage of whatever this is going on here.

Gary returns his view to the drone's thermal feed. Nicolas Nesbitt and Braid. There they are. The contrast of their body heat and the cool water makes the thermal images sharp—for thermal images—but still too blurry to even confirm an ID. Gary cannot see fine features, but he can see the two play. They are seated in inner tubes. Butt in the hole. Sometimes he spins hers with his foot. Sometimes she kicks water up at his face. Which is seen because his head jumps in splotches to a cooler color. He never kicks back. It seems the reason he spins her tube with his foot may be to keep her feet where they can't kick more water in his face.

The two have two hours. Two hours before they drift down to the bridge. Gary stays with them this whole time. A vigilance. He observes nothing else. Where the other analysts only see false-color tracking data, some vague motion, Gary sees grace. Virtue. Love. Or something like that. He's not sure. It feels like he is seeing something *right* with this picture.

But. But embedded is something very *wrong* with this picture. He has heard Cornbread behind him. Cornbread's orders are now to go ahead and just take the two out. Gone are the days when apprehending them alive for their intel was the goal. Gone are the days of taking them alive if possible. When the Apes boa down this time, they should just go ahead and kill the two.

What is more, Braid is already fading. As the two joust with their innertubes, her thermal color is converging with that of the cold water. Hypothermia. Or she's been shot.

* * *

It disgusts him. Gary. That some of his colleagues have eaten snacks. During the wait. As Nesbitt and Braid drift to the sea. Gary makes sure he will recall the names of each of the three. The ones who ate snacks. As Nesbitt and Braid drifted to the sea.

Or bridge. Not the sea, the bridge. As they drift toward the bridge. The impermeable section of the Ape perimeter designed to be the interception point. On the phone, when requesting the attack helicopter, Cornbread described the bridge as a catcher's glove. A catcher's glove with the power to obliterate anything that tries to drift by. Kill the two right as they come through the Ape perimeter.

A late bend in the river before the bridge provides a dramatic appearance of two night-time tubers in soggy monkey suits. Relaxed, butt in the hole, up until they round the bend and enter the bright light, a helicopter rising from behind the bridge to add a high and hungry beam. A whole bridge waiting for the tubers to come closer. And a whole line of stopped traffic to record it.

These days, Cornbread has a headset he puts on when he wants to possess one of his Apes. To say that he then becomes the Ape would be an overstatement. It's more just a matter of giving the Ape instructions from very close range. From inside the Ape's head, say. When time is critical and Cornbread becomes impatient with just riding on the back of the Ski-Doo, he shoves the driver out of the way, puts on his headset and takes control. He has learned to operate an Ape himself.

But even then, there's still an annoying delay. Because when Director Cornbread lowers himself into the Ape gunner up there in the whirlybird and starts rat-a-tat tat, splattering his metallic wad all over the water below…well the delay is really annoying; it should not be so hard to keep a bead on these slowly drifting targets!

He might have hit something. Because both tubes are popped, and the riders sank below the waterline. Cornbread further pummels the river. He covers the whole patch where they might be. And the helicopter drifts with this expanding ring, unloading kilograms of high-speed metal into the water. Anything still alive will have to come up to the surface some time.

There's an interruption. When Cornbread has embodied one of his Apes, he wants to be left alone to focus, concentrate. But some things are too important. He is notified by the handler he pushed off the Ski-Doo that since moments ago, there is an extra Ape on the bridge. One too many. And from the eyes of the other Apes, Cornbread can see that the extra Ape looks familiar. Except for the eye patch.

And, strangely, the extra Ape is shouldering an RPG. Aimed at the helicopter. An Ape beside him seems confused, like they maybe got different memos. Cornbread shifts back to his gunner Ape just as the helicopter explodes in the air. He jumps back to an Ape on the bridge. But that Ape has already been shot with his own gun. In the last seconds of his surviving Ape, Director Cornbread is aware of the one-eyed Ape asking politely. For the gun.

Splendidly Capable of Shocking Herself

Tatami Pallet

Gary Saar walks in as if he is inspecting a hotel room. He looks around and begins to unzip the raincoat he was given in the navy helicopter. The man in the uniform tells Gary that the captain will be with him in a moment, and then closes the door and leaves Gary alone in the room. Gary doesn't know much about such ships, but he doubts that this is the usual setup for meeting guests.

The room is small and sparse. There are three tatami mats on the floor and one porthole on the wall. Beside the door, four folded metal chairs hang like life rings on a ferry.

Abrupt...maybe even offensive. The man in the uniform opened the door for Gary but didn't enter the room himself. It was like he was sticking a bug in a jar. Gary is still processing this. If the man had taken even a short step through the door, the experience for both of them would have been much different.

Gary inspects the tatami floor. What is tatami? Rice stalks bound together? Okinawa? Another corn-fed yahoo dragging tea ceremonies back from his service abroad. How are they cleaned—swept? Vacuumed? Did the man in the uniform even have a choice in the matter? Was this rudeness stenciled on to him? Where's the captain?

Gary looks again at the chairs. The chairs hang on the wall by a rack comprising two hooks. Gary takes one of the chairs out of the rack and unfolds it—but only as a thought experiment. He rotates the chair in the air, flaps the seat open and shut a couple of times and then puts the chair back in the rack. Does each chair have four legs or does each chair have two legs? Why has he been called to a Legend-class coast guard cutter? Should they be called skids instead? Why should a chair have legs, anyway? Can there be legs that don't walk? Gary's focus bounces around the room as his eyes search for new stimulus. The ship is also called a National Security Cutter. Does that even make sense? What is this, a fucking sensory deprivation tank?

Gary closes his eyes for a short moment and then opens them again. The problem, Gary decides, is that chair *legs* are given their name based on how they look rather than what they do. Appearance rather than purpose. Form not substance. Such uncaring usage of the word once sentenced Victorian pianos to the equivalent of leg warmers, their sultry risers having been unfairly associated with the tentacles impious women used to gather sperm for their eggs: *leg* was a bad name.

Gary pulls the raincoat all the way off and searches for a name to capture the essence better. A pallet. Essentially a chair is just a pallet. One of a generic class of objects used for the purpose of keeping other, more valuable, objects from touching the ground. And for providing forklift access sometimes. Gary turns from the chairs to indicate the closing of his curiosity about them.

The door knocks lightly and opens. The captain comes in quietly with the gesture of somebody arriving at a yoga class late. He bends over to undo his laces and softly comes across the tatami mats in socks to where Gary stands in shoes.

"You must be Henry's man?"

The man's tone is soft and weird. Like he's meeting the neighbor's newborn or something.

"Yeah. Gary Saar."

The captain smiles and shakes Gary's hand. "There are chairs over there if you want to sit in a chair," he says, pointing to the wall racks as he sits down cross-legged on the floor.

Gary looks toward the folded chairs and then down at the captain. He tries to imagine a scenario where the visitor would now go get one of the chairs out of the rack and erect it beside the decorated captain seated on the floor. Such false freedoms are common. Gary sits down cross-legged in front of the man. His mind pauses during the adjustment of its blood supply and then is busy again—this time processing the possibility that the captain sits in this situation often: Indian-style on the floor, unaware of quantum theory and becoming ever more reaffirmed that he is objectively observing people's preference to sit on the floor. Rather than in folding chairs.

Captain Leroux quietly observes Gary. There is a reason why he has called him here, but he'll get to that in a moment; his guest seems distracted. "Pretty comfortable, isn't it?" The captain asks.

Gary responds, "What? The floor?"

"Yes. The mats, I mean. On a per-inch basis, I find that tatami separates me from ship metal better than anything else I've tried."

Gary looks at the captain.

The captain continues: "But, from what I'm told, they're hell to clean." He watches as Gary looks down at the shoes he hasn't removed. It's just a glance, but it appears involuntary, and that is the part that seems to interest the captain. Gary decides to take control of the conversation.

"Why am I here?"

The captain's smile is genuine but so is the recoil of his head, like he has just observed a pedaling preschooler roll over a snail in the driveway. He chooses to interpret the question in another way. "I guess that's a famous question that many have asked through the ages, Mr. Saar..." The captain follows with further sentences that pretend that there is no distinction between the fundamental *why am I here?* and the more irritated and pragmatic variety that his visitor must have intended.

Gary identifies the parallel but loses some attention. Existentialists are clowns in a dark circus tent fumbling around for the exit. Bleeding questions about the meaning of existence are ill-posed and have no formal solution. Not worthy of further thought. In any case, the captain speaks too slowly. Low bit rate.

"And some have even suggested that all those *why?*s are alike—no matter how big or small. Maybe like those fractal paisleys we've all seen in the science magazines." The captain suddenly stops speaking. He appears to notice something in Gary's face, and he leans forward to get a closer look. His voice is softer as he peers like a dentist through the bottom of his bifocals. "We're not great philosophers, so we have to pose the question more carefully...Mr. Saar, do you know why you are here?"

Gary is silent for a moment. He isn't sure whether he likes the captain or dislikes him. But he is pretty sure it is strongly one way or the other. In either case, he doesn't want to answer the question, so he throws the old man a koan. Standard evasive tactic. He answers a question with a question—while hiding the evasion in an implication that both questions share the same answer. It has just come to him but is still materializing. He's trying to twist the liar's paradox into a koan that pretends to provide an answer. He's midway through and starts to get tangled up in the internal consistency of what he's trying to do: a koan should illuminate the inadequacy of logical reasoning—and Gary's koan is turning embarrassingly reasonable. He can back out but instead just finishes the phrase he started and pretends like that's what he means.

Gary is surprised by the captain's quick response; parsing a logic matrix and finding it flawed doesn't seem to add any extra delay to the captain's response time. The captain points out the koan's logical flaw with a friendly gesture. Like he's pointing to a neighbor's low tire. But he thinks he understood what Gary meant, anyhow.

Gary decides that the captain's graciousness is rooted in a superior understanding of the nature of the dialog they're having.

"How was the ride in the chopper—pretty stormy out, eh?" the captain asks softly as he leans toward Gary. His eyes almost close, and he starts to move his head and torso through slow ovals.

"All right, I guess. Are you smelling me, Captain?"

"Please excuse me," the captain says in his dentist voice. "I don't mean to be rude. It's just that I'm getting older, and I can't trust my eyesight as much anymore."

Gary laughs nervously. "So how do I smell, Captain?"

"Gary, last night we pulled Braid out of the water." The captain watches Gary's face.

Gary can't speak. His mind and spirit have snatched the news and flown off somewhere to read it privately. Braid is captured? Is that possible? What does that mean, exactly? Gary doesn't yet try to answer these questions, he is merely collecting them to take with him on an emotional excursion.

Under other conditions, Gary might simply sit with the shock and let the significance finish raining over him. But his pale carcass has been left with the sniffing captain, and a decision is required before he can return. Is he happy? Is he sad? What is the proper expression to bring back and post on his pallid face?

Pursuit of GAIA and Braid has let light into his tent while each day the world makes progressively less sense. Following her path has spared him from mulling toward a destination of predictable stupidity—while society and environment crumble around him and human participation on the planet is being renegotiated. Otherwise, there is little to offer guidance, except perhaps that the "business as usual" model is surely a dead end. A bonfire of white-picket splinters.

Braid has been taken? Gary feels the reverberation of an existential crisis that recapitulates itself from the smallest scale of consciousness up to that of the scale of the planet. Gary suddenly feels that meaning in his own existence can be immediately invalidated if Braid can be caught. He suddenly feels that there is little hope for the planet if she is tried in a usual court. He suddenly sees that his own participation has been more than a futile token on a board game missing pieces. He suddenly sees that he has been seeing this all along.

The captain finds chapters on his visitor's face to read. He leans forward and peers at Gary through the bottom of his bifocals again. No doubt this news about Braid is very important for Mr. Saar. The captain removes his glasses and starts to clean them on his shirt. "But she escaped."

"She escaped?"

The captain is silent a moment. He moves his torso through slow ovals again.

"Yes, a guard noticed that she was missing from her cell."

Gary repositions himself on the mat and seeks a posture to match

that of the captain. He is silent several minutes before he asks, "How did she escape?"

The captain chuckles. "I don't know. I guess that's for you to decide, Mr. Saar." He switches to his dentist voice again. "Our brig isn't really set up to hold people like her. I guess the only question is how she got off the ship."

Gary casts his eyes toward the hanging chairs. He is in quiet contemplation for a moment.

"And you need me to figure out how Braid escaped?"

"Yes," the captain answers. "My crew is at your disposal."

Gary watches the weave in the tatami floor—the only thing separating him, on a per-inch basis, from ship metal. The individual fibers in the mat describing experiences of rice while alive and since. He stands up. The room, the mats, and the rack of chairs begin to spin, and he reaches for the porthole like it's a bathroom bar for the elderly. He sticks his face in the hole and ignores the room for a moment. It is stormy outside.

Gary turns around finally.

"I think, Captain, that if you have your men inspect the ship you will probably find that a fire hose on one of the decks has gone missing. And that one of the kitchen trash barrels has not made it back from the dumpster."

The captain relaxes his chin while he considers what he has heard.

"We don't really have barrels and dumpsters aboard. But we have the equivalent. What would she have done with a fire hose and a trash barrel?"

"I'd suspect that she made a boat out of them."

The captain brings a thumb and finger to his chin and slowly stands up from the tatami mats. His eyebrows become asymmetric, and he suddenly looks irreverent in the little room. "You mean with the hose wrapped around the top for flotation?"

"Yes, that's correct."

The two men stand in front of each other on the tatami-mat floor. The captain looks through the top of his bifocals and tries to understand better.

"And do you...do you suppose a little trash-can boat like that would be seaworthy in conditions like this, Mr. Saar?"

"No," Gary replies. "But she may have."

SPADED STRAWS

Gary Saar looks through the little window. The frosty buffer in between the double panes is there to keep his brain stem from understanding just how far above the ground he really is. The buffer is no more than a gap of air sandwiched between clear glass, but it efficiently reclassifies the light passing through it. Gary looks down from his incomprehensible height with the same calmness that a child watches a charging bull on television. What he's seeing isn't the real world but some abstraction of it. There's no fear of falling.

The sun is coming up and casts rays over the landscape below. The landscape reflects light with unusually Autumn colors. Along the jagged symmetry of the horizon the sharply serrated land line reaches down into the water. The snaggy forests, dead and despondent, reach up into the air. Both await erosion to smooth their forms.

Because the visual data streaming in through the frosty buffered window has been tagged as not quite real, Gary's brain processes it differently. First, the data is initially withheld from the more emotional and primitive parts of the brain that might mistake the data for being real and become overly alarmed. The tag on the data is there to explain to these impulsive brain parts that the data that they will be seeing are not quite line-of-sight data but, rather, they have been obtained through a periscope of sorts. In this case, objects in the mirror are further away than they appear. There's absolutely no need to flinch at the oncoming waves; the storm depicted is merely a reenacted dramatization for viewers at safe, periscope depth.

Because there's a pretty high penalty of embarrassment for flinching, the deeper brain learns the data tagging scheme and learns to not overreact. To be on the safe side, it learns to underreact. It safely ignores such flinch-free, abstracted data that has been obtained from tangling light rays up in a tube. It doesn't much care for this kind of data, anyway, and leaves it to be processed, pretty much solely, by the rational part of Gary's brain.

There is a firm historical (and, to a small degree, even prehistorical) basis of experiences underlying the logic of this compartmentalization in the brain. But Gary has decided that there are a number of things he needs to sort out, and that the only chance that he has of doing so is to start using his whole brain. He has even created a list of these things, and it has been through inspection of this list that he has arrived at the conclusion that he needs his whole brain to tackle this list. The items simply span too much of the range of the human condition to be tractable with his rational brain alone. Yes, he definitely needs his whole brain for this.

Gary expects this will be challenging, because he has become so accustomed to dealing with abstracted data that many parts of his brain have adopted a life of lassitude. Unless it's a *real* charging bull they just don't get excited. And it will be challenging for Gary to motivate these parts as they have an inherent difficulty feeling more nearness to an abstraction than a real, line-of-sight image (a prejudice that makes televised penguins more distant than the clear-night moon).

Gary needs to bear his whole brain down on his list of items, this list of items spanning the human condition. First on the list is the fact that Patricia is late. This is an item that since last morning has been periodically roiling up to the surface of his consciousness like a Band-Aid in boiling soup. It's the most important item on his list, but it's also fluidly mixed with the other items. In fact, much of the list is mixed like this, and Gary has little expectation for resolving it in a sequential, check-mark fashion.

The second item is that he just let Braid go—little more than an hour ago—although in that time he has been on a ship, a helicopter, and now a jet airplane, so it seems longer. Whether she's a real person or not—whether she walks and eats french fries, or whether she's just a coherent data pattern confusing his employers—Gary has just set her adrift in a trash barrel, and now he's wondering about the significance of his action.

The third item, much related to the other two, is the perilous situation of the planet on which he lives. Is this the end of civilization, or not? Gary has been busy with other things, and the situation has sort of snuck up on him. By the time he realized that climate and global change was *an* issue, it had already become the *only* issue. And now there it is, right below him: spruce forest holocaust. Gary pronounces the words "spruce forest holocaust" then thinks of cheery checker games that probably went on downwind of Auschwitz. He realizes he's probably been capable of playing such checker games, realizes he *has* played such checker games, and then decides that "spruce forest holocaust" doesn't have the right ring for drumming up interest in the parts of his brain he is presently trying to engage. It's a bit accusative and alienating, and he needs their help in analyzing these images—even if the images are buffered through a paned gap of air that makes all sights merely an abstraction. Dead trees out to the horizon. He needs to *feel* what this means.

Gary tries to push this data down into his limbic system. He tries to feel, feeyl, feeyul, the significance of these cortically processed results.

But it doesn't work. Honestly, he doesn't strongly care. Gary looks out the window, down at the dead forests stretching between horizons. He sees firewood.

Gary doesn't care, and this is unfortunate, because he has intuited that there is something tremendously important here to care about. But he just isn't finding the way of getting his deeper brain to emotionally attach itself to the abstracted data. Whatever joy or tragedy out there is buffered from him by a sandwich of glass and air. Gary Saar turns toward his peanuts for a break.

It's a stupidly large package for several peanuts. Gary clamps with his left hand and tears with his right. He knows the method, and he knows that the method is so well engineered for the anatomical configuration of his species that there's probably not another creature in the galaxy that can open our peanut bag as skillfully as we can.

He eats the peanuts, but with some disdain because of the poor ratio of peanuts to package. More energy went into making the packing than is calorifically available from the three peanuts inside. He shifts toward the window again and returns to his list.

Global Awareness In Action—GAIA. They're a self-subscribing group of activists who wish to increase awareness on the planet. And because they're self-subscribing, there's a burden on the individuals to determine on their own when they've become a member. Gary has heard that you don't join GAIA. You become GAIA. You are adopting a new state of awareness. By freeing Braid, Gary figures he's a member now.

He looks out the airplane's porthole. There's a fractal quality to the absurdity he sees: a telescoping level of variance in all that paisley nonsense. Somewhere down there in the dying forest is probably a squirrel shoving a nut into a hole of a dying branch in a dying tree overhanging an eroding coastline, the squirrel real busy with plans for Winter, a Winter that won't arrive, at least not in the way the squirrel is expecting. And there might be a space alien sitting in his space can and looking down at our planet's surface, looking at Gary pulling his nut out of a little bag. And maybe the space alien has the same thoughts one could direct at the squirrel: "So just what do you think you're doing? Where do you think you're going with all that?"

Gary decides that as long as the scene below him is an abstraction it might as well be a convenient abstraction. What use is an abstraction if it's not at least convenient? After some refocusing, Gary sees monkeys, many monkeys. Simian rascals. The monkeys are excited because they have lassoed a planet. They're crawling all over it like a swarm of ants. They seem to have it hog-tied.

The monkeys have little straws with sharp, spaded ends, like the kind that come glued to fruit juice boxes, and they're sticking the straws in the planet, sucking with opiate expressions, cheeks and eyelids wavering with the suction pressure in their straws. Some of the straws are sucking groundwater. Others are inserted a little deeper and have found pools of fudgy oil. Many of the monkeys are running around over the tied-up planet jabbing their straws in new places as the reservoirs of groundwater and oil fudge dry up. They're starting to have confused expressions; they can't seem to believe their accomplishment—any more than a swarm of mosquitoes would believe they've extracted all the blood from their host.

Perhaps through a different porthole is an abstracted pallet—a care package airdropped by God, for the monkeys and loaded with fruit-juice boxes. But the monkeys seized on the straws, not the fruit juice. Completely enamored with the spaded little straws, they ran off with them. With these, they found fudge. The fudge has such high calorie content that when they aren't sucking or searching for more, they're zipping around at hyperactive speeds to burn off the energy they've sucked up.

Gary is satisfied with the summary he has erected to describe the situation on the planet below him. He finds a fourth peanut he earlier missed and decides his portrait is reasonably complete. He has abstracted away all of the nonessential details and is left with the image of many monkeys mindlessly engaged in an oil orgy. All that nonsense is due to the fleeting accident of buried fudge. With their spaded straws, the monkeys have discovered a means of converting the fudgy goo into obnoxious gases, which they spit out of their tail pipes as they zing around with increased energy and the determination to stab their straws in new places. It's an absurd feedback loop.

Gary can't understand how such a serious situation snuck up on him. The planet's medical chart has been posted on the wall since decades and shows rising red marks never seen in a hospital before. All the monitoring equipment has been buzzing and beeping and flashing. But there's also a crew of conflicted night nurses invested in unplugging all that revealing shit. Still, the facts have always been there for Gary to see. If he wished.

A thought comes to Gary. It's a rare scenario that he regards first as hypothetical—until he realizes that there's statistically a near certainty it has occurred. He's thinking of old Germans playing checkers with their grandchildren. The kids want to know if they *really* killed all those Jewish people. The kids also want to know from their grandparents if they played checkers during the war.

As for the planet, judging by her complexion she doesn't look too well. But she has a lot of experience and wisdom wrapped up in her immune system, and Gary doubts she's really locked into that hog-tie the monkeys have imposed. Gary expects that any moment she'll lumber up from that ridiculous knot and start shaking monkeys off into outer space. But he's unsure of the details of how that will occur.

GAIA has obviously sculpted the name of their organization to emulate Gaia, the Greek goddess of the earth. Or the "Gaia" that in modern times has become the living superorganism, the living planet equipped with a homeostatic sense of self. GAIA probably sees itself as the human chapter of this superorganism, Gaia. GAIA probably sees itself as an off split group of Homo sapiens committed to reestablishing their loyalty and connection with the whole, a mutated branch with such an expansively dysfunctional tendency toward altruism, with such a long-range concern over the context in which their unborn grandchildren will one day find themselves, with such an imperative to question customary practices and experiment with new behaviors, that they are not even one bit surprised that they are regarded as freaks. It's a temporary and uncomfortable label that they are proud to bear—like the Webelos, the "we'll be loyal scouts," the awkward transition species between Cub Scouts and Boy Scouts.

Gary Saar finishes his second sachet of peanuts with regrets. The tiny snack is not about nourishment but rather some kind of entertainment that he can probably do without. The energy that went into the packaging of these peanuts, and the energy being used to fly them around in a jet airplane—was a thimble of nuts worth this? Gary is aware that this is not the most conspicuous example of spaded juice straws, but it is symbolically flagrant: who is he to expect peanuts way up here in the air like this? Can't he wait to get back on the ground for that sort of thing?

Gary Saar doesn't want to get sidetracked, and he's back ruminating over the list of things he needs to sort out that primarily roil around one item: Patricia is late. She told him this at breakfast, wearing a pair of his boxers and speaking through a lightly buttered English muffin so as to vulcanize the significance of her statement and keep it from splattering as a hot wad onto him, his orange juice, and morning paper. But however delayed, the whole message has arrived, and now he just needs to think about it.

SOLUTION SPACE

Patricia Concept sits with her knees to her chest, chin down and looking around her bathroom. It is overwhelming.

She decided to complete her analysis of the pool poems before presenting anything to her boss. IS white-washed the pool immediately when the poems were discovered. IS claims it didn't take any pictures before doing so. Access to the satellite images of the pool has also been tightly guarded by IS. And yet it seems that recently someone with high clearance has been leaking them.

There were thirteen logical clumps of poetry in Mrs. Nesbitt's pool, and Patricia finished analyzing twelve. Sharpening the letters and compensating for the distortions due to the satellite's oblique view of the pool walls was straightforward. It is the thirteenth tile, the wall of the deep end, that held her up. The satellite's perspective came in at such a grazing angle that there is no enhancement algorithm that can uniquely compensate for the distortion. Without injecting context, the tile is formally illegible. This is to say that the best that enhancement algorithms can provide are thousands of suggestions for word phrases that all equally fit the appearance of the dime-slot section of colored pixels that the satellite saw in the part of the pool just below the diving board as it passed overhead.

So Patricia Concept's analysis stalled while she inspected thousands of computer-generated suggestions. Most could be immediately dismissed; the computer offered up pathetic poetry as eagerly as the subset of quality. But there was still a large collection that Concept needed to consider more carefully. To narrow this set down, she needed to add the constraint that the poem solution match either the style of Anita Fray, or a different style she might attribute to Susan Nesbitt— since some of the retrieved images show both women painting from their air mattresses as the pool drained.

Susan's style may include the passages: "No lifeguard on duty," and "Don't pee in our pool...we don't swim in your john, " and "No diving in shallow end—risk of head injury." Anita's potential is less compact. Patricia is pretty sure that the thirteenth tile, the tile from the deep end, came from Anita's hand.

The statement of the problem is clear, at least; it is a simple non-unique inversion problem. Sort of like the "GO PIZZA" problem. This slogan can be uniquely converted to get the take-out restaurant's phone number, but the phone number isn't enough by itself to get the slogan: the space of slogans is bigger than the space of phone numbers. So the problem facing Concept is essentially to guess the restaurant's slogan from the solution space of possibilities.

To try to select the right one from the solution space, Concept has thoroughly studied Anita's style. Just like a pizza-slogan solution doesn't likely include words like "stale" or "cold" or the names of any number of insects, there are a number of constraints she can infer from context. But this is the problem that is troubling her. She found a candidate that fits Anita's style very well—she has even posted a picture of it provisionally at the deep end of her bathtub, and it is this she stares at as she sits with her knees to her chin.

Within a red cross, the thirteenth image hanging in Concept's deep end reads:

RE

FACE SOLUTION SPACE
II

It matches Anita so well in the wrong ways that it seems almost a decoy. Patricia had even fallen for it. Thought she had finally resolved the thirteenth tile. She could go to her boss now with the analysis complete. But then she made the mistake of considering it more closely. More deeply. She allowed fractals to blossom.

The Bigloo, as Concept understood it, is about the problems hanging over the world today. Not really just the environmental problem—this is more just a symptom—but rather the real problem seated in a lack of awareness, and the processes and parties invested in jamming awareness. At first, it seemed that as a second exhibit following her "Earth's Alert" in the Bigloo the career secretary, Anita Fray, wanted to say something like this in her poem on the deep end of the pool: *" RE: FACE SOLUTION SPACE (second memo)."* To Patricia, this sounds sort of like the "face it" people say when they really mean you should just concede.

It is subtle juggling of nuance, but Concept feels this interpretation doesn't fit in the pool. The Bigloo was about indication, and the pool is about action. The pool is about the resources under us for addressing the challenge overhead. And these resources, if Patricia's read is right, involve a complex system of planetary life with years of wisdom and experience that dwarf that of the recent Homo sapiens. A living, planetary organism that, through its long life, has seen asteroid impacts, mass extinctions, frost bite, sun burns, and every kind of fretful rash on its surface of specialized skin cells. A living planet that has experienced these illnesses not simply as a piece of driftwood experiences a stream, but rather as a planet with an intelligent immune system that has studied these events and recorded useful responses.

An intelligent planet with an immune system run primarily by microbes, the most perennial of which live far below the volatile conditions on the surface. The pool, the resources under us for addressing the challenge over us, is essentially the gene pool, the archive of responses that the planet's immune system has tested in the past. Another name for this, though unduly slanted toward macroscopic cells at the surface, is biodiversity.

Homo sapiens are just one type of specialized skin cell, and it could be argued that they present themselves to the planet as cancer, AIDS, or both. In any case, their part of the solution involves, above all, humility. No part of the solution space sees them as capable of fixing the problem—any more than a Nobel Laureate's most prized neurons might solve his fever. The best they can do is to stop doing harm, then get out of the way and follow the planet's lead. Maybe hand Gaia an end wrench, if she calls for it.

The pool describes the solution space—the possible slogans that might correspond to the phone number we've been given. The pool is about the solution, not the problem, and a poem that simply restates the problem doesn't seem to Concept to fit in the pool.

LEANING PARALLELOGRAM

Nicolas Nesbitt's only view of the world outside is through a high motel window. A high motel window that, from where he lies in a cast, appears instead as a leaning parallelogram. A leaning parallelogram that crops the world outside in such an unhelpful way that Nicolas prefers to regard the lean view as a small patch of nonsense randomly slit from a big mural that might have once made sense.

At an attitude of five liters below beer, and anchored to the bed by the cast, Nicolas sees the world as he sees the ceiling: as silly stucco specks. While, hidden in a pantry of a sympathetic motel, he recovers.

Anita Fray painted 'in' under the 'war' in 'awareness' in such a way that one wants to read the Bigloo as 'war in awareness'. Pretty succinct statement of the human existential threat on this planet. If you try to type what she painted, it comes out something like this:

The
aWareness....holyYamIholyYamIholyYamIholy…
In

But with the art Anita added to the type, the Bigloo can also be seen as a Sopwith Camel biplane towing a banner.

Now paint a circle Then a couple of brush strokes inside and she has cartoon continents. She populates the surface of the cartoon planet with a thin layer of fuzz. From very close one can see the fuzz is a globe-wrapping sequence of "…bitebackbitebackbite…" She leaves it to us to decide where to start reading the repeating sequence. That was in the Bigloo.

She paints a similar cartoon planet wrapped in fuzz in the pool. But the message this time is "…lateRlateRlateR…". Of the two immediate interpretations, Occam's Razor would slice for the repeating 'lateR' sequence. One repeating word requires less extravagant thought than two repeating words. Computer algorithms programmed for parsimony might find the 'are late' interpretation to be wasteful. Occam's Razor shaves it off.

But human minds seek messages. They let fractals blossom. They stop Occam a minute. Because once you see it, you can't unsee it. The 'R' in the sequence is built from an 'I' and a tilted '2'. So "...lateRlateRlateR..." can be fractally unpacked as a repeating sequence of 'I are too late'.

Similarly, an algorithm might not see the layers in "Dog Eat Dog". Might not see the uppercase ascendance of 'DED'. Might not think of the phonetic equivalence with 'DEAD'. Might not distill, finally, the soft suggestion that a dog-eat-dog world is a dead world.

Nicolas sleeps. Outside the high motel window, a lightning storm is in progress. The motel owner is Chinese and told Nicolas lightning rare. Almost never. And then grabbed a package of toilet paper and two bottles of bath tile cleaner before sealing Nicolas back in.

Nicolas hears the thunder booms outside and listens to the perspective touching ground under clouds that have reached a high enough potential to induce ionized pathways through a poorly conducting medium. Lightning then illuminating everything. But, keeping perspective, it's just the same thing as the static cling thing— like ordinary socks from the dryer after they've spun around a while together. It's mostly just a question of scale. Nevertheless, there's a mind-blowing aspect of realizing that the creature Gaia is splendidly capable of shocking herself.

As She Would Cross Herself

Patricia Concept discovers that the thirteenth tile is about commitment. She looks again through her naked legs, down at the bathtub drain with its "Part of a Party." Then she pulls her chin down and smiles at the two parentheses around her navel—her beautiful anterior superior iliac spines, the part of her Jiffy-Pop pan that will stay put.

Then back up at the wall of the deep end:

RE
FACE SOLUTION SPACE
II

Patricia sees it. She thinks she understands how to read the poem of the deep end now. Read without commitment, it's just a restatement of the problem. But read as she would wear it, read just as her finger would cross herself, the poem is the resolution of a mother.

ABOUT THE AUTHOR

Robert Tyler is an earth and planetary scientist. He specializes in dynamics, the study of motion, and does this from a motionless posture in a windowless office at a NASA center.

www.ingramcontent.com/pod-product-compliance
Lightning Source LLC
Chambersburg PA
CBHW021044130626
46552CB00005B/2005